Barefoot

AT SUNSET

Barefoot Bay Timeless #1

roxanne st. claire

Critical Reviews of
Roxanne St. Claire Novels

"St. Claire, as always, brings a scorching tear-up-the-sheets romance combined with a great story: dealing with real issues starring memorable characters in vivid scenes."

— Romantic Times Magazine

"Non-stop action, sweet and sexy romance, lively characters, and a celebration of family and forgiveness."

— Publishers Weekly

"Plenty of heat, humor, and heart!"

— USA Today's Happy Ever After blog

"It's safe to say I will try any novel with St. Claire's name on it."

— www.smartbitchestrashybooks.com

"The writing was perfectly on point as always and the pace of the story was flawless. But be forewarned that you will laugh, cry, and sigh with happiness. I sure did."

— www.harlequinjunkies.com

"The Barefoot Bay series is an all-around knockout, soul-satisfying read. Roxanne St. Claire writes with warmth and heart and the community she's built at Barefoot Bay is one I want to visit again and again."

— Mariah Stewart, New York Times bestselling author

"This book stayed with me long after I put it down."

— All About Romance

Dear Reader,

Welcome to Barefoot Bay Timeless...a brand new trilogy that celebrates the appeal of an older hero and second chances at love! Like every book set in Barefoot Bay, this novel stands entirely alone, but why stop at just one? Barefoot Bay is a whole world of romance, friends and family, and unforgettable stories, divided into bite-size trilogies so you can dive in to the water anytime!

The Barefoot Bay Billionaires
Secrets on the Sand
Scandal on the Sand
Seduction on the Sand

The Barefoot Bay Brides
Barefoot in White
Barefoot in Lace
Barefoot in Pearls

Barefoot Bay Undercover
Barefoot Bound (prequel)
Barefoot With a Bodyguard
Barefoot With a Stranger
Barefoot With a Bad Boy

Barefoot Bay Timeless
Barefoot at Sunset
Barefoot at Moonrise
Barefoot at Midnight

Want to know the day the next Barefoot Bay book is released? Sign up for the newsletter! You'll get brief monthly e-mails about new releases and book sales.

http://www.roxannestclaire.com/newsletter.html

Acknowledgments

As always, there's a team of professionals carrying me along from Chapter One to The End. Most especially, forever love and gratitude to Kristi Yanta, the Picky Editor who helps me to dig for emotional gold on every page. In addition, many thanks to keen-eyed copy editor Joyce Lamb, super-sharp proofreader Marlene Engel, super-talented (patient and determined) cover artist Kim Killion, and the world's most dependable formatter, Amy Atwell. Behind the scenes, amazing assistant Maria Connor keeps me sane. Extra love to the Rocki Roadies, the Roxanne St. Claire Street Team. (Want to join? We're on Facebook and have tons of fun.)

Barefoot

AT SUNSET

roxanne st. claire

Dedication

One day not so long ago, my brother, Dr. J. Zink, sat on my patio with tears in his eyes as he told me that he had found another soul mate, many years after he lost his beloved wife in the prime of her life. I will never forget the look of joy on his face, marveling that such a miracle had happened. "Who gets two soul mates in one lifetime, Rocki?" His question wrapped around my heart and inspired this book. So, this one is for Dr. J and my soon-to-be-sister, Sandra Nance. You two prove that a second soul mate doesn't only happen in fiction.

Chapter One

Mark Solomon had one question pounding in his brain as he strode across the lobby of Casa Blanca Resort & Spa. And not just the obvious one, which would be: How in the name of all that was holy did he get roped into being on a freaking high school reunion committee?

Because he *knew* how that had happened. The woman who owned this elite jewel in Barefoot Bay had tracked him down while he was parasailing in New Zealand. She'd offered some new breathtaking scenery and caught him in a rare moment of weakness. The straight whiskey kind of weakness. Oh, he'd said no at first, but then...

He reached into his pocket and thumbed the class ring he'd found in a safe-deposit box just two days after he'd gotten that call. *That's* how he ended up back on Mimosa Key for a high school reunion, arriving a week early to boot, to be at the final planning committee meetings. Because he never ignored his most trusted adviser.

Nor was he asking himself how thirty years had passed since he and a handful of eighteen-year-olds had ditched the prom to sneak booze into the only theater on the island for the opening of *Top Gun*. He didn't look, feel, act, think, or tire like a man at the high end of his forties. He could pass for ten years

1

younger, even though his thick hair had plenty of salt in the pepper. His age certainly hadn't stopped him from skydiving, hang gliding, snowboarding, or climbing Kilimanjaro. And the only "tire" he knew was usually squealing under him during a competitive Porsche street race.

No, the question plaguing Mark before he reached the conference room where he and a bunch of other graduates from years gone by were gathering, was short, direct, and usually posed by a woman with clingy claws.

A widower? Why haven't you remarried?

Most often, it was followed by some inane comment about a "silver fox."

God help him. *Someone* had better help him get through this reunion, because this was the one place where everyone once knew him not just as "Mark Solomon, quarterback, valedictorian, and all-around hot shot," but also as Mark of *MarkandJulia*, named Couple Most Likely to Last Forever.

Until "forever" got cut short.

But he hadn't been part of that power couple for sixteen long and adventure-filled years now. During those years, he'd figured out the ideal way to escape the past, and yet, here he was. In the middle of an island that was nothing *but* the past.

The doors to one of the conference rooms popped open, and a man walked out as Mark approached.

"I hope to hell you're going in here," the guy said, notching his head to the room behind him. "We need to balance the testosterone levels. There's only one other dude, and he's the strong, silent type."

"Mimosa High reunion?" Mark asked.

"That's it." The man offered his hand for a strong shake, his smile easy and natural. "Law Monroe," he said. "Class of...holy shit." He frowned and took a closer look. "You're Mark Solomon."

"Law...*Lawless* Monroe?" He felt his own smile pull at the recognition of the troubled youth who'd been thrust onto the football team Mark's senior year. He'd been expected to mentor the kid who'd never once been called by his real name of Lawson. But "mentoring" meant calling Law before practice to make sure he wasn't in the saddle of a motorcycle with a chick's thighs pressed against him.

Lawless was, what, three years younger than Mark? In amazing shape for forty-five, though. Plenty of ink on a tanned, buff body, but a good-looking, rugged guy with a spark in intense bottle-green eyes.

"You're not in the slammer?" Mark asked. "That's a miracle."

Law threw his head back and laughed heartily. "Not for lack of trying, trust me. Damn, I never expected to see you here. And at the planning session, too. Did Lacey Walker have compromising pictures or something? Why the hell would you be on the planning committee?"

"Two words: beachfront villa. How'd she get you?"

The other man lifted a sizable shoulder, shiny gray hair brushing his collar. "She gave me full responsibility for the food."

"The food?"

"Food's my thing. I'm a sous chef at the Ritz-Carlton across the causeway in Naples."

Whoa. "Impressive. And I've gotta be honest...not what I expected."

"Trust me, I was well on my way to exactly what you expected. But someone threw me in the kitchen of a restaurant about ten years ago, and I got my act together. How 'bout you? I remember you had an Air Force ROTC scholarship. Did you end up going overseas?"

He nodded. "Kuwait during the first Gulf War. Then I had a business, sold it, and now I travel the world."

Law gave his hand a la-di-da shake. "Nice. And..." His expression changed just enough for Mark to know exactly what was coming next. "I thought I heard that..."

He saved Law the awkward question with a quick nod. "Yeah," he said, sliding his hands into the pockets of his khakis. "I lost Julia about sixteen years ago. Cancer."

"Sorry, man." Law put a hand on Mark's shoulder. "I'd heard you guys got married right after graduation, and I always said if anyone would have made it, it would've been you two."

"Thanks. I'm sure we would have." He and Julia could have easily dodged the divorce odds, but not the long-shot odds of a thirty-two-year-old woman having a fatal allergic reaction to chemotherapy. Time to change the subject. "Did someone manage to tackle my best running back and make an honest man out of him?" he asked quickly.

Law puffed a noisy breath. "Your best running back, my ass. Your biggest headache, more like. I'm single. Chef's hours suck. That's the other reason I took Lacey's offer and cashed in on a long vacation. I needed a break." He threw a look over his shoulder. "Although I'm not sure sitting around a room with a bunch of women bickering over whether or not the theme should be a sundial or an iWatch to represent the past and the present was the break I needed." He pointed in the other direction. "I was on my way to check out the kitchen. Wanna come?"

Mark shook his head. "I should—"

The door opened behind Law, pushed by a tall man wearing a tight-fitting regulation fire department T-shirt and a semiserious expression of warning.

"Men, do not enter without full protective gear," he said,

holding up his hands with authority. "Or someone will volunteer you for something like flower arrangements which, God help me, I think I just signed up for."

"Why the hell would you do that?" Law asked.

The other man just shook his head. He had close-cropped hair and a dusting of gray around his temples contrasting with tanned skin that didn't look weathered enough for him to be much over forty. "Red sweater. Tight jeans. Brain fail."

"Red sweater?" Law frowned. "Wasn't her last name Endicott, as in, you know, money?"

"Yeah, that's Bethany Endicott." He half exhaled the name as if even saying it was too much for him. "I'm Ken Cavanaugh, by the way," the man said, extending a hand to Mark. "Class of '91."

"Mark Solomon, '86."

"Eighty-six?" Ken drew back.

"Graduating class, not my age," Mark joked.

"Still puts you five years ahead of me and three ahead of Law." He turned to gesture to the door. "Age before beauty, old men."

"And brains," Law shot back. "Since yours got fried into flower arranging."

"Point taken," Ken conceded. "In fact, there are exactly three men on a planning committee of about fifteen, so we gotta have each other's backs this week. It could get ugly. Uglier."

"How ugly?" Mark asked.

"Let me put it this way," Ken said, "I left when they were talking about something called the Dance of the Decades. With *us* as male dancers."

"Whoa." Mark inched back. "That's ugly."

"They keep saying how happy they are to have men on

the committee," Ken said. "It's like an estrogen bomb explodes every time Law or I say a word."

Law gave Mark a wry once-over. "Place is going to go up in flames when you walk in."

"It's okay," Mark said, putting a hand on Ken's shoulder. "We have a firefighter. Let's go. Remember, volunteer for nothing, ignore what they throw at us, and, for God's sake, *no one is dancing.*"

"He won't last ten minutes in there," Law whispered to Ken as they followed Mark.

"No shit," Ken replied. "Ten bucks says he's on the tablecloth subcommittee by two o'clock."

The two of them shut up when he opened the door, and so did the chatter inside—much of it loud and higher-pitched—from about a dozen or so women around a large conference room table.

The second or two of silence could have been awkward, but Mark crossed the room to an empty chair at the head of the table. "Ladies." He stayed standing and leveled a commanding look at women of all ages, sizes, and ethnicities. Not one looked remotely familiar, but it wasn't as if Mark spent time in high school looking at any other girl besides—

"Julia..." One of the women on his right stood, her word echoing the very name that hung on the edges of his brain.

"I'm Mark Solomon." He turned to her, not recognizing the woman with dark hair with one thick streak of gray running down the front and a serious, sad expression.

"Oh, I'm sorry. Julia was a good friend of mine and seeing you..." She sighed and extended her hand. "Allison McMurphy. My maiden name was Breyer." She held out her hand. "Do you remember me? Julia and I were co-captains of the cheer squad. I saw you last at her, uh..."

6

Memorial service, which passed in a blur. "Of course I remember you." He reached to give her a hug, a jolt of a memory rushing through him.

Coming to Mimosa Key was probably not the smartest move he'd ever made. He'd gone sixteen years without Julia, and each year had gotten easier and easier. He'd long ago numbed the pain of her loss and left the last stage of grief in an underwater cave dive in Sardinia.

But embracing a woman his late wife had called one of her best friends put some pressure on the tough skin of that scar. He hugged tighter.

"So good to see you," she said. "When Lacey told me you'd agreed to be on the planning committee, I admit I was stunned. I've heard you lead quite the jet-setter life now."

Is that what people called a life of freedom and adventure? "I was able to retire early, so I travel a lot," he acknowledged. "And I have time for…things like this."

"And I shamelessly begged." A red-headed woman with a bright smile and dancing eyes—Lacey Walker most likely—stood at the other side of the table. She offered a friendly salute in greeting. "We are so happy you—you three guys—are here." She gestured to the other men who'd found seats. "We have to have some representation from the boys in our classes, and it wasn't easy bribing, er, finding you."

The three men obviously had their reasons for accepting those bribes, and Mark's was a small ring in his pocket.

He laughed softly at Lacey's joke. "I don't think we qualify as boys anymore."

"No, you're definitely men." This came from a blonde he hadn't noticed, sitting on his left. She stood slowly, crimson lips curling up. She wore white, Mark noticed, so she wasn't the object of Ken's attentions. Though the woman was attractive in that Palm Beach big-money kind of way that usually meant high heels and high maintenance.

"Mark Solomon, I've heard of you. Libby Chesterfield, class of '89." She gave a secret point to her generous breasts. "Also known as Chesty Chesterfield," she added with a playful wink. "Oh, those Mimosa High nicknames do haunt you for the rest of your life."

The school had a weird tradition of awarding everyone a nickname. He'd been...he drew a blank. Of course, there must have been another nickname, but he remembered only the couple he was once part of.

MarkandJulia.

"Libby, sure. Nice to see you." Although, to be honest, he didn't remember Libby or her chest.

"So you two were in the same class?" Libby asked, looking at Allison, the first woman who'd greeted him. "Wow. I mean, you look good, Allison, but...*wow*." She raked Mark up and down and up again. "Now that is what I call timeless."

He managed a smile.

"That's it!" Lacey gave a quick clap and brought all the attention to the other side of the room. "Timeless! Forget clocks, watches, and sundials."

"Thank you," Mark muttered, making Chesty give a throaty chuckle and place a hand on his shoulder.

"I'm with you on the sundials," she whispered. "It's like we graduated during the Roman Empire, for heaven's sake. It was just the eighties, right?"

"There is no time," Lacey continued. "When we get together for the annual all-class Mimosa High reunion at Casa Blanca, time disappears and we're all young again."

"You're still young," Chesty whispered to Mark, adding a

squeeze, even though her gaze had shifted across the table…directly to Law.

"Timeless is perfect!" one of the other ladies said.

"I love it!" a few others agreed.

A petite brunette came around to where Mark still stood, since he'd been flanked by females and hadn't even sat down yet. "You are a genius. What is your name again? Mark? I don't think we've ever met, but then, this is only my fifteen-year reunion." She sidled in closer and pushed a wayward lock over her shoulder. "I'm Fiona, by the way."

Ah, man. Law was right. He wasn't going to last ten minutes. He had to get out of here.

"So, how can we bring the timeless theme to life?" Lacey asked.

"Don't look at me," Mark said, stepping back before he was forced into a chair and someone climbed on his lap. "I did my part."

In all fairness, he hadn't said a word, but he wanted to escape before the questions he didn't want to have to answer were asked.

Are you married, Mark? Still a widower? Why haven't you—

"Are you married, Mark?" Fiona whispered.

"Speaking of time, I'm out of it. Ladies." He nodded to the table, then looked at Law and Ken. Law was talking to one woman, but sneaking eye contact with Chesty. And Ken was trying hard to look like he wasn't staring at…a woman across the table in a scarlet sweater.

So much for manly solidarity.

"Great to see you all, and Lacey, you have my number. Call me in time for the next meeting."

"I will," she agreed. "But, Mark I have to tell you—"

He pulled his phone out of his pocket and looked at it,

despite the fact that it hadn't rung. "Really sorry, but I have to take a call."

He hustled out of the room, a low-grade resentment seething in him. Not against the women. Technically, he was fair game. And they all seemed...nice. Probably really good women. And he liked a good woman as much as the next guy.

But here, on Mimosa Key, Florida, he was profoundly reminded that none of those women was his soul mate, and once you've had that, all the lesser attachments were just...lesser.

He bypassed the lobby and took a side door out to the beach, the late spring sun blasting over the wide, white sands of Barefoot Bay. Gulls screeched, children ran in the surf, and vacationers lounged under the cheery yellow umbrellas along Casa Blanca's private Gulf of Mexico beach.

He kicked off his Docksides and held the shoes in one hand, oblivious to the heat of the sand or the occasional shell that stabbed his foot. Pain didn't bother him. He'd spent years on risky adventures that were rarely comfortable, and he'd yet to be inflicted with any physical pain that was close to the agony of losing the only woman he'd ever loved.

He shook off the unexpected punch of mourning, the feeling unwelcome and unfamiliar.

He didn't come to this island or this reunion to stroll down memory lane and cry into his beer because he'd lost his wife in the prime of their lives. He was here to chill out, to check out the changes in the town, and because...

Julia wanted him to come.

The truth, a small whisper in his brain, hit as hard as his foot on the stone path he took to get to Blue Casbah, the villa he'd checked into this morning. He rounded a thicket of flowering plants, the sickeningly sweet fragrance of honeysuckle mixing with salt air, and then he paused at the sound of a sigh. No, that was…what was that? An animal being strangled?

Very slowly, he inched past the hedge to peek at the walkway and small stone patio in front of the villa. A woman sat there, a roller suitcase and oversize bag next to her, her head in her hands.

Weeping. A full-out, shoulder-shaking shudderfest of misery unfolding on his porch.

Well, this was embarrassing. Mark looked left and right, dreading a resort guest passing by, then he took a step closer, dropping his shoes to make some noise louder than the gurgling and moaning coming from her throat.

But she didn't even look up, choking on the next sob.

"Excuse me," he said loudly.

She kept her face in her hands. "Go away!" she mumbled.

"But I…" *Want to get to my villa…where you're crying.* "Are you all right?"

"No. I am not all right." The words were garbled, teary, and spoken into hands that covered her whole face. "Give me five minutes before you drag me off, okay?"

Drag her off? "Okay." He took a few steps closer, trying to make sense of the scene. All he could see of her was long dark hair falling over narrow, hunched shoulders, jeans, and a white shirt.

"Would you, uh, like to cry inside?" Before someone got a very wrong impression.

Her head shot up. "Yes," she said softly. "I would very much like to cry inside. Inside *that* villa." She turned and pointed at the front door painted deep orange and trimmed in white. "In fact, that's the whole reason I'm here, a thousand miles from home, completely alone on what was supposed to be the happiest…" She grunted and stopped herself.

Brown eyes flecked with topaz and rimmed in red stared up at him, her cheeks little more than rivers of running makeup. Her face was shredded from tears, and her deep-brown hair spilled around her as if she'd combed it with a rake, the remnants of pink lipstick smeared around her mouth.

She'd almost be comical if she wasn't so...miserable.

"I swore I wasn't going to tell a soul my story," she finally said.

"Well, out here you're telling every soul." He pulled out his card key. "So you might as well come inside and weep."

She blinked at him. "You're not with resort security?"

He shook his head, then eyed her. "Should I be?"

"You're not going to take me in there and...rob me, are you?"

"It's my villa, with all my stuff in it. Maybe I should be the one worried about being robbed." But he was pretty sure the only thing she'd steal of his was some peace and quiet, and tissues. Lots of tissues.

"*Your* villa?" she asked.

"Well, this week anyway."

"Your villa for this week?" She choked the words, kicking the stone paver with her loafer. "Well, that's just perfect. I suppose you're here with your wife for a..." She narrowed her eyes at him, sizing him up. "Oh, I know. An anniversary in paradise?"

"No," he said simply. "I'm here alone."

He gingerly bypassed her on the step and walked to the door, sliding in the key card.

As he opened the door, he turned to find her watching him over her shoulder, distrust and uncertainty in those golden-brown eyes. She shuddered on the next pathetic inhale, and he held out his hand.

"Come on and make that noise inside. I have tissues. And wine."

A slight, unsure smile lifted the pink-stained corners of her mouth. "I like wine." Very slowly, she took his hand and let him pull her up, leaving her suitcases on the step.

Chapter Two

Emma had to see the place. She wasn't about to leave without at least placing her feet on the imported, cream marble floor or touching the posh furnishings or gazing out over the infinity pool that disappeared into the bay.

And don't forget the beach-facing bedroom balcony or the stunner of a bathroom with a Jacuzzi the size of a small country.

All designed for fairy-tale romance.

The copy on page three of the Casa Blanca Resort & Spa brochure still danced in her memory, torturing her. Oh yeah. *Fairy tale.* Those were the words that sold people on villas that cost this much. Not, you know, *real life.* But then, advertising copy wasn't real life...and who knew that better than the woman who wrote it?

Sniffing back some tears, she stepped in so she could fully wallow in her misery. Wasn't that why she'd dragged her suitcases along the path, gulping great mouthfuls of humiliation with the desk clerk's words still echoing in her head?

Oh, I'm sorry, that reservation was canceled by Mr. Kyle Chambers's secretary. Would you like to see the cancellation number?

No, but, damn it, she wanted to see the villa.

She'd hoped to find a kindly housekeeper who might let her take a peek inside when she'd marched over here after her failed check-in attempt. She was totally prepared to use her six degrees of separation trump card to get inside. *I'm with the ad agency that handles the resort...* Well, she had been with the agency, before quitting in shame.

But a housekeeper was nowhere to be found, and the villa was locked tight.

That was when frustration, sadness, and the total unfairness of life had kicked Emma in the chest so hard, she'd dropped onto the patio step and gave in to the first real sobfest since her fiancé broke their engagement.

This guy must think she was a total loon. She glanced at him, already soothed by his baritone voice and commanding presence, and grateful that he hadn't treated her like an unwanted piece of litter strewn outside his expensive accommodations.

She inhaled a quick breath as the impact of the place hit her. Here it was, in full three-dimensional living color, so much more beautiful than the photos they'd dropped into the brochure and on the website. The luxurious living area led straight to French doors that opened to a jaw-dropping, heart-stopping view of...that man.

No, no. *He* was not in the brochure, but could have been, easily. She'd know exactly what to ask the modeling agency to send, if they'd used a model: a gorgeous, confident man, maybe mid-forties, a little dusting of silver, a strong jaw, piercing blue eyes, and an air of authority and power. Yes, he'd be the perfect accent to the stunning villa.

Emma looked beyond her unexpected host to the turquoise waters of Barefoot Bay glinting in the late afternoon, warmed by pink clouds that heralded a spectacular sunset over the Gulf of Mexico.

At least, that's how she'd describe it if she had to write copy for that postcard view. Throw in a happy couple walking hand in hand, barefoot, of course. They'd be laughing or caught in that split-second exchange of an intimate touch and...

A sob bubbled up, and she choked it back with a noise that sounded something like a cross between a strangled burp and a hiccup.

Great, Emma. Just great. She'd never been a delicate crier. Hell, she'd never been a crier.

"So, what exactly did you mean by 'your villa'?" the man asked.

"I meant that it was supposed to be..." *Ours.* "Mine this week."

A frown creased his brow. "I was told there was a cancellation and that's why Lacey—the resort owner—put me in this, the last available villa. I would have taken a room in the main building, but that was booked, too."

"There certainly was a cancellation," Emma said. "A big, fat, nasty, embarrassing, gut-wrenching brutality of a cancellation." She wiped her face, vaguely aware that she must look like a red-faced freak, but honestly didn't care. "Can I see the bedroom?"

"Sure. It's through that doorway, to the left."

Maybe this was a little masochistic—okay, no maybe, this was truly self-inflicted torture—but she just had to see it. Taking slow steps to a vestibule outside a huge double-doored entrance, she peeked into the bedroom.

Yep. The photographer had nailed it. A king-size four-poster bed with a puffy white comforter and sheer drapes all around, giving it a secretive, seductive feel.

The pale marble floors continued in here, warmed by expensive Oriental carpets and layers of lush window treatments.

And the bathroom. She *had* to see the bathroom.

She crossed the room to a space that led into the spa-like sanctuary, drinking in a vaulted ceiling and blue tile trim that captured the Moroccan feel of the whole resort. Light bounced off the shiny floor, blinding her.

Just like she'd been blinded by...dreams and hopes and empty promises.

"Oh, Kyle. How could you do this to me?" She sighed and turned around, taking it all in, especially the magnificent tub surrounded by candles and a view out to the bay.

A tub built for...two.

"Seen enough?"

She startled at the voice behind her, low and close and as alluring as the surroundings. Looking up, she caught sight of the man in the mirror, pinning her with a look that fell somewhere between amused and annoyed.

No, mostly amused. And he had pretty eyes. If they hadn't already been that piercing sky blue that matched the villa, she'd have suggested the art department Photoshop them to exactly that color.

Then her gaze shifted to her own reflection, and she gasped. "Oh Lord." She put her hand to her mouth, laughing softly, because what else could she do?

She so did not match the cool and beautiful villa. "I look like I was dragged through a mascara factory."

He put a hand on her shoulder, slowly turning her to face him instead of the mirror. "Were you supposed to stay here this week?" he guessed.

She let out a breath and gave a weak nod. "Yeah," she managed.

"Special occasion?"

"Just, you know, a honeymoon. Is that special?"

"Oh." His eyes widened. "Usually, yeah."

She tore her gaze from him to take another longing look around. "Except there was no, you know…"

"Wedding," he supplied gently.

"No wedding," she confirmed. She heard the hurt and bitterness in her voice and wished she could hide those feelings, but they were out now. "Just a lot of frantic phone calls and canceled florists and returned gifts and sympathetic friends, and oh, that bitch at the dress place would *not* refund my money. And I woke up this morning, maybe a little hung over because last night was, you know, *not* my wedding night, as planned. Then I realized today would have been check-in day. I called, and the reservation hadn't been canceled, so I thought why not?"

"Of course," he said, as if that made perfect sense.

"Well, they do that in movies all the time, right? The jilted bride goes on her honeymoon alone and has…" She swallowed and looked up at him.

"And has…?" he prompted.

Wild sex with a hot guy.

No, no, good God in heaven, *no.* Except…*whoa.* He was easy on the eyes. "And has a chance to heal," she finished.

Silent, he searched her face for a moment, his gaze sharpening as if he read her thoughts, which would not be good. "You could use that wine."

He left her standing in the oversize Moroccan tile bathroom staring at her ravaged face.

Yeah, wine. To calm her jumpy nerves and misbehaving libido. Wine from the wine god who happened to be the lucky recipient of Kyle Chambers's cold, second-guessing

18

heart. Now, this man—whoever he was—knew her history, had seen her at her worst, and still offered wine.

Could anyone really be that nice? She'd think he had an ulterior motive, but one look in the mirror and she knew it couldn't be a hot seduction on the sand. Pity, more likely.

She closed the bathroom door and went to the sink, unwrapping some sweet-smelling goat's milk soap—made locally, exactly as she'd written in the brochure—to wash her face completely clean. She still looked pale and wretched.

Glancing down to the drawer in the vanity, she thought of a line from the direct-mail piece. *Every bathroom in Casa Blanca comes with all the extras, including a luxurious robe, fluffy slippers, and a supply of high-end cosmetics directly from our own Eucalyptus Spa.*

She tugged on the drawer handle and, sure enough, there was a blue silk bag with the spa logo embroidered on the flap. Inside, she found a never-been-used brush wrapped in sealed plastic, which was like heaven in her hair. And some powder, fresh mascara, and a light peach lip gloss.

The note inside said, "Enjoy your stay in Barefoot Bay. Kick off your shoes and fall in love!"

Ah, yes, the clever and ridiculously optimistic tag line that came with the Casa Blanca account and had to be incorporated in every ad, brochure, and web design. Emma might kick off her shoes and enjoy the company of a handsome stranger, but she'd never fall in love again. Never, ever.

Love was for idiots and fools and losers who bought what advertisers were shoveling out. Love was a fabrication used to sell stuff. Who knew that better than an advertising copywriter?

She cleared her throat and took one more look in the mirror. Better. Still bitter, but better.

And she sure could use that wine.

Jilted.

Mark thought about the word, and the woman who used it, while he sat at the table for two on the patio, enjoying the sight of the tangerine ball of sun slowly falling into Barefoot Bay. When the French door opened, he turned and tipped his head in silent appreciation of another sight equally as attractive.

She'd washed, brushed, and pulled herself together. Quite nicely, too. Her hair cascaded like a chocolate waterfall over her shoulders, her eyes bright, her skin clear, especially considering the tears. Thank God there were no more tears.

She walked toward him, giving him a moment to admire a feminine figure he hadn't really noticed in the middle of her crisis. Trim but curvy enough to appeal to him, with long legs in tight jeans, her bare feet adding a surprising kick of sexiness.

What kind of blind and stupid guy walked away from that before the wedding bells rang?

There might be more to that story. One thing he knew about romance gone south—and he did know plenty considering the business he'd been in for so many years—there were always two sides to the coin. Although this side was definitely fine.

"Feeling better?" he asked, pushing his chair back to stand as she approached.

A quick flash of her golden eyes told him the basic level

of chivalry surprised her. So the ex was a dick in all areas, he surmised.

"Better on the outside," she admitted. "And thank you again for letting a bawling stranger into your villa."

"It was silence you or face charges," he joked.

She smiled. "But you didn't have to listen to my tale of misery or share your wine."

He reached for the stemless bistro glass and offered it to her. "I have a soft spot for orphans and strays," he said. "I also like a nice sauvignon at sunset. I had the owner order a case of my favorite for the week."

She lifted her brows. "Fancy."

He laughed and met her glass in a toast. "Sorry. Didn't mean to rub it in."

"It's okay." She took a sip and closed her eyes as the mix of oak and vanilla hit her palate just as it hit his. "The view is rubbing it in enough."

"Please." He gestured to the other chair. "Relax. I'm Mark, by the way, stealer of your villa."

"Emma." She sat down and gazed out to the view with a low, sad sigh. "And you can't be held responsible for your good fortune and my bad choice."

"Hello, Emma." He tasted the name, like the wine, liking the feel of it in his mouth.

"Well, this place has lived up to its reputation, and I'm pleased about that," she said. "I knew I'd love it here, just like I knew every word I wrote was the truth. For once, I wasn't lying about the product."

The product?

She gestured toward the water. "Panoramic views." Then the villa. "World-class accommodations." Then him. "High-end clientele."

His confused frown deepened. "You lost me."

She set her glass down with a rueful smile. "I wrote the advertising copy for this place. I'm a copywriter for an agency in New York, at least I was until I resigned two weeks ago. That's when my boss, who was also my fiancé, walked into my office and said those four dreadful words no woman wants to hear when she's on hold with her wedding planner to finalize the tulip delivery."

Oh yeah, the guy was a monumental douchebag. "I don't like tulips?" he guessed with a smile.

"'We have to talk.'" She closed her eyes. "And you just know it's not about the copy for next week's new business presentation."

"That sucks."

She smirked at the understatement. "Anyway, Casa Blanca Resort & Spa is one of the agency's top accounts. That's how I knew about it and why I wanted to honeymoon here. This whole island is like a dream to me." She gave a soft snort. "So was the wedding, come to think of it."

"Oh man, now I feel even worse. You should have this place. You pulled strings and used your connections and—"

"No, no." She held up her hand. "I didn't. My ex pulled the strings, trust me. Including the one that canceled the reservation, except he hadn't done it yet when I called or I would still be in bed in Brooklyn licking my wounds."

"Didn't you tell them at the front desk who you are?"

"Nah. I'm just the pen monkey in the bowels of the creative department who'd never been to a place like this and couldn't stop thinking about it. For once in my career, I believed in what I was writing about. My other accounts? No, I didn't care if a checking account earned more interest at Community Bank or if All Green fertilizer really improved the grass. I don't believe that Colombian Cups coffee really has zero aftertaste. But is Casa Blanca Resort &

Spa really perfection in paradise? Yes. And there's something empowering about marketing the truth for a change."

She finished her speech with a good slug of wine, and Mark couldn't wipe the smile from his face. She was as refreshing as the sauvignon blanc and maybe as complex. And maybe, with the setting sun picking up flecks of gold in her hair and eyes, a little bit intoxicating, too.

"It was my fault, completely," she said, dropping her head back a little and giving him a tantalizing view of the long, lean column of her throat.

"A broken relationship is never anyone's fault *completely*."

"Oh, it can be." She peered at him through narrowed lashes. "But I meant assuming the reservation wouldn't be canceled at the very last minute was my fault. Being left holding a Vera Wang gown and a truckload of embarrassment? All on his skinny shoulders." She straightened her head and added a tight smile. "Sorry if I sound cynical, but I've spent the last two weeks realizing that the stupidest thing a human can do is buy into the dreams spun by marketing professionals."

"Says the person who writes ad copy for a living." He chuckled. "I imagine that could make you a little jaded."

"Jaded, jilted, and jobless—that's me." Her smile loosened as she held up the glass. "I like a wine that brings out my alliteration skills."

Laughing, he shook his head, enjoying this unexpected twist on his first day at the resort. "An alluring atmosphere for an afternoon of alliteration."

Her jaw opened with her delight as she raised the glass in a toast. "A-plus!"

They both laughed and took a drink, the wine and sun

warming him as much as the company. It made the whole concept of the event so much more bearable to be with someone. And not just anyone, but a woman with some...zing.

A woman who not only caught his eye, but made him laugh. So few had been able to do that since...well, since Julia.

She treated him to a wide, sweet smile. "Thank you for rescuing a massively crappy day."

He nodded in acknowledgment, tempted to tell her the feeling was mutual, but she might take that the wrong way.

"Hard to believe you've done all that for this resort and they couldn't find you another room or villa," he said instead.

"Apparently, the whole resort is booked solid."

"It's the high school reunion," he said.

"Really? What kind of high school can afford this swanky place?"

"Mimosa High, the local one. The owner is a graduate, and shortly after she first opened this place, she hosted a high school reunion on the beach, I guess to drum up business."

"Really? The business is booming, from what I hear."

"I don't know, but the idea caught on, and now she's having another. And word got out that the place is great, and it hasn't been here that long, so I guess that was enough to attract a lot of Mimosa High graduates."

"Including you?"

"Including me."

"So, you grew up on this island? You actually lived here?"

"Eighteen years before I moved away."

She gave an envious moan. "Why would you leave?"

He shrugged. "Life. Work." And too many memories to come back to.

She leaned closer, examining him. "What year reunion is it?" He could practically hear her brain doing the math on his age.

"All years, from five to fifty, since it wasn't that big of a high school. And I'm—don't drink before I say this now, or you'll spew—I'm on the planning committee."

She threw her head back and gave a hearty laugh, giving him another blast of attraction and maybe a little self-satisfaction that he'd taken her from sobbing to laughing in less than an hour.

"How'd you get dragged into that?" she asked.

"I'm still trying to figure that out," he admitted. "I guess I felt sorry for Lacey, who was having a hard time scaring up men for her committee."

"So I gotta ask," she said, leaning forward, her eyes gleaming a little playfully.

Oh, here it came. The inevitable question. *Where's the wife?* Followed by the conversation that would bring everything down. If only he had a wife handy, he wouldn't have to constantly make excuses for not having one.

"What is it?" she asked.

"What is...what?" What was the reason he was alone? He hadn't had enough wine to be that honest.

"The theme," she said. "Every reunion has a theme. Memory Lane or The Way We Were or Remember When. Something cheesy that will be in glitter glue on the ribbons tied around the favors."

He laughed with a combination of relief and genuine appreciation for her humor. "Damn, woman. You've done this before."

"Twice. Cheesy phrases are my specialty. So, what is it?"

"Timeless."

She leaned back and crossed her arms, nodding. "That's good. I like it. Especially for an all-class reunion. Timeless has a lot of potential."

"Glad the committee has your approval." He winked, getting another smile in return. "Remind me to drag you along to the next meeting." That would keep the vultures away from him.

"So that's why the resort is sold out without so much as a closet in the housekeeping bungalow for me to rent, huh? It's all Mimosa High's fault." She shook her head, then her eyes flashed. "Oh, I left my bags outside."

"I put them in the living room for you."

"Really?" She lifted her glass. "To gentlemen. A dying breed if there ever was one."

He toasted but lifted his brow. "Hey, you sound bitter again."

She sighed. "Can you blame me?"

"I don't know. What happened with skinny-shoulder guy?"

She closed her eyes and gave in to a very slight smile. "Heidi happened."

"Oof." Mark shook his head and felt his lip curl. "Cheaters are the worst."

"I agree, but he didn't cheat. Oh, that would have just slayed me completely. No, Heidi is his sister. He spent a weekend skiing with her and came back with cold feet, and not from too much time in the snow. I guess they stayed up all night talking, and she made him really think I was not his professional equal or some such nonsense."

"He told you that?"

"Not in so many words, but he danced around it enough for me to get the subtext. I guess I should never have dated my boss."

"You can't help who you fall for," he said.

She tilted her head, thinking. "I don't know if I would have described that as 'falling' as much as…sliding into it. Anyway, it was advertising," she said, as if that explained it. "And you know advertising."

"No, I don't know advertising."

"Built on lies. And affairs, though I've never had one. But it really is like *Mad Men*, only without the two-martini lunches."

"*Mad Men*?"

"The TV show."

"Never heard of it."

She drew back. "Where have you been for the last decade?"

"Mountains, rivers, cliffs, and deserts. Places that don't have television."

She eyed him for a moment. "I guess I can see that lifestyle on you. You've got that whole Ralph Lauren Goes on an Adventure vibe."

"Ralph Lauren?"

"Talk about selling an aspirational image," she said. "But, yes, advertising is an industry built on lies."

"Why don't you try your hand at something else now?"

"Because it's what I know, what I do," she answered. "Except…"

When her voice faded, he looked at her, silently inviting her to continue.

"According to my ex, I seem to be lacking ambition and skill because I've been in advertising almost fifteen years, and I haven't made the management ranks yet."

"The more you tell me about this guy, the happier I am for you."

She smiled. "I liked my job enough, even though it was

fairly low level. I liked the creativity. And I guess the late nights working on client crises."

"Late nights at work? Who likes that?" he asked.

"A single woman." She gave him a sad smile. "Then, after holding firm until I was thirty-eight years old, I fell for the mother of all marketing ploys: love."

He didn't know whether to laugh or reach over the table and shake some sense into her. "Love isn't a marketing ploy," he said.

She looked skyward with a cynical eye roll. "It is a 'key message,' as we say, used to sell long white dresses, overpriced flowers, dreamy honeymoons at places like this." She shook her head. "Truth is, I was perfectly happy before I got sucked into all of that, even though they have names for nearly forty-year-old women who've never been married."

"Smart, independent, self-sufficient, and able to set her own course in life?"

She put her hand on her chest as if his words had touched her heart. "Yeah, that's the spin we single girls like to put on it. Beats old maid who missed the boat because she was too…afraid to commit. Finally did, and wham, slam, good-bye, ma'am."

Laughing at her clever phrases, he stood to go to the wet bar and get the chilled wine. "Well, I'm really sorry I added to your mess by taking the last villa in Casa Blanca."

"It's not your fault," she assured him. "I don't blame you. I envy you the fine accommodations, but I don't blame you."

From the wet bar, holding the bottle, Mark studied her as she took in the view. For a second, he imagined that she belonged right there, on his villa patio, drinking, talking, and laughing. A sharp stab of longing hit.

Forget bringing her to a meeting. How nice would it be to have someone charming and smart and funny to take to the events this entire week? Someone who could help him ward off the hungry sharks. Someone who would make sure no one even *asked* about Julia. Someone...like her.

"Emma." He slowly crossed the space, holding the wine as an idea took shape. "I have an offer for you."

"An offer." She gave a tentative smile. "That sounds interesting."

"It might be. You want to stay here, right?"

"You giving the place up?" she asked.

"No." He sat down and held the bottle over her empty glass. "But I'll share it."

Her eyes widened, and she made a little grunt, putting her hand out to stop him from pouring. "I think we've had enough wine, cowboy."

"I'm serious."

She puffed out a breath. "Listen, you're gorgeous, with the whole silver fox thing going on, but—"

"I don't want to sleep with you."

She tipped her head and lifted a brow. "Just a platonic share, huh? You and me in the king-size bed with Scheherazade drapes and candles in the bath? Yeah, right."

Actually, the idea didn't pain him in the least. The more he listened and watched, the more he liked her and wanted her company. But what he needed was a woman to stop the questions he wouldn't be able to avoid all week. No one would bring up Julia with another woman in the picture. But it would have to be a woman who people believed was permanent, not a casual date.

He hadn't told a single person here whether or not he was single. He worked so hard to avoid the question that he'd completely succeeded.

"I don't want to sleep with you," he repeated. "I want to marry you."

Chapter Three

Emma whipped around, almost falling out of her seat. "*What?*"

"Just for this week, and this"—he gestured toward the beach—"audience."

"What in God's name are you talking about?" She blinked in dismay, her mind whirring with possible escape routes.

"Hear me out. I need someone to…deflect things so I can get through this week. You need your vacation in paradise. Come to a few events with me, say you're my wife, and I'll give you the master suite while I sleep on the couch and use the guest bathroom."

She could feel her jaw loosen and mouth grow wider and wider at each word. "Deflect things?" she asked, not sure the rest of his proposal—God, not another meaningless one—really sank in.

"I just don't want…questions," he said, shifting a little in his seat.

He didn't want questions? "From me? Too bad. You're getting them. Why would I agree to do that for you?"

"I'll tell you the story," he said. "And I think you'll understand."

Doubtful, but she reached for the wine and filled her glass. "I think I need this, after all."

He took a second to gather his thoughts while she took a healthy drink. "I graduated from Mimosa High in 1986," he began.

She did some quick math in her head and gave a low whistle, searching his face again. Yeah, he had salt-and-pepper hair, but his face was youthful, and his body was... *Don't think about that, Emma.*

"All throughout high school, I was attached to one girl. And by attached I mean..." He thought for a second. "I guess I don't know how to describe it to someone who thinks true love is a marketing slogan."

"Try."

He pinned her with his sharp blue gaze. "Okay, we married two months after graduation."

"High school graduation?" Her lips curled in a smile. "How'd that not-so-wise choice go for you?"

"Perfectly. She was everything I ever wanted, and I loved her with my entire body, soul, and being."

She drew back slightly, so not expecting that. Then what was the issue? "Please don't tell me she ran off with the bad boy from shop and is here with him and you want to show her how happy you are without her."

"I wish."

Frowning, she lifted the glass again. "Now *you've* lost *me...*"

"We got married at eighteen, and we were married for fourteen years."

Something in his tone—something dark and serious—kept her from making another joke or even a comment.

"She was diagnosed with cancer at thirty-two and died three weeks later from a rare allergic reaction to chemo."

"Oh." The word caught in her throat and, immediately, her eyes stung. "Wow. I'm sorry."

"Don't be, please. I've had all the sympathy I can take. Sixteen years have passed and I'm *fine*." He stressed the word, as if he'd said it so many times it was tattooed on his brain and heart. *Fine*.

"I'm sure you are," she said, sadness squeezing her heart. "It's so unfair, this life."

"There are no guarantees," he agreed. "But you go on."

She looked hard at him, drinking in the aura of strength he exuded. He'd gone on...alone. "So everyone at this reunion knew her?" she asked.

"Knew and loved her. Knew us. MarkandJulia were"—he smacked his hands together with a loud clap—"a single thing."

She dragged herself back to the bizarre marriage offer, not entirely making the trip from the loss of a wife everyone knew to...*that*. "I still don't get where you're going with this."

"Her name, of course, will come up a lot this week."

"And you want to avoid that?" she asked.

"That and the inevitable questions about my state of...widowhood. And those who'd like to change it."

"So you don't want to answer those questions or deal with flirty women enough that you'd fake a wife?" she asked, her voice rising in disbelief.

"I don't," he acknowledged. "I hate the questions. And I hate being asked why I haven't remarried."

And, of course, that's all she wanted to ask now.

"Sorry to break it to you," she finally said. "But I'm not the best emissary for the institution of marriage these days. Couldn't I just be your date?"

He shook his head. "A girlfriend is not an impediment to some women. Some...determined women."

Oh yeah. Who wouldn't want a catch like him? "Good-looking guy who likes orphans and strays? You're a package of silver catnip."

He gave a slow, achingly sexy smile. "I meet a lot of perfectly nice women, but…I'm not interested in anything serious or long term. Still, this would work if my companion has an official, permanent title."

She lifted one dubious brow.

"You'd have this great place to stay for the week."

There was that. But not at all what she'd expected when she got on that plane in NYC and flew to Florida. "It was supposed to be a romantic vacation in paradise," she said.

"But you came alone," he replied. "So you must want something out of this week in Barefoot Bay."

She wanted an escape, yes. Sun. Sand. But certainly not a man.

"I came down here to clear my head and get over what happened to me, but more than that, I wanted to experience the place. It's stuck in my head and heart, and I wanted to be here." She shrugged. "Of course, it would be nice to get to the point with my ex where I…"

"Forgive him?" he suggested.

She snorted. "Not want to stab his eyes out with a hot poker."

"A week in paradise could get you there and, you never know, maybe I can help you with that."

She rolled her eyes. "Now this fake marriage is going to make me forget him?"

"I only meant because my late wife and I started an Internet company called Seeking Soulmates. It grew out of a syndicated romantic advice column she wrote. We eventually turned it into one of the first Internet dating services, which sold to a much bigger and better-known service. In my career, I learned a lot about love, romance, and, of course, the elusive happily ever after."

Elusive? How about it didn't exist, except in the minds of people who were selling the dream, including Internet dating services? "I have to be honest, Mark. Internet dating is kind of my idea of the seventh level of hell. Talk about lies to sell more lies."

He inched a little closer. "I can help you, Emma," he said. "And you can help me."

He was crazy. He was gorgeous. He was...magnetic. How on earth had a guy in the George Clooney league of hot, loaded, and smart not been lassoed and branded by a woman in sixteen years?

"You're not going to like this," she finally said. "But I have to ask."

"Why haven't I remarried?" he asked, obviously knowing what she was thinking.

"Well, yeah. I mean, most men in your situation hook up pretty fast with wife number two."

He looked down at his glass, thinking for a moment. "She was my soul mate," he said softly, finally meeting her gaze. "And there was, is, and never will be any other woman for me. Ever."

Wow. Holy...*wow*. What...would that be like? Was it even possible to have that kind of love? What did it feel like, other than pure bliss?

She opened her mouth to reply, but a doorbell rang and stopped her. He hesitated a moment, then stood.

"Excuse me," he murmured, getting up. "Just think about it, okay?"

How could she think about anything else?

She listened to his footsteps in the living room, turning to the French doors for one last glimpse of the most extraordinary man—and offer—she'd come across in a long time. Her initial instinct, of course, was to run and hide.

Emma DeWitt always took the safe way out, and the one time she hadn't, it had blown up in her face. But this…

"Oh, hello, Lacey."

Lacey Walker. Emma had never met the woman, but she'd certainly heard about the dynamic resort owner who was one of East End Marketing's clients. And, after writing the "history of Casa Blanca" document for the stockholders' annual report, Emma had deep respect for the woman who had lost her home in a hurricane and used the opportunity and her windfall of waterfront property to build an exclusive resort. And married the architect.

No wonder she thought everyone should kick off their shoes and fall in love. She had.

"I just wanted to make sure you settled in okay, Mark." Lacey's voice drifted out to the patio. "And let you know how much I appreciate your agreeing to be here early and help with some last-minute details of the event."

Curiosity tweaked, Emma stood, slowly walking toward the door for a possible glimpse of the woman she'd written about.

"I'm fine, thanks," Mark said. "The place is fantastic, and I'm happy to be here."

"Even though you were only slightly attacked at the meeting," Lacey said with a teasing laugh.

So it was true, then. Poor guy. So in demand that he needed to create a significant other.

Although, Emma had to admit the idea had a surprising amount of appeal. It would mean a great vacation in paradise and…and…he needed help. How bad could he be, a guy who'd loved his wife that much? He'd been through a lot. The worst.

"It's all good," he said easily to Lacey.

Affable and kind. How could Emma *not* help him?

"Well, you haven't heard everything yet," Lacey said.

Emma stepped closer, their position in the entryway blocking her view of Lacey, but she could hear the exchange.

"Not sure I like the sound of that," Mark said with a nervous laugh.

"Well, you know that Robert's Rules dictates that when you leave a committee meeting, you are likely to be signed up to do things...all kinds of things." Lacey's voice was teasing, but not completely.

What had poor Mark been signed up to do? "Don't tell me. The tablecloth subcommittee."

Lacey laughed. "No, nothing like that. I think you missed this at the meeting, but the festivities at the reunion include a dance competition featuring songs from the different decades and choreographed routines. We're calling it Dance of the Decades, but it's a riff on *Dancing With the Stars*."

Nothing but silence for at least three seconds, and Emma covered her mouth to keep from laughing at what she imagined Mark's response to that would be.

"You know *Dancing With the Stars*," Lacey added.

Of course not, Emma thought. He didn't know *Mad Men*, either.

"So you want me to judge the competition?"

"No." She gave a nervous laugh. "You were signed up to dance."

During the long silence, Emma stepped just inside the French doors.

"Didn't Law Monroe and Ken Cavanaugh tell you I wouldn't do that?" he finally asked.

"Well, they left, too."

"Then they can dance."

"Well, it's kind of been decided by the committee. And at least half the women offered to help you learn the dance routine and, of course, be your partner."

Another silence.

Emma didn't know the man. Didn't know squat about him except what he'd shared with her. Yet, something urged her an inch closer. Sympathy for his plight, maybe. *Something.*

"The dance will only be a few minutes long." Lacey was speed-talking now, trying to convince him. "You know, a selection of songs from the eighties. That's your decade. We're doing five different decades and..."

Emma stepped through the doorway, and Lacey immediately noticed her behind Mark.

"Oh, hello," she said to Emma.

"Hi." Emma gave a slightly shaky smile. This was crazy...but...what had she just learned in the past ten minutes? Life was short.

"Hello." Lacey stepped around Mark and offered her hand. "I'm Lacey Walker, and I own the resort."

Mark turned, coming closer to Emma, a little confusion on his expression, but that might just be the aftermath of learning he'd been volunteered to dance. "Lacey, this is—"

"Emma DeWitt," Emma gave Lacey's hand a firm shake. "I'm Mark's fiancée," she added, the words sounding far too familiar. She'd been somebody's fiancée; she could play that role. "Nice to meet you, Lacey."

Emma looked up and met Mark's blink of surprise, seeing it morph into a smile and a conspiratorial wink.

Instantly, he slipped his arm around her and tugged her closer. "Yeah. My fiancée."

"Emma. How...lovely." Lacey shook Emma's hand and

looked from one to the other, her pretty brown eyes glinting with uncertainty and pleasure at the news. "So then I guess I only have one question," Lacey said.

Only one? Emma wondered. More like how, when, and why are you lying? She braced for the accusations.

"Do you dance?" Lacey asked.

Like a wounded water buffalo. "Of course, I love to dance," she replied, cuddling a little closer to Mark, which, she had to be honest, didn't suck. "So no need for him to have any other partner or teacher."

He added a little pressure with a strong, secure, and grateful arm around her.

"Wonderful," Lacey exclaimed. "We're having a little gathering at my house tonight for the planning committee and their spouses who are here, so we'll give you the rest of the details then. I just live at the north edge of the property. Can you make it?"

"Uh, Lacey, we're—"

"Absolutely," Emma said, cutting off Mark's protest. "I'm looking forward to meeting the other members of the planning committee."

"Yes, of course," Mark agreed, likely remembering that meeting people with Emma on his arm was the whole idea of this charade. "What time should we swing by?"

"Come on over in an hour or so for cocktails and dinner," she replied, reaching forward to Emma. "And, really, I'm so happy to meet you. So happy Mark found…you."

With a quick good-bye, Lacey left, leaving the two of them in a quick moment of silence, then they both burst out laughing as they slowly untangled their arms from around each other's waist.

"You got a pair, I have to say," he said between chuckles.

"A pair of left feet." She bit her lip and put her hand to

her mouth. "I have no idea how to dance. Plus, the eighties is not my era, silver fox. You have me by ten years."

"But you..." He reached out and took her hand. "Seriously? You'll do this for me?"

His hand was large, a little rough, incredibly masculine. Nothing like Kyle's smooth hands. Nothing like anyone's she'd ever touched.

"I'm doing it for me," she insisted, pulling her fingers out of his before she did something stupid and brought his knuckles to her mouth for a taste. "I want my week in paradise, and this is my villa. I'll take that offer and be your fiancée. Wife was pushing it, but I know all about being a fiancée." She leaned a little closer. "And I even have the hardware since Skinny Shoulders let me keep the ring."

"Emma." He took her by the elbows and pulled her closer. "I love that you're not afraid of adventure."

Not afraid of adventure? He couldn't be more off the mark. "I'm terrified of adventure," she admitted. "But you just want me to lie. I do that for a living, remember?" She smiled up at him, committed to the concept now. "I will put a marketing spin on this engagement that will keep all the she-wolves away, and in return, I'll..." *Fall right into your arms.*

Oh, Emma, don't buy into another lie.

"I'll bask in the sun and forget Kyle Chambers ever lived."

But he didn't laugh. He just held her a little too close, a little too securely. A little too much like a man who was about to kiss her.

"Which will be great," she said on a whisper, finally slipping away from him. "This will be great."

Almost as great as kissing him, but she would never do something that stupid.

Chapter Four

Emma slipped in some earrings, stepped back, and took a look at herself in the mirror, liking the way the cream-colored linen pants and sleeveless tunic fell, adjusting the long gold chain that pulled it all together.

She'd bought this outfit imagining romantic dinners by the water and slow strolls on the beach under the moonlight...with her *husband*.

The one who was plagued by icy feet and an even icier heart.

Okay, it was time to forget Kyle and think about this. What had made her do something as impulsive as agreeing to this?

Sometimes she did impulsive things when she was nervous. Like the day she started her job at East End Marketing and fought tears on the way into the office because being single was pressing down and starting to get so old. About half an hour later, she met Kyle Chambers, and the next thing she knew...she was talking herself into him.

That's not what happened today, she mentally insisted. Mark Solomon was just...a harmless old widower, right?

Uh...*wrong*. Old if you were blind and harmless if you

were wearing a chastity belt. Out there was pretty much the best-looking man she'd laid eyes on in years, with an impressive athlete's body, a good heart, and the ability to make her do something she hadn't done in days: laugh out loud.

The rationalization continued like a bad song she couldn't get out of her head. *What's the harm? What's a little lie to strangers? What difference does it make that he's hot as hell?*

He'd offered her a week in paradise for the small fee of a little white fib to a bunch of strangers.

Yes, it had felt strange to lie to the lovely lady who owned this place—who, fortunately, had no idea Emma DeWitt worked on the Casa Blanca account as a copywriter. Mid-level scribes didn't get dragged into important client meetings. Emma had hoped when she moved from a behemoth ad agency on Madison Avenue to a small shop in SoHo that she'd get more client interaction, but the only interaction she got was with the boss.

She squinted her eyes and tried to picture Kyle when he'd come simpering into her cube a few weeks ago after his spontaneous ski trip with a sister he hadn't seen in a year.

But the wedding loomed. The big day. White lace and promises, right?

She'd clung to the damn marketing like it was her life raft in a sea of singleness. It had all been so right...so right out of the movies, including the quirky restaurant engagement.

"That reminds me..." Emma snapped her fingers and reached for her handbag, hanging on the back of the door. Deep in the back pocket, she found the satin pouch she hadn't packed in her checked luggage. In the little bag, she'd placed the emerald earrings Mom had given her. There was a necklace of value, a gold bracelet, and...the rock.

Not a huge rock, but it did the job.

Sliding the engagement ring onto her finger, she waited for the weight of sadness that had pulled her down the day she'd taken it off, at Starbucks, surrounded by busy New Yorkers taking a break from a slushy rain.

When she'd held the ring out to Kyle, he'd shaken his head and said, "It's yours."

"But you're not," she'd whispered in response, making him avert his eyes and push back his chair and end the world's most uncomfortable coffee date in history.

History, she reminded herself. Kyle was history.

She closed her bag and slipped it on her shoulder, checked for lipstick on her teeth, and smoothed her hair one last time. Then she stepped out into the fading evening light of the living room, glancing around for Mark.

After moving her bags into the villa's only bedroom, he'd taken his belongings and stored them somewhere and must have used the guest bath on the other side of the little house. The villa had one bedroom, but the living room sofa pulled out and accommodated at least one more person, so it wasn't like he had to sleep on the *floor*, for heaven's sake.

A few butterflies fluttered in her belly at the thought, and then she spotted him back on the patio, leaning against the railing. And those butterflies soared.

He'd changed to tan linen pants and a pale, short-sleeved shirt that fit his broad shoulders tightly enough to show them off, but with enough drape to say he didn't care if anyone noticed his body or not. His hair was completely dark in the back, but the last bits of sunlight picked up the silver threads at his temples, giving him the look of a man with wisdom, experience, power, and class.

And a hella fine backside.

He turned as she came outside, studying her while she

rounded the pool and approached him, his gaze dropping over her with the same flash of appreciation she imagined lit her eyes.

"I have a question, Mark."

"Shoot."

"How recently did we get engaged?"

He lifted a shoulder. "How about a month ago? I was in..." Dark brows knit as he thought about it. "Indonesia? No, Bhutan. The Sacred Rivers. Let's say we hiked to the Tiger's Nest Monastery, and I popped the question three thousand feet above Paro."

She choked a laugh. "Well, that makes getting engaged at Daniel in New York sound pretty pedestrian."

"Good restaurant, but not very romantic."

She rolled her eyes. "Okay, Bhutan it is. Three thousand feet off the ground because we were so in love, we were floating on air."

"You *are* a copywriter."

"To the bone," she acknowledged, lifting her left hand to wiggle the ring. "And I can fend off evil predators."

He reached for her hand to take a closer look. "So this was dessert at Daniel?"

"Actually, the appetizer. So we could spend the dinner planning."

He nodded, angling the ring to check it out. "I might have gone a little bigger, but not ostentatious."

"Do you think these people will judge?" she asked.

He lifted his shoulder. "I don't know. I don't talk to any of these people."

"Then why did you come?"

He started to answer, then stopped, catching himself. "I just did," he said. "You ready? We can walk up the beach to get there."

She didn't move, slowly crossing her arms. "No."

"What? You changed your mind?"

"No, you can't lie to me."

He frowned. "I'm not lying. You really do walk up the beach to get there."

"That's not what I mean. Just now, when I asked you why you came to this reunion, you said, 'I just did.' That's a lie."

He opened his mouth to argue, then closed it again.

"Am I right?"

"Possibly," he said after a second's hesitation. "Does it matter?"

"Why you came? No. Honesty? Yes. Very much. In fact, it's my deal-breaker. In this villa, when we are together, it's one hundred percent honesty or nothing at all."

He leaned closer and glanced side to side as if someone might be listening to him whisper, "You do realize you agreed to lie to every person you meet this week."

She caught a whiff of his aftershave, spicy and masculine, giving her an unexpected pull of attraction. "But I'm not lying to you. I can't do this if we dance around our conversations and tell each other half-truths. It's the truth, the whole truth, and nothing but the truth between us."

He studied her face for a long time, his expression changing, but she couldn't quite interpret his thoughts. "All right," he finally said. "No lies, only truth with us. I promise."

And she believed him. Not sure why, but Emma was certain Mark Solomon was a man of his word.

"Then answer the question," she said. "Why did you come if you have no friends or acquaintances at this reunion?"

He turned away, the hint of a smile lifting the corner of his mouth. "You're going to mock me mercilessly."

"And you would deny me that opportunity?"

He smiled at that. And then he reached into his pocket

and pulled something out, his fist closed around it. "For sixteen years, I've periodically received...guidance from my late wife."

"Like messages from the great beyond?" She had to work to keep the disbelief out of her voice.

"Exactly like that." He turned his hand over and opened his fingers to reveal what was in his palm. A ring with a bright red stone and writing on the side. A woman's ring, she realized, with a gold and black '86 on the side.

"Her class ring?" she guessed.

He nodded, his smile wry enough to tell her he saw the humor and irony and maybe a little bit of foolishness. "Lacey contacted me while I was in New Zealand, asked me to come and be here a week early to help with the planning. They were desperate to get men on the planning committee, and no one had said yes yet."

"But you did."

"Not at first. Hell no. I flat out refused the committee and the event, and not because I think I'm too good or too important or too busy, like a lot of the other men had said." He gave her a serious look. "I didn't want to open up wounds that have long closed and healed."

"Or at least scarred," she added, deeply suspecting that his grief wasn't truly *healed* yet.

"Completely scarred and numb," he agreed. "Anyway, I left Auckland and flew to New York, where I keep a small apartment. I had some papers I had to pick up from my safe-deposit box. When I was in it, I lifted up an envelope, and this ring fell out. I totally forgot I had kept it with some of Julia's things."

He held the ring with two fingers and angled it so they could both see it.

"And that was the message? Finding her ring?" Bit of a

stretch, Emma thought, but hey, she'd never been a widow.

"I had a flash of a memory from the day the rings arrived and we both put ours on. She was so excited. We were outside eating lunch, and she held the red stone to the sun and said, 'I'm going to wear mine forever. I'll be the only person at the high school reunion who still wears her Mimosa High ring.'"

Emma didn't say anything, watching his face as he relayed the story. No sorrow or grief, just a look of warm appreciation. Like he was grateful he'd had that moment with her.

"When Julia suggests something, I usually listen."

And maybe he was a total nut job. "How often does she, uh, talk to you?"

Laughing, he pocketed the ring. "And she mocks."

"Not mocking, just…it's a little out-there, don't you think?"

"It is, but it doesn't happen that often. Once every couple of years, something will hit me hard, especially when I have a decision to make. And if I listen to her advice, my choice usually turns out to be the right one."

"When was the first time?" she asked, fascinated by this romantic illusion.

"When I had the offer to sell Seeking Soulmates, the company we started together. I had no intention of selling, because we were profitable and I enjoyed running the business. Being a workaholic had kept me sane after Julia died, even though I didn't realize how burned-out I'd become."

Emma eyed him, seeing a man in his prime of health and life. She couldn't even imagine him burned-out. "So how did she deliver that message?"

"I'd fended off about six offers from larger companies because I just knew she wouldn't have wanted to sell to a huge conglomerate that would bury or kill the concept, no matter how much they offered. Then, I was approached by LoveInc.com."

"Ahh." She immediately recognized the name of the largest Internet dating site. "The 'love only happens if you take the chance' people. Kind of a lame tag line, if you ask me. And they *are* a huge conglomerate."

"Not back then. The owner had vision and millions in stock options before a public offering. The cash wasn't great, but his ideas for the company were. I was immediately tempted, but uncertain." He looked out to the water, which had settled into a million shades of twilight blue, but Emma couldn't take her eyes off him.

"So how'd she convince you to do it?" she asked, guessing that had to be where he was taking this story.

"I was in midtown, on my way home from a meeting with the LoveInc people, and it started to pour. Cabs were short, but I managed to snag one at the very same moment as a woman. I offered to let her have it, but she asked where I was going, I told her, and our destinations were close. She suggested we share."

Of course she did, Emma thought. Who wouldn't want to climb into a cab with George Clooney's blue-eyed brother?

"Her name was Julia," he said, his voice a little lower. "She looked nothing like my late wife, but she was very excited because she'd just gotten engaged. I asked how she met her fiancé, and she said—"

"LoveInc.com," Emma finished.

"Yep. She said it was the best experience, and if she were going to buy stock in a company, it would be that one. Those were her very words."

"Maybe she was an investment banker working on the deal and wanted you to buy in."

The corner of his mouth lifted. "You are a cynic. No, she was just a girl named Julia who needed a cab and unwittingly delivered a message that I should sell the company and take the stock offer. And that decision…"

"Made you a rich man."

"Beyond my wildest expectations," he confirmed.

Of course, that probably would have happened if he hadn't accidentally met a girl named Julia who raved about her online dating experience, but she couldn't help be charmed by the idea of a man who listened to his wife…even from the grave.

"So what do you think your late wife would have to say about the whole fake fiancée to fend off offers and questions idea?" Emma asked.

He thought about the question—really thought about it, she could tell—and then said, "I'm not sure."

"Maybe we'll find some seashells that spell out 'good idea, Mark' on the sand."

He laughed. "You're mocking."

"Ya think?"

He put an easy arm around her and guided her toward the villa. "So you're the fiancée who makes fun of me."

"I could be."

"I like that." He tightened his hold, pulling her an inch closer.

I like *that*, she thought. The realization made her slow her step, and he matched the timing, looking down at her.

"What is it?" he asked.

"Nothing."

He leaned back and raised his eyebrows. "Didn't you just set rules for complete honesty? Something is wrong, I can see it."

Nothing was wrong, but the reaction in her body when he

pulled her closer was...unexpected. And powerful. And stimulating.

And the last thing she wanted or needed was a man who made her feel *stimulated*.

"I don't know." She glanced away, his gaze a little too intense for her. "This whole thing is...spontaneous. That's not how I roll."

"You jumped on a plane to go on your honeymoon alone," he reminded her.

"And look how well that turned out."

"It's not too bad..." He brushed some hair off her cheek, the graze of his knuckles on her skin just making everything worse. "So far."

Her eyes shuttered at the touch and his deep voice.

"But I promised platonic," he added. "You have my word on that."

Too bad, whispered a devil in her ear. "Still, the whole thing scares me a little," she admitted.

"What part?" he asked.

"The part..." She looked up at him, almost immediately lost in the depths of crystal-blue eyes. "The part when it starts to feel like it's not pretend."

He looked into her eyes for the longest time, saying nothing. She could feel her pulse pound and her breath catch, hear the squawk of a distant gull and the splash of water, smell the spicy, woodsy scent of him and feel his warmth.

That would be *this* part, right now, she thought, as every sense was overloaded and time stood still.

"You know, I have a theory about fear," he said. "Any fear can be conquered by facing it head on. Just staring it right down and doing what scares you most. Three times."

"Three times?" she asked.

"That's the magic fear-beating number," he assured her.

"I had to parachute out of planes three times before I could deal with the sheer terror of it. First time I went rock-climbing? Same thing. Anything that comes with inherent risks needs to be faced down three times."

"So, how would that work here, exactly?"

"Depends on what you're scared of. Telling people a lie? Being trapped in a villa with me? Wanting to—"

"Kiss you," she whispered.

His eyebrows raised. "That's what you're afraid of?"

She swallowed and managed a nod. Afraid to do it…afraid that it might never happen. "I mean, out in public, if we're going to get people to believe we're really engaged, then we'll probably…kiss."

"You're absolutely right," he agreed. "So you know what we have to do."

"Three times?"

He smiled slowly. "Fast learner. I like that." He inched closer. "I like that a lot."

"On the mouth?"

"That's usually where I go first, but we can start with a peck on the check and build up, if you like."

"Okay…but…wait." She put a hand on his chest, wishing it weren't so hard and that she didn't want to press down so much. "How did you do this? How did you get me from 'gee, is this the smartest move?' to mouth-kissing?"

"I told you, face your fears." He lowered his face and brought his mouth a slight centimeter from hers.

She leaned into him and kissed his mouth very softly, barely touching, just the slightest whisper of a kiss, just enough to…melt. And thank God there would be two more after this.

Chapter Five

Heat sparked at the mouth-to-mouth contact, shooting a lightning bolt of arousal through Mark, shocking him as if he'd stuck his finger in a live socket.

What the holy hell was *that*?

Besides…nice. He felt his eyes close and his head tip to feel a little more of her lips against his, enjoying the sudden rush of pleasure that rolled through him. He broke the kiss and instantly went for number two, a little deeper and a lot longer.

Kiss number three included a brush of their tongues, swirling against each other until he felt pressure on his chest.

That was her hand, slightly fisted, unintentionally grabbing some of the material of his shirt.

He finally broke the contact, cursing himself for not insisting on five or six, or a dozen, attempts to conquer her fear.

Emma stayed exactly as she was, in the classic pose of a well-kissed woman, head tilted back, eyes closed, lips slightly parted. All he wanted to do was kiss her again.

He put his finger on her lips instead of his mouth and went for casual. "Okay, got that out of the way."

"Yeah." When he lifted his finger, she replaced it with

her own, lightly touching like a person checks a tender spot for pain. "Out of the way."

"So, we're good now?" he said.

"Good. Great. Just…" She eased back and looked at him as if her eyes were just focusing. "This is a really, really, *really* bad idea."

"You think?"

"I know." Stepping farther away, she shook her head a little. "I don't want…I can't…I'm not going to…I just got out of…"

He smiled. "I get the idea, Emma. I swear I'm not suggesting anything like that."

"Like what? Like that kiss? 'Cause, come on. You felt it. I felt it. We both felt the little earthquakes of trouble in that kiss."

Not so little, he mused.

She let out an exasperated breath. "I just wanted a place to stay and lick my *wounds*, not a *man*."

He laughed softly.

"I just need to figure out the rest of my life, Mark, and you seemed so nice and like you were in a bind, and I wanted to stay here more than anything, and it all made some sense until…"

Until that kiss.

"Look, Emma, if you want to bag this whole idea, that's fine. You can still stay here in the villa, and I'll just have a fiancée in the background, or we'll come clean with Lacey and go our separate ways." It stank, but he sure as hell wasn't going to force her into it if she was uncomfortable.

She nodded, sending a stab of disappointment into his belly. "I really think I should go home tomorrow." Taking a few steps away, she managed a smile. "You're really nice, Mark. Like, way too nice. The last thing I need is…kissing."

She started around the pool back into the house. "The *last* thing."

"Mark! Mark Solomon!" A female voice floated up from the beach, a few feet away on the other side of the path. He turned to see a woman he didn't recognize loping closer. She wore a bright pink beach cover-up, strapless, to the ground, her short dark hair spiking in multiple directions, which was probably not supposed to look like a cat that fell into hair gel, but did. "I missed the meeting today, but I heard you were here."

He frowned as she came closer, no name coming to mind, vaguely aware of Emma slipping out of sight.

"It's me! Margot Hutchinson!"

No recollection. None. "Hey, Margot." He fought the urge to turn to the villa and call Emma back.

"You do remember me! I thought you might. We had social studies together, though I'm a few years younger than you."

She flashed a pretty smile. Not as pretty as the mouth he just kissed, however.

"How are you?" he asked, hoping he hid the complete lack of interest in his question. Because the only thing he was interested in right now was the woman who disappeared into the villa. He had to convince her leaving was a bad idea.

"I'm better now that I heard you need a Dance of the Decades partner!" Margot came as close as she could get to the raised pool deck of the villa without actually climbing up to reach him. "You might remember I was the captain of the dance team, and I have my own studio in Tampa now. I'm a ballroom expert and..." She finally stopped and looked up, her smile turning to a serious look of intent. "We could win, Mark, I know we could. And I want to win."

"Win," he said, stealing a glance over his shoulder at the villa. *Why did you leave me now, Emma? I need you.*

"Hey, listen, Mark," the woman continued. "I know it's been a while, but I was so sorry when I heard about Julia all those years ago."

And there it was. Exactly what he wanted to avoid.

"I think about Julia all the time," the woman continued. "Every time I hear *Like a Virgin*. She and I used to have gym class together, and we made up a little dance to it." She lifted her hands and did a little boogie. "Touched...for the very first time," she sang. Off-key. "That line always made her blush, and I bet I know why." She let her voice rise in a little singsong tease.

Really, Julia? You dropped that ring in my lap to get me here...for this? So he could have inane conversations with Margot Whoevershewas?

"I figured you'd be at Lacey's tonight," Margot powered on. "But I didn't want to wait to ask you, because you'll be in huge demand. I heard Libby Chesterfield making noise about you, but she isn't a dancer. I'm a professional!" She punctuated that with the widest, whitest smile and outstretched arms. "Mark and Margot, what a team, right? What do you say?"

"I say..." Shit. That's what he'd say. Just...*shit*.

"Mark? Honey? Are you ready?" Emma's voice came from inside the house, floating over the pool like a warm, welcome breeze. "Shouldn't we leave soon?" She came outside, just as fresh and beautiful as the first time, only now, there was a truly conspiratorial spark in her eyes. "Who are you talking to, sweetheart?"

He turned to the woman on the path, noticing the smile had quickly faded.

"It's Margot...from the committee."

"Margot Hutchinson," the woman supplied. "And you are..."

Emma breezed around the pool, her dark hair fluttering as she walked. "I'm Emma DeWitt, Mark's fiancée. It's nice to meet you, Margot."

Margot's jaw dropped a little. "Oh, hi. Emma. Mark's...wow. I don't think anyone knew you'd gotten engaged."

"It's a pretty recent development," he said, sliding an arm around Emma as she got next to him.

"A month ago," Emma said. "In Peru. At the Sacred Tigers...monastery...nest. Have you heard of it?"

Mark bit his lip to keep from laughing.

"No." Margot's gaze slipped over Emma, checking her out. "Um, congratulations," she added, her bubbly enthusiasm waning.

He glanced at Emma again, a mix of admiration and sympathy. She didn't have to do this for him, but every time someone got close to his tender spot, she jumped in for the save.

"You sure you still want to go tonight?" he asked Emma. "I thought you weren't...feeling well."

"And let you go alone?" She gave a playful nudge. "Not a chance. I just got too much sun. Will we see you at the dinner party, Margot?"

"Yes, definitely." The woman took a few steps backward, obviously embarrassed and bewildered. "You'll be Mark's dance partner, I take it?"

Emma dropped her head on his shoulder, a move that felt ridiculously natural. "Of course."

"Great. Then...see you in a bit. Bye!" She tried for bright as she walked off and Emma gave a little wave.

When she was out of earshot, he turned to her. "What changed your mind?"

"I don't know, I just..."

"Truth, Emma."

She looked back at the villa, a frown on her face, then back at him. "You'll be shark bait if I don't circle you in these waters. I can't stand to see a grown man eaten alive."

"You pity me? Is that the truth, the whole truth, and nothing but the unvarnished truth?"

She hesitated, then shook her head. "I really liked that kiss," she whispered, so soft he barely heard her.

Pulling her closer, he kept his voice just as soft. "I liked it, too."

Chapter Six

"How did we meet?" Emma asked as they left the villa and turned onto the stone path that led to Lacey and Clay Walker's home at the northern most edge of the resort.

"Good question," he said, taking her hand as they walked. The gesture was perfectly harmless; the quiver in her belly that it caused was not. "We'll get asked that a lot, and we should have the same answer."

"We could say online through LoveInc." She leaned into him. "Keep that stock price high."

He gave a soft choke. "Not in a million years would I meet someone online."

"Isn't that like Mrs. Fields not eating carbs?"

"It's like Mrs. Fields not eating poison cookies. There are some serious whack jobs out there."

"Says the man who asked a perfect stranger to marry him twelve minutes after he found her lurking outside his front door."

He laughed, pulling her hand to bring her closer. "You're funny, you know that?"

"Don't change the subject, George. How did we meet?"

"George? It's Mark. If you can't remember my name, we'll never pull this off."

"George, like Clooney. You remind me of him, except for the blue eyes. Hasn't anyone ever told you that?"

He rolled those blue eyes, which she took as a yes. "Okay, how we met." He thought for a moment, glancing at her as if he were trying to imagine where he'd meet a woman like her. "I met you on a plane. It's where I spend half my life anyway."

"But I don't. A subway would be more appropriate."

"I haven't been on a subway in ten years."

Of course he hadn't. "Well, that's where you'd have found me, but okay. Let's live your exciting life and not my boring one. A plane it is. Flying to Paris? And we spent the week there and fell in love?" As if *that* happened to anyone in real life. "You know, we strolled the Champs-Élysées, sipped coffee in bistros in between shopping and museums, and kissed for the first time under l'Arc de Triomphe?"

He gave her a quizzical look.

"What? Too cliché for you?"

"I'm just wondering if that's your idea of a dream romance."

"I don't have an idea of a dream romance because I don't believe in romance."

"Oh, that's right, the cynical advertising writer comes out again. I have a better cliché. How about we were skydiving, and your parachute almost failed, so you clung to me, and by the time we hit bottom, *wham*."

"Oh!" She dropped her head back, laughing. "So not cliché. Unless you're falling in love with James Bond. But I can't skydive. What if someone asked me a technical question?"

"You'll handle it about as well as you handled the Sacred

Rivers and the Tiger's Nest Monastery. In *Paro*, not Peru."

"Whoops. So let's stick with the plane to Paris for our first meet," she suggested. "But be sure to say we sat in first class."

"Why not?" he teased. "Go big or go home."

"And how long ago did this happen?" she asked.

"How whirlwind of a courtship was this?"

"The week in Paris," she replied.

"We got engaged after a week?"

"Go big or go home," she reminded him. "Plus, we don't want to have too much history together. We'll get tripped up. And people might wonder why they haven't heard about this on Facebook or something."

"Facebook?"

"Please don't tell me you..." She caught him laughing. "Okay, you know what Facebook is."

"But I've never been on it."

"It's like you stepped out of the last millennium. Do you have a cell phone?"

"Of course. But, honestly, when I sold the company, I checked out. My goal is to put my feet on every country in the world, climb the highest mountain on each of the seven continents, and conquer El Capitan before I'm fifty." He threw her a grin. "Clock's ticking, but I'll make it."

"Those are lofty goals, for sure. Beats 'stay out of the unemployment line' and 'stop renting before I'm fifty.'" She returned his grin. "Clock's ticking, but I have twelve years, although if I stay in New York, that last one will never be reached."

"Have you considered moving?"

She shrugged. "Advertising is kind of based in New York, but if I could, I'd live somewhere warm and clean and affordable. Like..." She swept her hand out. "Mimosa Key."

Her voice caught with the longing. "But I doubt there are too many ad agencies in Barefoot Bay."

"So start one."

She snorted softly. "You are fearless. So I guess it makes sense that you 'adventure' for a living, if I may use that as a verb."

"You may not. I *travel*," he corrected. "And I happen to enjoy extreme sports."

"Sounds more like you escape and enjoy risking your life."

"That's just semantics."

"Semantics are my life, remember? I work with words for a living." She sighed. "At least I did."

"Hey." He gave her hand a squeeze. "Don't think about that this week. You'll get a job because you're too good not to."

Holding on to that infusion of confidence—and his incredibly strong and secure hand—they rounded the path past the last of the villas, the one called Rockrose, and caught sight of a beautiful two-story hacienda built on a rise to overlook the bay on one side and the rolling fields of a farmette on the other.

A few cars were parked in the circular drive, and some people gathered on the side lawn.

"Mark, you made it," a man called from the group and broke away to greet them. He looked close to Mark's age, with thick hair with a good shock of silver on the sides.

"Okay, Em," Mark whispered, giving her a squeeze before they separated. "Fiancée game face on."

She squared her shoulders a little and gave him a quick smile. "Paro, not Peru."

The man reached them and gave Emma a killer smile and

outstretched hand. "You are definitely not a Mimosa High graduate. I would never forget those eyes."

Nor would she forget his, which were intense and direct and the color of fresh sage. "I'm not, but I still want to come to the party."

"You better," he teased, giving her a flirtatious up and down.

"Law, this is Emma, my fiancée."

Law's brows rose in surprise. "You didn't mention a fiancée this afternoon."

Because he didn't have one this afternoon.

"You didn't ask," Mark replied, sliding a strong and secure arm around her shoulder. "Emma, this is Lawson Monroe, but we called him Lawless."

She laughed at that. "I bet there's a good reason why."

"So many I don't know where to start," Lawson said, slipping his hands into the pockets of khaki pants.

"Start with why the hell you let me be put on that dance thing," Mark said.

"I tried to tell them you didn't dance, but your name was at the top of the list."

Mark glared at him, a little playful, but not completely. "You better be dancing your ass off."

"Me?" As he lifted his arms, a little bit of ink peeked out where his corded forearms weren't quite covered by the rolled-up sleeves of a blue chambray shirt. "We're in the same decade, dude. You own the eighties, and I mean that in the nicest possible way. Those ladies couldn't get your name on the list fast enough." He added a wink for Emma that made her wonder just what went on in that meeting.

"What about Ken? He could do the nineties."

Law shook his head. "Red Sweater wasn't dancing and,

don't tell our friend we're on to him, but I'm pretty sure she's the only reason he's here."

Mark swore under his breath. "Remind me to find better backup next time."

"Why'd you leave?" Law asked, then looked at Emma. "Dumb question. I'd have ditched that thing, too, if someone so pretty was waiting for me at home."

"Thank you," she said with a tip of her head. "And that's where I was, sitting on the front porch, waiting for him to come home."

Law laughed, but probably didn't get the real joke like Mark did, who secretly squeezed her shoulder.

"So why are you on this nearly all-female committee?" Emma asked Law.

He looked around with that swaggery confidence women loved, and it worked well on a body that had to call the gym a second home. "I needed some time on Mimosa Key," he said. "Got some plans for the place."

"That sounds interesting."

"If Law's involved, his plans include a bar, multiple women, and probably the cops."

Law gave him a tight smile, shaking his head. "One out of three, my man. I've changed most of my wicked ways."

"You're wicked enough to let me get dragged into some decade dance."

Law gave Mark a slap on the shoulder. "I'll make it up to you by buying you a drink."

"They're free," Mark said.

"Exactly. Bar's in the back."

"Of course you'd know that," Mark mumbled.

Law leaned closer to Emma to whisper, "Some things never change. I'm looking for trouble, and Mark Solomon is trying to keep me out of it."

"Oh, you know Mark," she said. "Orphans and strays."

"Anyone in trouble, really," Law agreed, the comment making her smile. At least she was "engaged" to a good guy this time.

Law motioned them to the lawn that wrapped around and fed into a patio area, where another twenty or thirty people mingled.

"Were you two classmates?" Emma asked as they walked.

"I'm *so* much younger than he is," Law said.

"Three years." Mark slid him a look. "Although it might have taken him eight or ten to graduate."

"Made it in four, big guy, and rocked a D-plus average. But I'd have dropped out if this guy"—he gave Mark's shoulder a solid slap—"hadn't taken me under his big ol' football shoulder pad and got me out of a few brushes with the Collier County Sheriff's Department."

"More than a few," Mark reminded him.

Law nudged them and gestured to a group of people. "Look, Solomon, someone older than you."

A very old man with gray Einstein hair and a full suit and tie sat in an oversize wicker chair, holding court with a number of people leaning in to hear his every word.

"Is that Wigglesworth?" Mark asked with disbelief. "Holy hell, I can't believe he's still alive."

"Barely," Law said. "He might not have any teeth left, but I'm still afraid of his bite. I hear he still hangs around the school, too, looking for dress-code violators and troublemakers."

"Your people," Mark joked.

"Who is he?" Emma asked. "The dean?"

"He was not only our principal," Mark said, "but one of the last living founders of Mimosa Key, a group of guys who built the first wooden causeway back in the forties and claimed a lot of the land, making a mess out of county lines and such. He started Mimosa High and ran it with a steel rod, literally, all the way through to the late nineties, when he retired."

"He's ninety-six years young." Law gave Mark a teasing nudge. "Go stand by him. You'll feel like a kid again."

"Go get us drinks, rookie," Mark shot back.

"Only because your fiancée is gorgeous, but then I'm taking off."

"You have somewhere better to be than at the reunion planning committee dinner?" Mark asked.

"Headed down to the old TP."

Mark made a disgusted snort. "The Toasted Pelican? I seem to recall picking you up one night when you got kicked out for sneaking some beer."

"Pelican Piss, the finest brew of Mimosa Key."

"Is that place still there?" Mark asked.

"It's not only there, I heard from the woman next to me at the meeting that the ownership changed recently."

"So the beer improved?"

"Actually, I heard the place is empty half the time, and I'm hoping it might be for sale."

"Are you looking for a bar?" Emma asked.

"Law Monroe is always looking for a bar," Mark jabbed.

"Not anymore, my friend. I haven't had a sip of booze in almost eleven years. But that doesn't stop me from wanting to get out from under the chef at the Ritz and open my own gastropub."

Mark slowed his step, nodding. "That's a brilliant idea."

"Glad you think so, 'cause I'll be hitting you up for investment cash if I make this work," Law said, only half teasing, Emma suspected. "Wine, beer, or a margarita?" he asked, inching away toward the bar.

"Wine?" Mark asked Emma. At her nod, he gave Law's shoulder a pat. "See if she has a nice sauvignon blanc for us. And thanks. We'll go inside and find Lacey."

As they started toward the house, a woman came darting up from the right, her eyes on Mark. "Hello there, handsome."

Emma felt him subtly put pressure on her hand, and she gave him a quick *we got this* look.

The woman strode closer and opened her arms, her expression expectant. She looked about his age, her hair blond and short, a pair of bright pink glasses on her nose. "Don't tell me you don't remember me, Mark Solomon."

If he didn't, Emma couldn't tell, as he smoothly got the woman to reveal her name, and introductions were made all around. Within minutes, a few others approached the group and it grew. After the tenth introduction, Emma lost track of the names and started to settle comfortably into her role as Mark's fiancée.

Law Monroe delivered drinks, a few flirts and jokes, and disappeared with a quick hug to Emma and a promise he'd see her during the week. In the group, conversation was light, easy, and fun...and not a single person mentioned Julia.

But who would when Mark played the engaged man better than, well, the last man Emma had actually been engaged to? He touched her whenever she was near, a casual brush of her arm, an easy hand on her back, and once, the lightest finger to push a lock of hair over her shoulder when he made an introduction.

Every move was possessive, sexy, subtle, dizzying. And fake. She had to remember that.

For dinner, they took an outside table with two other couples and a single woman who introduced herself as Beth Endicott.

"Endicott?" one of the men at the table said. "Like the development company?"

She gave a smile and smoothed back a lock of butterscotch-blond hair. "Ray Endicott is my father."

"That man single-handedly put Pleasure Pointe on the map," another person said.

"Oh, I don't know about that," Beth said.

"But your family owned most of the south end of Mimosa Key and sold thousands of residential parcels over the last forty years, right?"

"He did." She busied herself with her napkin.

"Are you in the family business?" another woman at the table asked.

"Not really," Beth said absently, sipping wine as her attention veered from the conversation to someone or something across the lawn.

Emma followed her gaze, where it landed on a man who was just coming into the party, his commanding good looks and height drawing more than a few eyes. Another one with a great body. Only, something about him looked more wiry and less gym-toned than Law Monroe. His hair was more pepper than salt, and his dark gaze was intense as he scanned the party, obviously looking for someone.

"Oh, there's Ken Cavanaugh," Mark stood, spotting the same man. "Excuse me while I end his life slowly and with great pain."

"Why?" Beth asked, her eyes wide in surprise.

"Because he was not supposed to let them sign me up to dance, which means he broke the bro code."

"Ken?" She shook her head. "That doesn't sound like something he'd do. He's a firefighter, you know."

"I do know, which means he has a guy's back for his

profession, and still he let mine get stabbed. I'll make him miserable first, and then let him eat with us."

He left to walk over to Ken, and Emma could have sworn Beth Endicott sat up straighter and her blue eyes sparked at the idea of the firefighter joining them.

"Oh, I know that guy," another one of the men at their table said, taking a look at the new arrival. "Captain Cav. That's what they call him at his station in Fort Myers."

His wife admired the view as well. "Oh yes, I was talking to him today at the meeting. Very nice guy. What do you want to know about him?"

"Everything," Beth said under her breath.

The woman leaned closer, clasping her hands under her chin. "Well, I can tell you this. He is divorced, but very much single. And, he's on the market."

"The market?" her husband asked with a small choke.

"The market," the woman confirmed. "In fact, he told me that the one thing he wants most in this world is a family, and he doesn't have one yet."

Beth stared at her, and Emma could have sworn some color drained from her face. "He said that?"

"Not in quite so many words, but yes. We were talking in a group about where all our lives have gone since high school." She shot a tight smile to her husband. "Of course, I told them how happy I am."

"Of course," he agreed dryly, running a hand over his shiny dome. "You love your old, fat, bald husband."

"I do and—"

Beth put her hand on the woman's arm. "What did he say?"

The woman glanced as if to check to be sure the center of her gossip was still out of hearing range. "He said his biggest regret was not having kids yet," she said. "He said he'd love to have a family, and I told him he most certainly can."

The husband harrumphed. "With a much younger woman."

"Donald, that isn't true anymore. Women have babies in their forties, right?"

Beth didn't answer, but her gaze drifted back to the man in question and softened to something akin to sadness. Then she looked down at the untouched plate of food in front of her.

"Oh, here he comes," the other woman said as Mark and Ken walked closer. But Beth didn't look, Emma noticed. She was folding her napkin and pulling her phone out of her purse.

"Your fiancé is pretty nice-looking, too, Emma," the chatty woman said. "I think I heard the collective sound of single women's hearts breaking all over the island when Lacey told us Mark is engaged."

Then mission accomplished, Emma thought as she laughed lightly. "I consider myself quite lucky," she said, taking a sip of water and hoping that was suitably vague.

Mark returned with the other man, the two of them laughing about something, but Emma noticed that the moment "Captain Cav" spotted Beth, his expression changed. Laughing with Mark morphed into...intensity.

"Hey, Beth."

Like no one else was at the table.

"Hello, Ken." She suddenly looked at her phone, which had not buzzed, dinged, or vibrated. "Oh, I have a call. Excuse me." She smiled at Ken. "This seat's open."

His face fell with obvious disappointment, but he recovered instantly, letting Mark do a round of introductions, reminding Emma that the chatty woman's name was Linda and her husband was Frank. They all kept up the small talk, but Ken was quieter than the others, except for a few jokes with Mark and answering Linda's many questions about life at his fire station. The minute everyone was done eating, Ken excused himself and disappeared.

"Dance of the Decade planning is next!" Linda announced, elbowing Mark's side. "You two better win for the eighties!"

"There's a meeting about it?" Mark asked with a groan.

"Can't miss that," Emma said, leaning back. "We promised Lacey."

He pushed up and pulled Emma's chair back for her. As he did, he put a hand on her shoulder and leaned close to her ear. "You're killing this, by the way," he whispered, his breath warm and mouth wonderfully close.

You're killing me. "Thanks," she whispered, standing up and out of his touch before he felt her shiver.

Just then, Lacey came up to their table to invite them to the patio to talk about the dance program.

"We're on our way," Emma assured her. "As soon as I swing by the ladies' room."

Lacey sidled up to her and gestured her toward the house. "It's through the family room, Emma," she said. "Come on, I'll show you."

"Thanks, I'm sure I can find it."

"I'm going that way." Lacey stayed close as they walked across the patio and into the house, greeting guests as she passed, but as they reached the counter bar in the kitchen, Lacey stopped and put her hand on Emma's arm. "Can I talk to you for a second?"

"Oh, sure..." A sudden warmth rose up in Emma's chest, somewhere between a full-on blush and a blast of liar's fear. Was this going to be about Julia? A few questions about Emma's engagement? She felt completely confident in the "game" when Mark was next to her, but didn't want to blow it with a mistaken fact, even though Lacey was younger than Mark and not in his class. She still might have some kind of personal knowledge that could throw Emma's game.

"What is it?" Emma asked.

Lacey's golden eyes searched Emma's face, all the sparkly warmth fading.

"Can you explain why you were trying to check into the resort today for a reservation under another name that had been canceled?"

Emma stared at her, that heat in her chest intensifying, knees weakening, and palms suddenly damp.

"And when the clerk at the front desk told you the reservation was canceled, you started crying?"

Emma blinked, speechless.

"And that one of our security personnel reported you rolling your two suitcases to the villa, but when they went back to check, you were inside with Mark?"

She felt like a stowaway discovered by the captain, dragged out of a storage closet, and thrown onto the deck for all to see.

"You see," Lacey continued, her voice very soft, private, but dead serious. "We have security cameras at the front desk, and I always review them at the end of the day so I know who our guests are."

"That is...smart." And something she and Mark had never even thought of.

Lacey lifted her brow, waiting. No accusation, but no sly grin of shared conspiracy, either. Could Emma trust her? Or would their little secret be blown, making things even worse for Mark?

Considering she'd already lied openly to Lacey once, telling her the truth now would make them both look bad.

"I was so confused," Emma said quickly. "You know Mark and I have been traveling so much, all over the world as he does, and we flew in on separate flights because he was in..." She gathered a breath. "Somewhere I can't even remember, but he told me the villa was Blue Casbah, and I saw that on the reservation list over the clerk's shoulder, and I read the name... Chambers, was it? Anyway, I thought maybe Mark had registered under an alias, because he does that sometimes."

Oh Lord, only a copywriter could lie like that on demand.

"That makes sense, sort of," Lacey said. "But you were so upset."

"Oh, the wedding planning is killing me," Emma said. "I'm so tense. It's so close. We haven't known each other that long, and you have no idea how much I've looked forward to this vacation. This resort! It's fabulous."

"Thank you. We're proud of it."

"You should be! Ever since Mark brought the brochure home, well, I've practically memorized it! 'Sweeping views of soft sandy beaches and sunsets that will melt your heart and your stress.'"

Lacey finally smiled. "You think we went overboard with that?"

"Not one word. It's genius."

"Oh my God, Lacey, you snagged her!" A woman came out from the hall, presumably leaving the bathroom, her eyes bright with just a touch too much wine. "You know that every woman here is dying to talk to the future Mrs. Solomon."

"Well, here I am," Emma said quickly, insanely grateful for the diversion. "Emma DeWitt. What's your name?"

"Karen Stevenson, class of '82. Congrats on getting the ungettable."

Emma felt her smile freeze and her unstoppable chatter suddenly dry up.

"You know," Karen said, lowering her voice and getting closer. "Mark spoke at Julia's memorial service here on Mimosa Key and, honestly, the women were circling like hawks, but I knew he wouldn't be one of those men who gets remarried in a year. Or ever. You know why?"

"Karen," Lacey said, putting her arm around the other woman's shoulder. "I don't think Emma needs to hear the details—"

"Oh, she needs to hear," Karen insisted with that slightly wrong emphasis fueled by an extra glass of wine, or three. "How else will she know what she's up against?"

"What am I up against?"

"Karen," Lacey said more firmly. "Go drink some coffee and get ready for our meeting. We're discussing the dance contest over dessert, and I know you have opinions on…everything."

Karen shot her brows up, crinkling her forehead and spearing Lacey with a harsh look, but Lacey very subtly guided the other woman out of the kitchen. "Now, please do me a huge favor and round up the wayward guests so we can have a quick discussion about the dance contest."

Karen glanced over her shoulder, taking the hint, but sending one last look at Emma. "He'll never really be yours," she whispered.

"Karen!" Lacey scolded.

"She ought to know the truth. I'd want someone to tell me if I were going to marry a man who—"

Lacey gave her a solid nudge toward the sliders, just as her husband, Clay, was walking in. "Honey, help Karen pull together the schedules and possible playlists for the dance contest, will you?"

They shared a look that only happily married people managed, somehow exchanging hours of dialogue and information with nothing but a quick gaze and flicked eyebrow.

Clay guided Karen out with ease, leaving Emma standing with Lacey.

"Well," Emma said with a quick laugh. "That was awkward."

"Not at all," Lacey assured her. "Karen's so green with jealousy she blends into the grass."

"Does that mean you aren't going to tell me what I'm...up against, as she put it?"

"You're not up against anything except the stress of a wedding," Lacey said kindly. "If you want to spend a few minutes with our on-site wedding planners, just for a second opinion on things, I can arrange that for you."

The offer was so kind and sincere, it tweaked Emma's conscience. "Maybe," she said. "But I think I have things under control."

At Lacey's dubious look, Emma added, "Kind of under control."

But she sure wanted to know what she was up against, fiancée or not.

Chapter Seven

They left the party with an address of a local dance studio and a schedule of rehearsals for the next week. Oh, Mark left with one more thing, too, he thought as he took Emma's hand and led her to the beach instead of the path.

The strongest desire to kiss his fiancée.

"Where are we going?" Emma asked as they reached the sand and he stopped to kick off his shoes.

"Back to the villa."

"The path is faster," she said.

He shot her a sideways look. "The beach is empty and the moon is full."

"Aren't you a smooth talker?"

"Hanging out with a copywriter," he teased, scooping his shoes off the sand.

But she didn't make a move to slip off her sandals. "Makes me wonder…what I'm up against," she said.

"Not up against anything." *Yet.* "Come on, kick off your shoes."

"And fall in love."

He inched back. "Or walk on the beach."

She gave him a playful tap. "It's the resort slogan, big guy. No worries. I couldn't fall in love again if someone paid me a billion bucks. Bought that load of hooey and had to clean up the mess with a shovel."

"It's dangerous, you know."

"Love?"

"Mixing those bitter pills with wine."

She smiled. "Nope, I switched to water when the meeting started. Wanted to have a clear head when we had to discuss whether to dance to *How Will I Know* or *Caribbean Queen*." She added a playful elbow to his side. "Some horrific music you eighties kids had."

He gave her a look. "Beats the *Macarena*, nineties baby."

"But we had timeless classics like *Livin' La Vida Loca*. And *Believe* by Cher."

"Case made," he insisted, bending toward the sand to slide his hand over her calf, the thin material of her slacks giving him a chance to feel a feminine curve.

"What are you doing?"

"Taking off your sandals so you'll walk on the beach and get sand between your toes. We have to come up with a list of songs for tomorrow that we can discuss with this choreographer guy."

She lifted her foot to help him slip one shoe off and toed the other one. "Did you get another sign from your late wife or something?" she asked.

He stood slowly, shaking his head. "No, why would you ask?"

"Because you're all into the dance contest, like you really care about winning. Thought maybe they mentioned your song or something and you thought it was a woo-woo message."

He narrowed his eyes at her, fighting a smile. "I do believe you are mocking me *again*."

"I do believe I am. I don't mean to be disrespectful, honest." She took the sandals from him.

"But you think it's a—what would you call it?—a *load of hooey.*"

She smiled at the echo of her own words. "What I think is that your signs are coincidences and wishful thinking brought on by warm memories of days gone by. It's incredibly sweet that you think your late wife is whispering directions, but I honestly don't think it works that way."

Not worth arguing with a jaded pragmatist. He knew when Julia sent him messages, and that was all that mattered. "To answer your question, there were no signs from beyond, but the whole committee is so excited about it, and it's the highlight of the reunion." He leaned his body into hers. "And I like my partner.

So let's count our blessings that I wasn't in your decade, because then we'd be dancing to Britney Spears or Boyz II Men, whoever the hell they are."

"Whoever..." She choked and kicked the sand as they stepped on it. "God, now you sound old."

He took her hand, as much out of desire as habit now. No, mostly out of desire. Her fingers were strong but small, and so soft.

"I may sound old, but I don't feel it." Not out here in the moonlight with a pretty woman and a warm buzz from a perfectly enjoyable evening. "And, by the way, compliments on your acting skills."

"So you said at dinner. And speaking of dinner," she added, "what's the deal with Beth and Ken? She was so interested in him and then ran off like a scared rabbit."

"I don't know, but he can't think straight where she's involved." A warm, comfortable feeling settled over Mark. It had been a long time since he did a post-mortem on party gossip with a woman.

"Couldn't help but notice. Did they go to high school together?"

He laughed. "I think so. He doesn't say much, but I can tell he's amped when she's around. That's why I brought him over."

"He's *amped*?" She jabbed him playfully with an elbow. "Hey, Mark, 1986 is calling. They want their expressions back."

"Nobody says that anymore?"

She just laughed. "Not sure anyone *did* say it."

"Anyway, I was doing a good deed for a friend, like you're doing a good deed for me. Which worked, by the way, since not one person cornered me, offered sympathy, tried to introduce me to a single woman, or slipped me a phone number." He pulled her a little closer, fighting the temptation to kiss the top of her head in gratitude.

"Well, lucky you, because I got cornered, and good."

"By who?"

"Lacey Walker."

He slowed. "Why would Lacey corner you?"

She didn't answer right away but sighed softly. "She saw me check in. Knew I got turned away. And had some security guy check out your villa...and I was already inside."

"What?" He stopped walking. "Oh God, Emma. What did you say?"

"I'm not sure exactly, but it was a big, fat cake of lies that I iced with butter cream bullshit and stuck in a candle of distracting suck up for good measure."

"Damn." He lifted her hand and grabbed it between both of his. "Sorry for the embarrassment."

She gave a charming laugh, looking up at him so that the moonlight made her eyes look like sparkling topaz. "Are you always this kind and caring?"

His brows furrowed at the compliment. "You're doing me a huge favor and, honestly, I should have thought that through. Of course they have security cameras behind the front desk."

"I think we're fine," she assured him. "And we were interrupted by another member of the Mark Solomon Fan Club."

"Stop," he said. "There is no such thing."

"Don't go all modest on me," she teased. "I heard enough about the captain of the football team, valedictorian, most likely to succeed, and winner of a full scholarship to the University of Miami that I signed up to be the next president of that fan club."

He gave another grunt and looked at the night sky. "Let me put that all in perspective for you, Emma. The football team was three and eleven my senior year, the competition was not tough academically, I was a big mouth with a lot of friends who voted on those things, and the full scholarship was not free. It was ROTC, and I left college and went straight into Desert Storm."

"All that and he's humble, ladies and gentleman."

The compliment, as subtle and slightly underhanded as most of those he got from her, warmed anyway. "Just honest," he said.

She leaned into him, silently telling him she liked that, too. "So you fought in...the first Gulf War?"

"I went to Saudi Arabia after college graduation in 1991. Air Force. A captain when I left." He looked out to the water, wondering if he should tell her the war might have been hell for a lot of soldiers, but being away from his young wife had been the worst part. "I didn't see much action, so please don't think of me as a hero. That was a quick war, and I worked in satellite communications. When I got out, I got a job with a small tech firm in Melbourne, Florida, over on the east coast. But the real fun was..." *Working with Julia.* Again, he hesitated to say it, though.

"Being married?" she suggested for him.

He couldn't help stroking the slender, soft fingers he held. Talking to her was so *easy*. "Yeah, and building Seeking Soulmates. We were living in this crappy house, but it was on the beach, and every night I'd come home from work, and she'd read the letters that had come in from all these torn-up people with broken hearts, and we'd write the responses." An old punch of grief hit him, not with much force, more like a soft tap on the shoulder from an old friend.

"You would write them, too?" she asked, surprised.

"No one knew, of course. But it was...fun." Mostly because he and Julia would drink cheap beer and toast to what a solid, happy marriage they had compared to the rest of the world. "Anyway, my tech skills were building, and soon enough, I turned her business into something profitable on this little-known avenue of technology at the time called the Internet."

"Wow." She rubbed her arm a little.

"Are you cold?" he asked.

"No, I just got chills. That's a great story. What a wonderful life you had together."

"Until I didn't," he said quietly.

This time, she squeezed his hand. "Of course," she said, and he could have kissed her for not saying she was sorry. She had, earlier, which was polite.

But she knew no one was to blame for cancer or chemo killing his wife. It just happened.

"And you have carried on remarkably," she added.

"I have carried on," he corrected. "Once I sold the

company and then LoveInc went public, I had enough money to live well for the rest of my life. That's when I dedicated every waking moment to chasing speed, jumping out of planes, hanging off rocks, and gliding through the air on nylon wings. Or as you called it, escaping and risking my life."

"The way you describe your life, it's not adventure or escape. It sounds like a death wish to me."

He closed his eyes and slowed his step. "Not a *wish*," he said. "But I..." He couldn't finish. She'd never understand.

"But you don't care if you die, because you think she'll be there waiting for you on the other side."

Or maybe she *could* understand. "It's just that I've already known true happiness and have accepted the fact that no other emotion will come close. And since I'll never feel the bone-deep bliss of that kind of love again, why not get that thrill falling from twenty thousand feet and hoping the chute opens? If it doesn't, then..."

"Then you'd be out of your misery," she said softly.

Right. "Let's talk about something else."

"Because I'm right?" she asked.

"Let me put it this way," he said. "I wouldn't welcome death but it doesn't scare me. Nothing scares me."

"Lucky you. So many things scare me."

"So you've said." He stroked her cheek and brushed some hair back, letting the silky strands slide through his fingers, nearly sighing at how good it felt. "What, besides kissing me, scares you?"

"Oh, some really dumb things."

"Name one."

She cocked her head to think. "Oh, let's see. One of my worst fears is making a left turn across three lanes of traffic with no light."

He laughed. "You're just in the wrong car. Drive my Porsche Carrera and you'll scream across those lanes."

"I'm no fan of heights, either. Especially bridges. I didn't even like that causeway that gets on this island."

"I jumped off that causeway a hundred times when I was a teenager."

Her jaw dropped. "There could be sharks in that water!"

"Don't bother them, they won't bother you." He tickled her earlobe with his thumb. "What else, fraidycat?"

"Biscuit cans."

He thought for a second, then barked a laugh. "Like breakfast biscuits?"

"You know, those kind that come in a tube that you have to slam against the edge of the counter?" She drew back and held her hand out, miming the act of thwacking a canister. "I'm always sure they're going to pop all over me."

He tossed his head back and laughed from his belly. "And champagne, too?"

"Of course. I never open the bottle."

"I'll open them for you." He pulled her a little closer, barely aware that he'd wrapped one arm around her waist. Well, not barely. He was fully aware of the warmth of her body close to his and the bow of her back under his hand. Completely aware of the sweet floral scent that hung over her and how pretty her mouth was when she laughed at herself, which she did a lot.

"Is that it?" he asked. "No other freakish fears?"

She thought about it. "You know, the usual. Closed shower curtains, escalators, stray dogs, huge flocks of birds, entering an empty house at night."

He cracked up. "Those are usual? What deep, dark childhood horror caused these fears?"

"I don't know. Well, I guess some of them I do. I had a

car accident when I was sixteen, the week I got my license."

"Making a left turn?" he guessed.

"Across three lanes of traffic. No injuries, except my psyche." She gazed up at him. "Are you always this awesome and intuitive?"

"I just don't want to make it onto your list of fears. Markphobia would be debilitating."

Her breath caught again, but not with a laugh. This time, it was the soft intake of breath as she looked up at him. "Truth be told, I *am* a little scared of you."

"Uh-oh. I'm right up there with closed shower curtains and biscuit cans and stray dogs."

But she didn't smile. "Am I supposed to feel that fear after those three kisses?"

"Maybe we need more. This case seems serious." He lowered his head, half expecting her to jerk out of his arms, make a joke, change the subject, but...she didn't.

Instead, she met his kiss and slightly arched her back. Her lips opened and invited him deeper, the warm, wet, sweet kiss somehow both tentative and anxious. Their lips met like they'd been created to do this and only this, opening enough to invite each other's tongue to touch.

He flattened his hands on the small of her back, easing her into him, feeling his body already respond, part of him— the lower part—wanting to press harder against her. But way up in his brain, he knew that would send her skittering away.

Still, he had to feel more, had to stroke her back and let their tongues touch and twist, and give in to a little groan of pleasure when all his blood rumbled and his body heated to life.

Finally, they mutually broke the kiss, with exquisite reluctance.

She closed her eyes and leaned her forehead against his chin with a sigh. "See?" she whispered. "Terrifying."

He laughed softly, wrapping his arms all the way around her. "Like free soloing up the side of a two-thousand-foot vertical granite wall."

She dropped her head back. "Free soloing...like no harnesses or clips?"

"Not a single one."

"You are fearless."

"I like that better than having a death wish." But she wouldn't be the first to suggest that his endless search to fill his days with dangerous adventures was his way of testing fate. "But the only wish I have right this minute is to do that again." He dipped his head.

"Well, we don't have an audience, so you better not."

"I don't need an audience," he said gruffly, stealing another kiss on her temple. "Just because our engagement is fake doesn't mean we can't kiss." He moved his lips down.

She drew back. "Kissing becomes making out, then making out becomes couch groping, then couch groping becomes..."

"A trip to the Jacuzzi for two."

"Exactly!" She gave him a playful push backward. "And then the Dance of the Decades is the horizontal mambo. Is that what you want?"

More than his next breath. "Oh, no, of course not."

Her eyes turned to slits. "You told me platonic."

"I did, and I meant it." He backed up, holding both hands up in surrender. "I won't do anything to make you uncomfortable."

"Too late," she murmured, taking his hand and bringing him back.

"You're uncomfortable?"

She shot him a look. "Hot, bothered, and seriously uncomfortable."

"Sorry." But he wasn't. "I promise, no stripping down or making out or couch groping, whatever the hell that is."

She gave a low grunt. "As if you don't know."

He draped an arm around her and started walking slowly toward their villa. "Pretty sure I skip that one with most women."

She fell into step with him. "You find a lot of companionship on those adventure treks?"

"Some," he admitted. "Nothing that, you know, matters." As soon as he said it, he regretted the statement. He felt her stiffen slightly, like her guard had just risen to protect her.

And who could blame her?

They crossed the sand in silence, reached the path, and finished the short walk to Blue Casbah.

He used the card key to let them into the dimly lit villa, and she separated from him and turned, backing toward the bedroom.

"Good night," she said softly, holding out her hand. He wasn't sure if she wanted him to take it so she could pull him along with her or not.

So he closed his fingers around hers, lifted her hand, and kissed her knuckles lightly. "Good night, Emma."

She stood still for a long moment, not pulling her hand away from his mouth, but just looking at him, her expression unreadable. Then, without a word, she took a step forward, pulled her hand from his lips, and replaced it with her mouth.

This kiss was light, sweet, and gave him a shocker of a rush, like falling into thin, clear air or finding the sweet spot on a black diamond run.

But before he could slide deeper down that steep slope, she broke the kiss, gave him a smile, and disappeared into the bedroom, closing the door behind her.

She didn't lock it, because she knew she didn't have to. He'd be on the couch, groping nothing and no one, and probably not doing much sleeping at all.

Chapter Eight

"**W**ake up, Sleeping Beauty. I got you a present."

Emma rolled over and blinked into the morning light, yanking herself out of slumber. For a moment, she didn't know where she was or who was pounding on the door.

Oh yeah, her fake fiancé.

"Hang on," she mumbled, pushing back the comforter and stepping out of bed, tugging the sleep shirt down to cover her thighs. *Sort of* cover her thighs. "What time is it?"

"Seven fifteen. Up and at 'em."

She scowled at the door and pushed her hair off her face. And breathed into her hand. Oh hell no.

"One sec." Good God, it was early. Wasn't she on vacation? He probably climbed a mountain and jumped out of a hot air balloon before sunrise, and she…was so not a morning person.

In the bathroom, she swished with mouthwash and dared a look in the mirror. A little sleepy, a little tousled, but not horrible. Not as bad as when he'd found her snorting like a pig in pain on the step yesterday. And she wasn't trying to impress him anyway, right? They were just doing this…charade together. *Right?*

"Right," she whispered, padding to the door and opening it.

Oh, not right. It wasn't fair he looked that good at this hour.

"Greetings, sleepyhead." He stood inches away, wearing nothing but loose-fitting shorts that hung low on his hips and absolutely no sign of a shirt. Abs. Pecs. Shoulders. Dusting of hair.

"Oh man," she muttered.

"I'm an early riser," he replied.

She forced her gaze north and blinked at his right hand, extended and holding a…a canister of biscuit dough?

"And you want breakfast from this night owl?"

"I don't care if you bake them or not, but you're opening this."

She retreated a few inches. "You want me to wake up at dawn's early light and…face my fears."

"There's no better time." His smile widened, and he reached for her hand, turning it palm up to place the cylinder in her grip. "Come on, against the counter in the kitchen. Three times."

"Oh, that sounds…" *Sexy as hell*. "Noisy."

"You're going to pound it until it pops."

She burst out laughing as he pushed her into the main living area. "It's too early for innuendos and puns."

From behind her, he leaned closer, his lips in her hair. "Not too early to stare down what scares you and make it bow to you."

"I'm not really that scared of a can of biscuits." That bare chest, low voice, and warm breath, though? Definitely making the knees a little shaky.

"Then bang it."

She bit her lip and looked up at him. "That sounds very, um, dirty."

"Banging the biscuit tube? You Gen-Xers. What'll you think of next?"

She laughed again, because how could she do anything else? "You want me to open this right now?"

"Before you even think about it. Just do it."

"Is this some kind of weird adventure-seeking ritual you mountain-climbing, car-racing, parachuting types do? Get each other out of bed and jump off a cliff just to see if you can?"

He covered her hand with his. "You're procrastinating."

"You're crazy."

He lifted a brow and looked at the can. "Three...two...one..."

She inched back, cringing, and held the can to the counter's edge. This was ridiculous. This was stupid. She glanced up, falling into ice blue eyes.

"Then...bang."

And, just like that, she wanted to. Not just to conquer her silly little hang-up, but to show him how brave she could be.

Closing her eyes, she held her breath, lifted her hand, and thwacked, jumping backward into him with a tiny shriek when the pressure popped.

"You did it." From behind, he wrapped both arms around her. "Want to try another one?"

She wanted to turn and kiss him. Couldn't she work on *that* fear again? "Do I have to?"

"Two more times and you will reign over those biscuits." She heard a plastic bag rustle. "I cleaned out the local convenience store and received a dressing down and inquisition from the old lady who still owns it and remembered me. All so you could conquer Mount Biscuit. You're welcome."

She glanced into the bag he held open next to her. Sure enough, five cans of Pillsbury Flaky Layers rolled around in the bag.

"We can't just waste these biscuits," she said.

"Exactly what the sourpuss owner of the Super Min said. I assured her we won't waste a bite. Don't make excuses, Emma. That's what fear does to you."

"We can't eat thirty biscuits."

"Of course not." He pulled out another canister. "We'll bake the three you're going to open and drop them off at Heaven's Helper, the food bank in town. My mom used to volunteer there, and they'd love a donation."

Was he for real? "You want to bake bread for the homeless?"

"After you conquer biscuitcanphobia." He put the tube in her hand. "Go ahead. Give it hell, Em."

Em. The way he said the single syllable made her almost moan out loud.

"All right. Here we go. Hell for Heaven's Helper. How's that for a headline?" She grabbed the tube, but this time, she didn't close her eyes or step back.

She held her breath and slammed it against the edge of the counter, her shoulders jerking when it popped.

"Way to go," he cheered. "Two down, one to go."

"Why not?" She snagged the biscuit container from his hand, spun around, and whacked it so hard the biscuit dough almost fell out. Fearless. Smiling, she turned to him. "That was fun. I believe I am officially cured of this particular phobia."

"That's my girl." He opened a few cabinets, locating a

baking sheet, oblivious to the gooey, great way being *his girl* made her feel. "Can you preheat the oven?"

She just stared at him. She really shouldn't want to be his girl. That was a recipe for disaster, not biscuits.

"Uh-oh. Don't tell me you have a fear of ovens."

She finally looked away at the stainless built-in, touching the screen to preheat. "Not afraid of ovens."

Just...*heartache*. Not that he would intentionally hurt her. A man this fundamentally good? No. But if she let herself start feeling things she shouldn't be feeling? Yes.

And she had every right to be afraid of that.

"You want a cup of coffee?" Mark asked, indicating the countertop coffeemaker, definitely on the wavelength where she should be.

She shoved her fears aside and considered the question, automatically curling her lip. "I'm kind of a coffee snob, but at this hour? I'd drink motor oil to get started." Pulling the biscuits out of one of the open containers, she started placing them on a cookie sheet.

"There's a coffee bar in the lobby if you require a toasted cinnamon caramel whipped peppermint swirl with salt and cream and your name on the side."

"Ohhh, someone doesn't like Starbucks."

He laughed, finding a cup. "I like coffee in a tin cup around a fire before a good climb into the mountains."

"After sleeping in a tent. How lovely."

He leaned into her from behind. "Don't knock what you haven't tried."

"I think I'd be scared of sleeping in a tent outside. Bugs and snakes and bears, you know? She finished lining up the biscuits on the tray, then accepted the freshly brewed cup he handed her.

"And the occasional brown recluse in Death Valley."

She closed her eyes. "No."

"I killed it with a canteen," he said calmly. "You never did answer my question last night. Why do you have all these random fears?"

She added cream and a heaping teaspoon of sugar, thinking about the question. "I don't know. My mom was always sure disaster was right around the corner and, for her, it was. Disaster in the form of my dad's next tall tale and...*diversion*."

When the oven beeped, she slid the biscuits in and finally took a first sip of coffee, which she reluctantly had to admit wasn't bad. Probably because it was made by the gods. Well, a god.

"So Dad was an issue?" he asked.

"Just a liar and a cheat, if that's an issue." She went around the counter and settled on a stool. "It was for my mother. It is for me."

He nodded, his hands around a mug of steaming black coffee, his blue eyes locked on her. "And have any of these fears you have actually blown up in your face? Have you nearly lost a limb to a biscuit can?"

She felt the smile threaten. "Look who's mocking now."

"I'm just curious where this all comes from."

She thought about it for a moment, realizing she'd never analyzed herself that much before now. And she certainly had never been with a man who showed so much interest.

Not even her real fiancé.

"One of my fears came true," she said, surprised at how easy the admission rose. "The fear of walking into an empty house at night."

"What happened?"

"I found my dad on top of the next-door neighbor."

His jaw dropped. "Gross."

"On so many levels, you can't even imagine. But he couldn't lie his way out of it when his thirteen-year-old daughter was the witness. At least my mom finally filed for divorce."

"Wow." He put the cup down and studied her. "That must have wrecked you."

Again, the fact that he actually thought of it in terms of what the event did to her touched her. Folded her heart in half, to be honest.

"The divorce wrecked my mom more," she told him, easily opening up on a subject she normally kept locked and hidden. "But mostly because she would have happily gone on believing his lies because she had a good life with a lot of money and friends. All of that dried up at the hands of a slimy divorce attorney."

"So now you don't trust men," he said, as if it was so simple and he'd figured her out.

"I trust men," she replied. "It's liars and cheats I don't trust." The oven beeped as the aroma of buttery biscuits filled the kitchen.

"I'll have to remember that," Mark said.

"I doubt you ever lie or cheat, Mark. You're too busy taking in strays and making biscuits for the poor."

He smiled at her. "You sure do know how to package things to make them seem better than they are."

"It's my gift," she said, sliding off the stool. But something told her she wasn't making Mark better than he was. He was really that good.

Setting the bar so high for other men that all they'd ever do was walk under it.

"Get dressed, Em. We need to swing by Heaven's Helper on the way to the dance studio."

"The fun never ends." She tried for sarcasm, but failed. For once, she didn't feel sarcastic. She was up early, facing fears, smiling at her home brew, and writing off men she hadn't even met yet.

Man, she was in such deep trouble.

Chapter Nine

"Some things never change," Mark mused, looking out the window of the sedan that had picked them up in front of the resort to bring them to their morning dance lesson. "The Super Min being at the top of the list."

Emma dipped down to share his view out the window, taking in a small beach town that mixed genuine old-school tropical charm with a few contemporary touches. "That gas station convenience store where you got the biscuits?"

"Yeah." And where he got grilled by Charity Grambling, who remembered every detail of his and Julia's life. He finally shut her up by pulling the fiancée card. Which meant his "engagement" to Emma would be all over Mimosa Key in a matter of hours.

"The whole place is so quaint," Emma mused, looking around. "But not in a 'let's build a quaint town to attract tourists' way. It feels so genuine."

"That's Mimosa Key," he said. "Real old-school Florida."

The driver, a soft-spoken retiree named Al, eyed Mark in the rearview mirror. "I take it you're here for the Mimosa High reunion?"

"I am," he confirmed.

"Move away long ago?" the driver asked.

"I left after high school, and my parents moved off the island about twenty years ago. I've been back once or twice to visit since then."

"I'm not a local," the driver said. "I moved down here after sixty-eight years of Pittsburgh winters. But I've been talking to a few of the folks here for the reunion, and apparently a lot has changed, especially since the resort opened."

"Barefoot Bay sure has changed," Mark agreed. "There was nothing but a few houses up there. And east of that, there was an old goat farm some ancient Italian guy had and lots of canals and mangroves."

"Goat farm's still there, but it's a whole little petting zoo touristy place now and part of the new baseball stadium. Have you heard we have a minor league team, the Barefoot Bay Bucks?"

Mark nodded. "I did hear that. Have they started playing yet?"

"Exhibition preseason games. In fact, there's one later this week, on Friday afternoon. You can bet I'm taking that day off."

Mark turned to Emma and gave her a nudge. "I love baseball. We should go."

She agreed easily, the sunlight and playfulness of the morning still making her eyes spark and making him more and more certain this whole "engaged for the crowd" thing was a good idea. The sleeper sofa sucked, but everything else was good.

"We didn't tell him about these," she whispered, tapping the plastic container full of biscuits she held on her lap.

"Oh yeah." Mark leaned forward. "Before you go to the

dance studio, can you swing by Heaven's Helper? Assuming it's still there."

"It is." The driver raised his eyebrows in the rearview mirror. "Don't get a lot of Casa Blanca guests who want to go to the food bank and thrift store."

"Well, we do." He gave a wink to Emma. "My fiancée had a hankering to make biscuits."

She lifted one shapely brow. "Hankering?"

"Too old-school?"

"Too...cute." She turned away with an eye roll, as if it pained her to admit anything he did was *cute*.

"Here we are." The driver pulled into a small parking lot, and Mark turned, sucking in an audible breath that he covered with a cough. What the hell had he been thinking coming here?

He recognized the bittersweet taste of grief as it rose up with surprising insistence at the sight of the small wooden sign that said Hope Presbyterian. He'd only been thinking of Heaven's Helper, the tiny storefront across a side street from the church.

He hadn't really been thinking that coming to "the Helper," as his mother had called the operation that served the homeless on the mainland and a few struggling folks on Mimosa Key. This also put him in front of Hope Presbyterian—the very church where he and Julia took their vows again after they'd infuriated two families by eloping. And where he'd said good-bye to her sixteen years ago in front of a weepy gathering of a few hundred people.

Damn it.

"You okay?" Emma's question, along with a tender hand on his arm, pulled him out of the instant fog.

"Fine, why?"

That brow lifted again, but not in humor or sarcasm. More like real concern. "You sure?"

"Of course."

But she just looked at him. "Hey, the honesty thing isn't just for the villa. It's for whenever we're alone."

The driver had gotten out of the car to get her door, so they were alone. "It's not important. I'll tell you later."

Al opened Emma's door, and she turned to get out, taking the plastic container with her but eyeing Mark before she stepped out of the sedan. He recognized her look. It was very much like the challenging glare he'd given her when he playfully handed her a biscuit tube to open so she could fight her fear.

But this was different. This was no little lighthearted phobia.

He got out of the car and let out a slow breath while his gaze traveled across the street to the church. It had a Spanish vibe, like much of the island, with a red clay roof, yellow stucco walls, and big brown double doors...doors he and Julia had burst out of to a spray of flower petals. Doors he'd last pushed through fighting tears and hugging friends.

What in God's name had he been thinking coming here?

"I'll wait at the car," Al said.

Mark fixed his gaze on the cottage that housed the food bank and a small thrift store, pointedly not looking at the church.

"You said your mom volunteered here?" Emma fell into step with him, holding the biscuits close to her chest, the way he wanted to hold his personal pain.

"Yeah, when I was a kid and in high school. That was our church."

She glanced past him to look at the church, quiet for a moment. "Where did your parents move?" she asked.

"Over on the mainland, near Tampa. After my dad retired, they wanted to live near my sister and her kids. Where are your parents?" he asked, wanting the subject off him and his family and his youth and this church.

"My dad's in California, but my mom still lives in upstate New York, where I'm from. Skaneateles. Ever heard of it?"

"Sure. The lakes are pretty up there. Any brothers or sisters?"

"No siblings." She slowed her step and looked up at him. "Will you tell me why you tensed up when we pulled into this lot?"

He surprised himself when he felt his lips curve in a smile. "You won't let it go until I do, will you?"

"You know me well."

"About as well as you know me, which is pretty impressive, considering we met yesterday."

He kept his gaze on the tiny food bank/thrift store cottage, remembering coming here as a kid after school to see his mom and get a treat from Mrs. Reinhardt, who always had jelly doughnuts under her counter. She got the previous day's unsold sweets from the local doughnut shop and kept a treasure trove for special guests, like him.

"I think I know," Emma said as he pulled the door open and held it for her.

"You think—"

"Mark Solomon!" An older woman stood up from behind a counter, holding out her hands in exclamation. "I heard you were on the island!"

"Mrs. Reinhardt." He felt his face light up at the sight of a woman who'd been like an aunt to him when he was a kid, still able to see that younger version in her bright blue eyes, not the gray-haired, crinkly faced lady she'd become in the past forty years. "You're still working here?" he asked.

She had to have left her seventies behind a few years ago.

But here she was, stocking cartons for the hungry.

"Of course I am!" She came around the counter and threw her arms around him. "I'll leave when they bury me next to my dear, sweet Fritz." She gave a squeeze and leaned back to look at him. "Oh, if you're not still the best-looking man on this island and possibly in the state."

He put his hands over hers and laughed. "And you're still a flirt."

"Only with you." She patted his shoulder and glanced at Emma. "Hello."

"Mrs. Reinhardt, this is Emma, my..." Holy crap, he had to lie to this sweet old woman now. He never imagined she'd be here.

"I know who she is," she said, throwing another embrace around Emma. "The whole island is talking about your engagement. Emma DeWitt, is it? Oh my word alive, look at you! So pretty and sweet. Welcome to Mimosa Key, future Mrs. Mark Solomon!"

Mimosa Key really was the world's smallest island for news, Mark remembered. Of course the news would spread past the reunion and all over the island. He really hadn't thought this idea through, but had to live with it now.

Emma seemed unfazed by the affection, returning the hug and laughing easily at the *Mrs.* moniker that was just hung around her neck.

"Now, Emma, I'm sure Mark has told you all about me," the woman said, adding a playful wink. "As if he remembers the old church ladies."

"Of course I do, Mrs. Reinhardt," Mark assured her.

"Oh, hush up with that Mrs. Reinhardt business, Mark. I see plenty of snow on your roof. You can officially call me Carla now."

All those years growing up on this island, and he'd had no idea that was her name.

"We brought biscuits for the food bank," Emma said, holding out the plastic container and getting a wide-mouthed, open-eyed look of astonishment.

"And she has a heart for the needy!"

Emma slid a sideways glance. "Honestly, it was Mark's idea."

"Oh my dear Mark." She took the biscuits and beamed at them. "There's a surprise for you under the counter."

Smiling, Mark stepped around her work area and, sure enough, there was a box from The Donut Hole, one of his favorite places in Mimosa Key. "Jelly?"

"Of course," she said. "You know what my Fritz used to say. Life is like a jelly doughnut. Sometimes you get all the good stuff in the first bites, and sometimes you have to plow through the dough before you hit the motherlode!" She gave a hoot. "Oh, that man had the sayings."

Mark remembered Fritz, who'd been quite a bit older than his talkative wife, and vaguely recalled his mother telling him that Fritz had died maybe fifteen years ago. He must have been in his own fog then.

"Oh, our Mark was always such a delight," she rattled on to Emma. "Why, I remember when you got...I mean, the last time I saw..." Her words faded, and she gave him a look he easily interpreted: sympathy, pity, and here came the tears.

"But he's happy now," Emma interjected, and immediately, Carla's expression morphed from agony to joy.

"Yes! Yes, he is, and that is simply wonderful. I mean, it's...*wonderful*."

What was wonderful was how skillfully Emma deflected that conversation.

"But can I just say it took you long enough?" Carla added in a hushed whisper.

"I was waiting for…" He put his arm around the narrow shoulders next to his and gave Emma a grateful squeeze. "Perfection."

"Oh my word." Carla put both hands over her mouth. "I can't contain my happiness. What does your mother think? Have you met her yet, Emma? We used to be the dearest of dear friends, but you know, the only way people keep in touch nowadays is on that darn computer, and I just can't be bothered with all that Face business." She turned back to Emma and gave her an unexpected hug. "Like an angel, you are. Such a gift. Straight from God to Mark."

Over the thick shoulder, Emma looked up at him, a mix of tease and torture in her golden-brown gaze. "Thank you, Carla," she said, giving a little eye roll to him. "I don't know if I'm from God, but I'm happy to be here."

"From God," she insisted, turning her attention to Mark. "When's the big day?"

He glanced at Emma, not wanting to contradict anything she'd say.

"We haven't set a date yet," she said easily.

"Then let me know when you do, and I can put it in the church newsletter. Everyone will be so happy for you, Mark."

He promised they would and talked some more before they left. When they hugged good-bye, Carla whispered, "She's delightful, Mark. I'm happy for you."

Guilt squeezed, and he almost told her the truth, but bit it back, giving her a kiss on her gray hair instead.

As they walked back to the car, Mark took Emma's hand, which was free of the plastic container now. "You're really good at this."

"Told you. I lie for a living."

"You're not just lying."

She laughed. "I'm superlying?"

"You're making sure I don't have to handle conversations I'd rather avoid."

"Wasn't that the price of my villa in paradise?"

He gripped her hand a little tighter. "I didn't think we'd be seeing people like…that. Damn near family."

"Well, you grew up here, Mark. You're bound to see people you know well."

He'd planned to avoid any of that, too, including his old house…and Julia's. He'd stayed in touch with Julia's mother, but she'd died a few years after her daughter had. Mark had sadly lost touch with Julia's father after that. The last time they'd talked, Wayne Coulter sounded down in the dumps. Talking to a sad old man who'd lost his only daughter and then his wife was just another thing Mark preferred to avoid.

"The real problem is going to be the next time you have to face Carla and tell her we broke up," Emma said. "But don't worry, you can tell her it was all my fault. Don't slip off that pedestal on my account. Just say I dumped you."

He hesitated on the next step. "That sounds…" He looked to the side, and his gaze fell on the church, the kick to his chest almost stealing his breath. "Sad."

"The story of our breakup or the sight of the church where you got married?"

He looked at her, astonished. "How did you…"

"Am I right?"

Of course she was. "Julia and I went to the mainland and got married by a Justice of the Peace, but her parents wanted a wedding, so we had a small one here." He blew out a slow breath. "And had her memorial service in the same church."

"Oh." She touched his shoulder, a gentle, sympathetic pressure that actually helped. "So why did you want to come here today?"

He smiled at her. "You made me forget."

For a long moment, she looked at him, then she lifted their joined hands. "Why don't you come with me now?"

"To the car?"

"To the church."

He stepped in the opposite direction. "Why would I do that?"

"Face your fears, coach. And since I'm nicer than you, I'll only make you do it once."

Slowly, he shook his head. "This isn't the same as a little tube that pops when you hit the counter."

She squinted her eyes to challenging slits. "I thought you were fearless, Mark Solomon."

"I...I..." He looked at the church doors. Not *that* fearless.

"You don't have to, but I'd like to see the church. And..." She held his hand close to her mouth and pressed the lightest kiss on his knuckles. "It might help you."

"I don't need help," he said. "Let's just go learn how to dance. That, I need help with."

She shrugged off the joke. "Your call. I understand."

Maybe she did. He wasn't at all sure how he felt about that.

Chapter Ten

T wenty minutes at Allegro, the dance studio that was upstairs from the local florist, and Emma decided that Mark had effectively squashed the emotions and memories that had plagued him when he'd seen the church. And while she'd love to take credit for that, she knew the real reason was the next challenge in their brief courtship: a whirlwind of a dance instructor named Jasper Vonderleith.

If Jasper were a product and Emma had to sell him, she'd be digging through the thesaurus for more ways to say *big*. Because he was larger—brighter, louder, and bolder—than life.

Hovering somewhere in his mid-twenties, the wiry, heavily tattooed dance instructor sported hair like a yellow cockatiel, multicolored fingernails, and a gold tooth that glinted when he smiled, which was often.

"We're going to tell a story," Jasper announced not long after they settled into a warm studio where sunshine poured through oversize windows along one wall and bounced off three mirrored ones. "One these people will never forget."

Leaning against one of the mirrors, Mark crossed his arms and narrowed his eyes at their instructor. "Just so we're clear, this is for a high school reunion," he said. "Not a reality TV show."

Jasper sucked in a noisy breath, shocked. "We are in competition, my friend. With..." He flipped his hand and pointed toward the mirror on the other side.

"With ourselves?" Emma guessed.

"With Tiffany Jones, a child—a mere babe in the dancing woods, I tell you—who arrived here not two months ago, rented the next studio, and has her eye on my client base. Especially the ones I, you know, scare a little." His eyes grew wide as he gestured to his Crayola box self. "At this very moment, Tiffy is on the other side of that mirror teaching a couple from the *sixties*." He leveled steely gray eyes at Mark. "So they're not only from the sixties, they are *in* their *seventies*. And they live locally and are part of her *borrrring* ballroom classes she started on Wednesday nights, so this is one big advertisement for her business."

"Are we your only couple?" Emma asked, hoping Jasper wasn't going to put all his competitive energy into them.

"I have the eighties and the whatever you call those unfortunates born in the oh-somethings."

"Millennials?" Mark suggested.

"Aughts?" Emma added.

"Pains in the butt," Jasper said. "Tiffany has the sixties and seventies and, like it or not, the precious old factor is going to be in their favor." He sighed as though not happy with the dance draw. "The know-it-all nineties folks are choreographing their own, of course." He looked Mark up and down. "Are you sure you're in your forties?"

"Quite."

"Well, at least we have the beauty factor with both of you," Jasper said. "*You* didn't graduate in the eighties," he said to Emma, his tone accusatory.

"Know-it-all nineties," she quipped. "And I didn't go to Mimosa High."

"That's okay. If you're with him, you qualify. Let's dance and win that ten grand. You get to keep it all, and I get bragging rights."

Emma let out a low whistle. "That's a decent prize. Who put up that much money for a dance competition, anyway?"

Jasper rolled his eyes. "One of the Mimosa High alum is a hedge-fund billionaire, and he proposed to his dream girl, who was a maid at the resort, at the first reunion on the beach."

"Really?" Emma asked. "What a romantic story."

"So *Pretty Woman*, don't you think?" Jasper asked. "Anyway, those two put up the cash as a nice gesture, promo for the resort, and to get more people to come and be excited for the event. And you could win it! If you can dance, that is."

Emma and Mark shared a look, but Jasper was studying his clipboard.

"Now, we are required by rules to play seven different numbers from—"

"We're dancing to seven songs?" Mark practically gagged on the question.

"Not the whole song!" he assured them. "Just enough to get the message and tell the story. And here's the story." He held out his clipboard like he was presenting the Hope Diamond. "Would you like to read it, or shall I tell you?"

"Just tell us," Emma said.

"Well, I understand you two are recently engaged— muchas congrats, by the way—and so who better to tell the story of meeting, courtship, and forever love...eighties-style?"

Who better indeed?

"We open with Blondie. *Call Me*," Jasper said.

"Wait," Emma said. "We have a list. We came up with songs."

Jasper somehow managed to lift one brow while the other tilted down in the most hilarious *you've got to be kidding* look she'd ever received.

"I'm the choreographer."

"We're the talent."

"You're the dancers," he corrected. "We've yet to decide if there's any real talent involved."

Once again, she glanced at Mark and somehow knew what he was thinking. No talent, and if they used Jasper's playlist, maybe they could blame their loss on him.

Jasper checked his clipboard. "Okay, *Call Me* will kick it off with a little something fast and furious and—get this—we use one of those giant brick cell phones and Mark can strut across the stage like Michael Douglas in *Wall Street*. Won't that be *fabulous*?"

"My dad had one of those phones," Mark said. "It was...cool."

"Well, now it's a museum piece, so don't drop the one I managed to find," Jasper said. "We'll start with a little back and forth, really using your jazz hands—"

"Our what?" Mark asked.

Emma stepped forward. "We probably aren't your top-level jazz hands...types," she said. "Maybe something a little less technical."

"When those antiques across the hall will be doing the Twist?" Jasper waved off the protest. "You'll learn. Then we move into *Your Kiss Is on My List*, Hall & Oates. You know what that means."

Mark kissed the air in Emma's direction, and she tapped her face as if it hit the mark.

"Yes!" Jasper snapped his fingers and pointed at Emma. "Playful! That's what I want. Playful, romantic, sexy, and fun. That's what the eighties were!"

"They were?" Emma laughed. "I thought they were all about shoulder pads and the Rubik's Cube."

"No," Mark said, shaking his head and getting them both to turn. "They were playful. And fun. And...romantic."

Damn. They were also the ten years when he met and married his soul mate. Immediately, Emma stepped closer to him, feeling protective and determined not to let this little stroll down memory lane take him to a place that hurt. Not after seeing how his expression changed when he saw that church.

"We'll just dance and have fun," she said.

He gave her a warm smile. "I always have fun with you," he assured her, the compliment surprising her.

"Okay, lovebirds," Jasper said, clapping. "Focus. After Hall & Oates, we're going into something a little slower and waltzier. I want to know what love is..." He started to sing.

"I want you to show me," Emma finished.

"Excellent," Jasper nodded. "Then, the eighties anthem."

"*Livin' on a Prayer*?" Mark suggested, lifting his hands in a classic air guitar pose. "We had a band in my garage."

That earned him a look of sheer disgust from the dance instructor. "*What a Feelin'. Flashdance*. Leg warmers and torn shirts, remember?"

"I may have slept through that one," Mark said, making Emma laugh.

"Three left," Jasper continued. "And this is where it gets even better."

"Don't know how it can," Emma said dryly.

Mark slipped his arm around her and gave a gentle hug.

"There's at least one bottle of wine waiting for us as a reward."

"Wine? I'm going to need to swim naked in a vat of tequila."

His smile grew. "We can arrange that."

Her whole body weakened at the sexy promise.

"Do you mind?" Jasper demanded, getting their attention, though they both fought a laugh. "We shall then, if you two aren't busy planning your evening activities, move into the big crescendo. We have Huey Lewis doing *The Power of Love*, then a slow, sexy ballad with *Endless Love*, and then, the *ultimate* eighties dance song, *The Time of My Life*—"

"No."

Emma startled at how sharply the word came out of Mark's mouth. Jasper looked up, too, already exasperated, but Emma instantly read the change in Mark's expression.

"No," she agreed immediately. "Not that one."

It had to have been their song. She just knew it. And she'd take this colorful bird down with one hand if she had to, but they weren't putting Mark through that.

"What?" Jasper practically screamed. "First of all, you don't have a say, no matter what you were told by some planning committee. Second of all, it's *Dirty Dancing*, you two. This is the *eighties*. This is the essence of the eighties! Jennifer Grey and Patrick Swayze and..." He started moving his hips and running his hands down the back of an imaginary partner. "You can't *not* have *Time of My Life* in an eighties homage celebrating dance!"

Mark just stared at him, silent, but Emma was already gearing up for battle, her hands fisted as she stepped forward, her mind whirring.

"I have a better idea," she said quickly. "A perfect idea, guaranteed to get a win."

Both men stared at her, and she suddenly felt like she was in the middle of a brainstorm session at the agency and everyone had a good idea but her. She had nothing.

A quick look at Mark and she dug deeper. "The way to win is to get the rest of the place involved," she said, giving her hands a confident clap.

Jasper scowled. "You're the ones on the stage dancing."

"That's what everyone else will do," she scoffed. "We need a song that makes everyone emotional and...and...happy." Especially Mark.

"Patrick Swayze doesn't make you happy?" Jasper countered.

"That song is not right," she said, grabbing his clipboard. "How about..." She scanned the page and then smashed her finger on it. "Oh my God, this is the song, Jasper. Right here. *That's What Friends Are For*." She shoved the clipboard back at him. "Can you imagine? Everyone will stand. Sing. Sway with their arms around each other."

"S-S-Sway?" Jasper could barely say the word.

"Of course they'll sway! By then, they'll be good and toasted. And we will win."

Jasper's lip curled. "Dionne Warwick?"

"We'll *win*," she insisted.

"But this is a love story," Jasper fired back. "You can't end with a song about friends!"

"We're friends," she said, indicating Mark, who still hadn't spoken or taken his eyes off her.

"But you're *lovers* in the dance. And, I assume, in real life."

Mark finally stepped forward, putting a hand on Emma's shoulder. "I think she's right."

"Of course you do. You're going to be her husband. You have to say she's right."

"He doesn't," she replied. "But I am. Jasper, people are seeing friends for the first time in years at this thing. A reunion isn't about love, it's about *friendship*." She threw up her hands. "Game over, baby."

Jasper just stared at her, the face of defeat. "Okaaaayyy." He dragged the word out. "I guess it has more or less the same beat. For *swaying*." He rolled his eyes dramatically. "As long as we win."

Mark looked down at Emma and pressed a kiss on her hair. "Thanks," he said.

They didn't get a chance to say another word, because the music blasted, and Jasper went into full choreographer mode, dragging them through move after move, sighing mostly in disgust, pushing them together, pulling them apart, and finally getting them to remember the simplest of simple steps.

Two hours later, Jasper snapped off the sound, and Emma was surprisingly disappointed that all the contact and laughter ended.

"Download these songs," Jasper said. "Practice at home, perfect those steps, and I'll see you back here at least two more times this week. God knows, you'll need it."

Emma looked at Mark, expecting an argument, but his eyes glistened and his tanned complexion glowed with exertion when he nodded several times. "We'll be here."

Jasper looked up from his notes, eyes flashing. "Someone's had a change of heart."

"That was fun," Mark said with a shrug, pulling Emma into him with no music or reason. "Didn't you have fun?" he asked her.

Fun? Understatement of the year.

For one thing, she'd forgotten that Kyle Chambers existed. She didn't think about the fact that she had no job or was spending the week in a crazy pretend engagement with a man who made her laugh and twirl and…forget.

"Yeah," she agreed. "I had a blast."

They said good-bye, promised to practice, and stepped into the cool, dimly lit hallway. Almost immediately, Mark turned to her and put both hands on her shoulders, holding her in place with a light touch and intense gaze.

"How did you know?"

She swallowed. "You're kind of transparent with your own fears."

"I don't have fears."

She tipped her head. "Not that you admit to. I like our replacement suggestion. Friends are…good."

He slid one hand under her jaw, palming her cheek, lifting her face to him. "You wanted to protect me."

"Just doing my job to help you avoid the things you want to avoid."

He scanned her face, his blue eyes searing her as they searched every inch as if he couldn't quite figure her out but didn't want to stop trying. The intensity was enough to make her almost step backward.

She held her ground and was so insanely aware of how close they were. Of how he smelled like sweat and spice, of how tiny salt-and-pepper whiskers shadowed his hollow cheeks, of how much she wanted to kiss him. The desire was pulling her under like a powerful rip current.

"Doing your job?" He closed the space very slowly, getting closer and closer until his lips were right over hers. "Give the woman a promotion," he whispered.

And down she went. "Give her a kiss, instead."

A flicker of surprise flashed in his eyes. "Conquered that fear in a hurry, did you?"

"Maybe. Better test me."

He did, pressing his mouth against hers, so soft his lips tickled hers, then a rush of pressure and pleasure as he upped the ante and opened his mouth over hers. Emma couldn't stop herself from lifting her hands and laying them on his shoulders, feeling the strength in his muscles and the warmth of his skin through his thin T-shirt.

She couldn't help angling her head and offering her tongue while her hands moved up and around the sturdy column of his neck. His flesh was still damp, and she could feel his pulse thumping under her fingers.

His hand spread on her cheek, taking control of her face and the kiss, drawing the softest whimper of surrender from her throat.

"So, how about we take on another fear of yours with something bigger and badder?" he asked. "Something faster and more dangerous?"

She melted. "Okay." And then she got her wits back. "Wait. How big and bad? How fast and dangerous?"

He just smiled, all slow and sexy and sweet. "You gotta trust me, Em."

And off she went like a lamb to the slaughter. A very happy lamb.

Chapter Eleven

"This baby is sheer perfection." Mark sighed happily.

They'd gone back to the resort, showered, changed, had lunch, and instructed the Casa Blanca driver to take them to the exotic car rental in Naples.

After all that, Mark finally had what he wanted in his hands—the wheel of a gleaming silver 2016 Porsche 911 Carrera S, the heady need for speed already heating up his veins.

"It's pretty nice," Emma agreed, sitting lightly on the leather as if she didn't really want to settle into the low seat and see how a car like this would ride.

Smooth and fast and sweet, that's how.

"Pretty nice?" he choked softly. "If I showed up at the next Porsche Club of America race in this, they'd hand me the trophy without racing. But that wouldn't be any fun. Look at this jewel, Emma."

She gave the sleek dashboard a touch. "Fancy."

"Yeah, but who cares about that? Under that hood? Four hundred and twenty turbocharged horses. The tach hits 6500. You can go zero to sixty in under four seconds."

"*You* can," she fired back. "Please do not think for one second that I'm driving this thing at high speeds."

"Sure you will. I even got the automatic for you."

"Was that a huge sacrifice?"

Actually, it wasn't. In fact, without hills and curves in the road, the Sport Chrono version was better, and a stick was a waste. "What would have been a huge sacrifice was that Ford Taurus you suggested on the way over."

She laughed. "Well, it seemed sensible if all I need to do is beat the fear of left turns."

"Sensible is stupid." He threw her a smile. "And you look damn good in this car."

A slight flush deepened her cheeks, and she gave him a playful tap. "And you look like you were born to drive it."

"I was." He pulled on a seat belt, a low-grade heat of anticipation rolling through him. "Sadly, we're not autocross racing today, although I'd love to. But we can take a joy ride along the beach, maybe find some back roads near the Everglades and some challenging left turns for you."

He fired up the engine and took a minute to listen to the music of German engineering.

"Did you race when you lived here?" she asked.

"Oh, no, I didn't start taking driving seriously until a few years ago. I met a guy who was in the PCA, went to a weekend race, and I was hooked. Bought a 911, though not this nice, and when I can, I race. Ready?"

She checked her seat belt with a tug. "I guess so."

"Come on, Em. You're going to love it. I've never had a racing partner."

She gave him a quick, questioning look. "Never?"

"I've always flown solo," he said, getting a warm, surprised smile. "Until today."

"Then let's do this."

He rolled out of the exotic-car rental lot in the heart of high-end Naples, revving the engine enough to make the

115

hairs on the back of his neck dance. "Oh yeah," he murmured, reaching for her hand. "And holding your hand is another good thing about the automatic."

She curled her fingers around his, and he lifted their joined hands to his lips. Why *hadn't* he ever had a racing partner, he wondered fleetingly. This was way more fun with a beautiful woman at his side.

But his passion for racing had developed in the last few years, so he'd never shared it with Julia. Or any woman...until today.

Why would he want to start now? Because he met someone who wasn't just a distraction...but a real attraction? That was a first. That was...

Not supposed to happen. He'd never wanted to share life or time or anything meaningful with someone who wasn't Julia.

But today, he felt differently.

Brushing off an unexpected twinge of guilt, he drove into Naples traffic, already seeking traffic breaks and the chance to change lanes to warm this puppy up for some real driving.

The Carrera drove like a dream, screaming to get wide open, and he found a few straightaway roads that gave him a chance to test the speed, but mostly they cruised up and down the tony store-lined avenues, enjoying the salt air whipping through the car and testing its handling.

Emma asked a lot of questions and, without even thinking about it, he talked a lot about the car, the racing club, and his love of the sport.

Until he realized she was just trying to make him forget the real mission today.

"Hey, I'm on to you," he teased, easing through traffic to a side street. "Don't think I'm not."

"What?" She feigned innocence.

"All these questions. Like you really care about torque peak and active suspension management."

She laughed, busted. "I do. That's how I write ad copy, you know. I pick someone's brain who's extremely knowledgeable, and then I turn that into words that make other people want to buy whatever product is being sold."

"So what would you say about this car?"

She thought about that for a second. "Well, a picture of you driving it might sell it to anybody who can afford it."

"I thought you were all about words, not pictures."

She studied him as he pulled off the main road onto a side street. "A simple headline, I think. Your hand..." She reached down and brushed a light fingertip over his knuckles, the whisper of a touch kicking him in the gut. Lower. "Just like that on the gearshift."

"This is an automatic and that's just for show." He tapped the stick that rose up from the console, its purpose little more than to put the car in park and drive and have a place to rest your hand...so a beautiful woman would touch it.

"My ad would definitely be for a manual transmission, then," she said. "Your hand, a close-up, the Porsche logo. Headline..." She spread her hands through the air to highlight her next words. "Sex on a Stick."

He wanted to laugh at the innuendo, and marvel at her quick thinking, but all he could do was react to the blast of heat that had very little to do with the engine or handling.

He cleared his throat. "And the rest of the ad?"

"The copy? Not much. Just something that would tap into the fact that men want to take the ride behind the wheel. And women want to take a different kind of ride."

He slid the Porsche into a parking spot in front of a café. "A different kind of ride?"

"With the driver. It's probably not news to you, but sex sells. The sooner you bring it into the copy, the better."

He turned to meet her gaze, captured by the teasing spark and that little bit of seriousness he saw there. "How about you?"

She swallowed visibly. "Me?"

She was only a few inches away, her eyes bright, her lips parted...the word *sex* hanging in the air like it was part of the breeze.

She put her hand on his arm. "I'm ready."

Really? "Emma..."

"Can we do it with the light first?"

With the lights on? Is that what she meant?

"At least that way I can get the feel of the car before I attempt a left turn without a light."

Oh, of course. Left turns. "Sure." He reached for the clasp of his seat belt. "Time to make left turns," he said, his voice surprisingly gruff as he climbed out.

And cool the hell down.

What just happened? Emma sat in the car for a few seconds, her cheeks warm. There was an awful lot of dancing around kisses and sex talk and things that...she couldn't stop thinking about. Had no business thinking about.

Her door opened, and she turned to see the lower half of Mark Solomon standing there, khaki pants on a half that was every bit as divine as the upper half. Narrow hips and waist, strong thighs, and...if she didn't know better, a little rise in the crotch.

Her mouth actually watered.

Great. She'd turned him on with ad copy about a gearshift. Which Kyle would have...

Kyle? What was she thinking about Kyle for while staring at a much nicer lower half?

Mark dipped down. "You scared?"

Not of left turns.

"Of course not." She automatically took the hand he offered and slid out of the seat. She let him pull her to a stand right in front of him, suddenly aware of the late afternoon sun pressing down and the light in the blue eyes that looked deep into hers. "I mean, I won't be after I make three left turns, right?" she said, trying for a lightness she didn't actually feel.

"That's the plan." He let go of her hand and stepped to the side to let her pass. "Fears are conquered."

She didn't answer, but rounded the front of the car to get into the driver's seat. It was still warm from his body, and that...didn't help things.

Holy hell, the man turned her on top to bottom. How was she supposed to get through a week of this? The more time they spent together, the more they talked, the more she stared at him and touched him and sneaked in a few kisses...the more she wanted more.

"You look awfully serious," he said, pulling his seat belt on.

"I thought we were just, you know, having a little fake engagement here, and the week has turned into some kind of active fear management therapy."

He laughed softly. "Active fear management therapy? Never heard of that."

"I just made it up."

"Of course you did, word girl." He gave her a nudge.

"Come on. Just a single touch, right there, and the engines will scream."

She slid him a look. "Does everything have to be so sexual?"

"Says the woman whose winning headline is 'Sex on a Stick.'"

"I meant…" She took a breath and slowly exhaled. "With us."

He met her gaze with one that was direct and unwavering. "Does that scare you, too?"

"To death."

She waited for him to scoff at her. To give her some kind of assurance. To tease about their fake engagement or offer a three-point fear-conquering technique. But his expression remained perfectly serious. "Me, too," he admitted softly.

"Oh." She barely whispered the word. "Well, there's always active fear management therapy."

He gave a slow smile. "Or we could just give in and see what happens."

She knew what would happen. She was already imagining the feel of his hands, the weight of his body, the thrill of his—

"But for now, let's make left turns, Em."

She forced herself to settle down and focused on the driving.

Within minutes, she forgot the chemistry and electricity arcing and sparking between them. She forgot that rise in his khakis and that look in his eyes. She forgot the ache to get closer and the confusion that brought.

Because, for the first time in her life, Emma was one with a machine. And pretty much anything she'd ever done prior to that was forgotten.

"Oh my God," she exclaimed as she found a stretch of

road with no traffic for a few blocks. "Can I open it up a little?"

"Not too much unless you want the Naples police bearing down on you," he warned her. "You like this, don't you?"

She stole a glance to her side. "*Like* is the wrong word. It's more like…a driving orgasm."

He barked a laugh. "Ten minutes ago you were complaining about the sex talk."

"I'm serious!" She broke when approaching a light, feeling the rumble of, what had he said, four-twenty horsepower? She had no real clue what that meant, but it felt…solid and thrilling and *hot*. Like a little too much power under her hands and way too much need to exercise it.

"Is this why guys like driving so much?" she asked.

"This is why guys like driving ninety-thousand-dollar Porsches so much."

She gave a whistle.

"Slide into the left lane, Em. It's time."

She let out a little exhale but followed his order. There was a light and not a lot of other cars on this section of the boulevard. She didn't enjoy making left turns with oncoming traffic, but with a light, this would be a breeze.

"I got this," she assured him, making the turn easily.

"I thought you were scared."

She shrugged. "That wasn't very tough, and this car? Oh my God, I'm in love with this car."

He laughed heartily. "The same thing happened to me the first time I was in a 911. It's really a religious experience, isn't it?"

She couldn't argue that. "Should I turn here and then make a left back onto Gulf Shore?"

"Not yet. A few more roads, then you'll have to make that left with no light."

Damn. But the car made her feel totally in control, so she followed orders and made the turn. And another. And another.

"Had enough? The turn to the causeway is about half a mile from here."

She shook her head and changed lanes with confidence. "Enough? I can't get enough. I hope you don't expect to get behind the wheel of this car again all week."

"Damn, woman, you drive a hard bargain. I love to drive the car, but I kind of enjoy watching you do it more."

She threw her head back with a satisfied laugh. "This is so *awesome!*"

"So are you," he whispered, but she heard him even though the words were whipped by the wind. She gave the steering wheel a squeeze in response and hit the accelerator, cruising onto the long bridge that connected Mimosa Key to the mainland.

"I thought you hated bridges," he said when they were almost at the halfway point.

"There's a bridge?" she joked. "I thought we were just flying."

She concentrated on the view that spilled out in front of the silver sloping car. The sun was dipping low, casting a gorgeous orange glow on the wide body of water dotted with white pleasure craft. Salt air filled the car, and the engine revved loud as they reached the top of the bridge and the commanding view of the tropical island of Mimosa Key in the Gulf of Mexico.

"Let's cruise all over the island," she suggested as they passed the harbor and reached the small town center.

"You sound like my high school buddies."

"Yes," she said, excitement growing. "Let's go to Mimosa High. I want to see this place everyone is talking about."

Instantly, she felt him tense. "And take the chance of running over a texting teenager? Better go back to the resort."

She kept her eyes on the road, silent for a few more beats. "We're alone now."

"I'm aware."

"You have to be honest."

"I am."

She threw a quick look at him, but he was staring out the window at the water below.

"Running over teenagers is not the reason you don't want to go to Mimosa High."

"You know the reason."

"So, why am I the only one forced to face fears this week?" she asked. "I think it would help you to—"

"I didn't ask for this," he said sharply, making her suck in a quick breath. "I mean, obviously I asked for your company and am enjoying the hell out of it, but I had no agenda to…to…let go of the past."

"And I had no agenda of conquering fears," she replied. "I thought I was getting a vacation in paradise and maybe some advice about getting over my ex, since you're a professional relationship adviser or something."

"Are you thinking about him?" he asked.

Not for one freaking second. "Not really," she admitted. "Which is nice. You should try it."

She could feel his eyes on her, but she kept her attention on the road ahead, navigating her way through town.

"What precisely does that mean?" he finally asked.

Taking a slow inhale, she smoothed out her thoughts so they'd make sense. "It means that you will benefit from the same kind of happiness if you let go of the memories that are weighing you down."

"They don't weigh me down. I treasure them."

"As you should," she agreed. "But if you treasured them instead of dreading them, you wouldn't avoid places like the church or your high school."

He didn't answer for a long time, long enough for her to reach the empty beach road that headed to Barefoot Bay.

"Now you can open it up a little," Mark said. "This is a safe road."

She pressed the accelerator and watched the speed increase, along with the zing in her blood. It didn't last long, but it made her whole body vibrate and ache for more. She slowed down and pulled into the entrance to the resort, breathless from the speed, but still waiting for his response.

"Park anywhere?" she asked.

"Right along here should be good."

She drove down a lane and found a spot on the end, pulling in and reluctantly putting the car in park.

"I don't want this to end," she admitted on a sigh.

That made Mark laugh again. "I've created a monster."

"I don't mean the car." She turned to him, still clinging to the wheel, wishing she hadn't pushed him so hard. It wasn't her place at all, despite the easy friendship they were developing. "I mean, I don't want to end the fun we're having. I didn't mean to force you to think about things that make you unhappy."

He didn't answer, and she vowed to keep this light and fun.

"And I think you promised me some wine…" Her voice drifted as her gaze caught movement over Mark's shoulder. A man, walking toward them, slowing to look at the car. He was so…familiar.

He lifted his hand to shield his eyes from the setting sun,

staring at them, right into Mark's open window. Right into the car.

Mark glanced back, following her gaze. "It does get attention."

She opened her mouth to reply, but the words were caught in her throat, so impossible to speak that she completely lost her voice.

The man kept coming. Closer. Intent. Staring at the car…or inside it. Ten more feet and he'd see her.

"That's…" She croaked the word.

Mark turned again, just as the man stopped a few feet from the car, staring. "It's like a beautiful woman," Mark said. "Men can't resist—"

She grabbed his head and pulled him into a kiss, angling her face not to intensify the kiss, but to hide. She just had to hide until he passed.

Through her thrumming pulse, she heard, "Nice wheels," and a low whistle, but Emma pressed so hard into Mark's face that neither one of them could breathe. Or be seen.

Finally, she broke the kiss, and a very surprised Mark stared at her. "Like I said," he whispered, "the car's magic."

She closed her eyes and slowly turned to see the man retreating from view, walking into the resort. "My ex is here."

Chapter Twelve

Mark poured her wine and let her talk. And for forty-five minutes, Emma spewed her disbelief, concern, and fury at the man who killed her driving buzz.

"It has to be something with the Casa Blanca ad account," she said, taking a healthy sip of the sauvignon. "Why else would he be here?"

"Maybe he's looking for you," Mark suggested, the idea so obvious he couldn't believe she hadn't assumed that first.

But she shook her head. "He doesn't have anything else to say to me. It's all been said."

"Maybe he changed his mind and wants to give it another shot?"

She closed her eyes as if the thought pained her. "No," she said simply. "I'm not interested."

"Then why couldn't he be here for the same reason as you? To take advantage of the resort."

"He was the one who canceled the reservation. I suppose he could have business about the account, but I really need to be sure I can avoid him."

"Why avoid him?" Mark asked. "You have every right to be here."

"With my fiancé?" She blew out a long exhale.

"Unless he's going to the reunion events, he doesn't have to know."

She pushed her hand through her hair, moaning a little. "I really don't want a confrontation."

"Why should there be one? He broke off the relationship, not you."

"I know." She ran her finger over the rim of the glass, staring at the water, distant. "I just want to know why he's here."

Mark could understand that, and her concerns. And clear reasoning wasn't doing a thing to make her feel better. Still, he kept trying. "Unless they had another sudden cancellation, he's not staying here," he said. "So you don't have to hide for a week."

She gave him a pleading look. "I don't want to see him."

Mark couldn't make the guy go away, and he couldn't seem to make Emma feel better.

But he had to try. His mind flashed back to her stalwart defense of him, her determined fight to get that song changed because she wanted to help him, and he knew he had to try to get her what she wanted. Information? Surely he could do that.

"Listen," he said, pushing up. "You take a swim, a shower, maybe drink some more wine. Let me do a little recon."

"You'd do that?" She looked up at him, her eyes bright and her color high. Just like it had been in the car, but this didn't get the same physical reaction in him. Instead of wanting to jump her bones, he wanted to help her. The need to do something for her, to fix the situation and see her smile—not wry and rueful, but real and happy—burned in him.

He reached out his hand and caressed her cheek, the

smooth skin delicate under his fingertips. "I would do that and more."

Her jaw loosened a little. "Why?"

Because he liked her and already had a soft spot for her in his heart...the only thing of his soft around her lately, that was for sure. "Strays and orphans, remember?"

She turned her face so that her lips brushed his palm. "I'm your stray this week." The kiss was light, barely air, and kicked him hard in the chest.

He smiled. "Prettiest one ever. And, hey, I'll order dinner from Junonia while I'm over there, and we can eat out here tonight. Just the two of us."

"That sounds perfect," she said. "No lying to Mimosa High grads or hiding from my former fiancé."

He bent over and kissed her on top of the head. "Save me some wine."

"No promises."

Still smiling, he walked the distance from the villa to the main building of the resort without even glancing at the sunset over the gulf to his right. The arrival of Kyle Chambers threw a monkey wrench into their charade, but Mark wasn't worried. He just didn't want to lose the magic that had been building with Emma.

Magic.

Man, it had been a long time since he used that word to describe something he felt for a woman. Why was she so different? Was it just the right time and place or...right woman?

There'd been plenty of "right now" women over the years, but something about her was...more.

Maybe it was just the chemistry, which was real and tangible. Hell, if that bonehead Chambers hadn't shown up out of the blue, Mark had a feeling he would *not* have been sleeping on the sofa bed in the living room tonight.

Stepping into the marble-tiled, air conditioned lobby, he glanced around, fairly certain he'd recognize the guy again. Definitely skinny-shouldered, dark hair, glasses, smooth-faced with the kind of goatee that screamed craft-beer-drinking hipster.

No sign of him at the desk or around the lobby. Of course, he could have checked into a room, but Lacey had told Mark they were booked solid when he'd gotten the last available villa. He could talk to Lacey, but he didn't want to send up any red flags, especially since she'd already questioned Emma at the party last night.

On a hunch, he headed toward the patio, pausing at the doors to scan the outdoor dining area. Almost immediately, he spotted the same guy he'd seen in the parking lot, now sitting at a table alone, looking at his phone.

Mark studied the man that Emma had been ready to marry. His shoulders weren't *that* skinny, but he had a lanky build and long limbs. Maybe six feet, forty-ish, decent-looking, he supposed.

Certainly not the monster Mark had imagined, but still a dick based on everything he knew. Suddenly, the man looked up and stood as Lacey Walker headed in his direction.

So it *was* an ad agency thing that brought him here. Emma would want to know that, and Mark realized he could easily round the bar and take a seat close enough to hear their conversation but not be seen by Lacey.

Without giving it much thought, he went outside, followed that plan, and sat less than five feet away, although his back was to them and Lacey was turned the other way. He was half tempted to take out his phone and fake-text to sneak a picture for Emma.

She'd like that, but Lacey's words snagged his attention as he casually flagged the bartender.

"I really appreciate you coming all the way down here, Kyle, and how important this is, but I simply don't have time this week."

"I had to, Lacey," he said. "I couldn't just lose the account without a fight."

Lose the account? Mark leaned back a few centimeters, listening to the reply.

"You haven't lost the account," she said. "I just think it's time to do an agency review. Casa Blanca is growing, and our needs are changing and—"

"That's shorthand for East End getting fired," he said.

During her long silence, Mark quickly ordered a club soda and settled in to hear more.

"Can I at least ask why?" Kyle asked.

"I'll be straight with you: The three proposed ads you sent last week were bombs," she said. "I don't know what happened in creative, but the copy wasn't what I've come to expect from East End. It was lackluster. *I* could have written better copy."

Mark knew what had happened; Kyle's superstar copywriter quit with a broken heart two weeks ago. He stole a glance over his shoulder and could see Lacey getting up already.

"I hired you because the creative sang," she said. "I know you came down here to save the account, but we have a huge event, and I need to deal with that. I wish I could offer you a room, but we're booked solid."

"Then the advertising must be working," Kyle replied, a mix of dry humor and hope in the comment.

"I'll be making a short list of agencies to invite in to pitch, and I promise East End will be on it. Okay? I'm sorry, but I really have to go. Thanks, Kyle."

She stepped away, brushing past Mark as he turned on the barstool.

"Oh, hello, Mark!" Her voice was lighter and brighter as she greeted him. "How'd the dance lessons go today?"

"Surprisingly fun," he said.

"I'm so glad. Oh, I'm pulling together a group to go to the Barefoot Bucks exhibition game later this week. Can you and Emma join us?"

"Absolutely. We were thinking about going to the game anyway. Thanks, Lacey."

She clasped her hands, pleased with his answer, her bright smile growing. "Perfect. I'll see you at the next meeting." She gave him a quick hug and took off toward the lobby.

Less than ten seconds later, Kyle Chambers had moved to the bar, his gaze on Mark.

Mark acknowledged the look with a jut of his chin.

He took the stool next to Mark with a low sigh. "You know the owner, huh?"

"I'm here for an event she's hosting."

Heaving out a breath, he signaled the bartender, then glanced at Mark's half-empty club soda. "Can I get you one?"

"No, thanks, I'm good."

"Wish I could say the same," Kyle said glumly, holding up his empty beer glass for a refill.

"Sorry to hear that," Mark said, even though the bastard deserved what he had coming to him. Still, maybe he could get more details for Emma. "Work or women?"

He snorted. "I'm good with women," he said. "In fact, my girlfriend is on her way down. They may not have rooms here, but I got a suite at the Ritz in Naples, so screw Casa Blanca and it's no vacancy thanks to my company's great advertising."

Mark hadn't heard much past girlfriend. *He has a*

girlfriend already? "I'm sure you guys will love the Ritz."

"I don't plan to leave the suite, if you get my drift."

Classy. "How long have you been together?" Mark asked, trying for casual.

He scratched the back of his head, thinking. "Six weeks, maybe?"

What? Mark looked hard at the guy. "That's...a decent amount of time." For someone who was supposed to have married another woman two weeks ago.

"We had to keep it on the DL for a while because I was getting out of another relationship."

A low-grade anger bubbled up, and Mark took a gulp of his club soda. "Really."

"Hey, I wasn't married. Close, though. In fact, I was engaged and just a couple of weeks away from getting married, but..." He shook his head and took a fresh beer with a nod to the bartender. "When I met Rachel, whoa. Wow. Fireworks. That ever happen to you?"

"Have I ever dumped my fiancée after cheating on her with another woman?" He couldn't keep the disgust out of his voice. "No. That's never happened to me."

Kyle eyed him hard, then shrugged off the obvious judgment. "Hey, no one sees it coming, you know? Wham, it's love."

"How'd your former almost-wife take this news?" he asked, already imagining that she wouldn't take it well when Mark told her the real reason this clown dumped her.

Kyle hesitated before answering, holding the glass close to his lips. "I just told her I had cold feet," he said. "No reason to break her heart."

Except you did. "Really big of you," he said.

"Whatever, pal." Kyle pushed the stool back. "You've never walked in my moccasins."

"They'd be too small," Mark mumbled.

Kyle stood, glaring at Mark. "Sorry I talked to you, man."

"Not as sorry as I am."

Kyle leaned a little closer, and Mark didn't even flinch. He could have this skinny prick on the ground with one well-placed kick. "Look, you don't know a thing about my situation."

That was where he'd be wrong. Mark leveled a vile look at the guy.

Kyle shrugged again. "I shouldn't have gotten my meat where I get my bread, you know."

Screw class. He might have to make this joker eat his hand.

"But I did," Kyle continued. "I got caught up working late nights, and the next thing you know, one thing led to another, and getting engaged seemed like the right thing to do for a good woman, but for the wrong reasons."

"So why not tell her the truth?" Mark challenged. Because, damn it, now *he* would have to.

"Hey, I'm in advertising. My whole career is built on making things sound and seem better than they really are. I didn't know things were that serious with Rachel. I thought we were just, you know, hooking up."

What a son of a bitch.

"But then Rach and I went on a ski trip…"

Rachel…not his sister, as he'd told Emma.

"As soon as I realized where things were going, I broke it off with my fiancée."

Douchebag. "You're a great guy. So thoughtful."

"What the hell difference does it make to you?" Kyle asked, not too dumb to miss the sarcasm.

"None at all," Mark lied, standing up, his hand fisted. One more word, and he'd have to pummel the prick.

Mark walked away, ending the infuriating conversation. All the way back to the villa, he tried to decide how much to tell Emma. Should he break her heart all over again and tell her the truth? Or spare her the pain and be as much of a liar as the chump she almost married?

No, he wasn't going to break her heart. He couldn't do that to her.

Chapter Thirteen

Emma listened to Mark's recounting of the conversation he'd overheard with mixed emotions.

"So he's losing the business," she said, running her finger over the top of the crystal wine glass as she thought about…the fact that Kyle wasn't here to find her.

She didn't want it to hurt and, really, it didn't hurt. Just stung her pride a little, that was all.

Mark put his hand on top of hers. "Losing it because the copy's gone downhill. That should make you feel better."

She gave him a tight smile. "There is some revenge, yes."

"She was clear there were no rooms or villas available, too. So no chance of running into him."

"Thank God." She imagined the conversation and how brutal it must have been for Kyle to find out East End was losing that account. She didn't want to care about him, but the loss would be tough and maybe deep if it meant laying off someone at the agency.

"Did he say anything else?" she asked. "Anything about—"

The villa doorbell rang, and Mark pushed his chair back. "That's dinner. And, I'll try to remember."

"No, no." She waved her hand. "It's fine. I know enough."

When he left, Emma took another sip of wine and looked out over the evening sky, the remnants of another perfect sunset glowing over the sand.

Kyle was history, she thought. And tonight was…perfect.

Mark came back, and she chatted with the waiter who set up a formal table with a cloth and candles and delivered a glorious dinner under glass domes. While they talked, she noticed that Mark stood off to the side, looking out at the water, his broad shoulders more tense than she'd seen them.

Well, he did just go on a spy mission…*for her*.

After the Junonia waiter left their villa, they sat across from each other, the aroma of spicy shrimp and jasmine rice drifting up from the plates. Emma took another sip of wine and leaned closer.

"I have to say something." She put her hand over his and gave a squeeze. "You sure know how to turn a bad scene into a great night. This is the second time in two days that you transformed my unhappiness into a perfect time. Thank you, Mark."

His smile was just a little tighter than she was used to. "My pleasure."

"Spying on my ex was a pleasure? Why do I think you're lying?"

"I'm not lying, I…" He let out a breath, picking up his fork but not diving in.

"What is it?" she asked, definitely sensing something wasn't right. "Was it my being a pain about going to the high school today? Because I'm sorry if I came on too strong."

"No, not at all."

She eyed him longer. "But you seem really bothered by something."

"I didn't like that guy," he ground out. "You're so much better than he is. What if you hadn't figured that out?"

She swallowed, embarrassed and surprised how much his opinion mattered. "Well, then I guess I'd be another statistic and end up divorced, or I would have worked hard to make it a decent marriage."

"Did you really love him?" he asked.

"I...I..." She inhaled deeply, enjoying the aroma, but not the truth. "I live in New York, which is no easy place to be single. I'm staring down the barrel of thirty-nine, and every year, the pool of available men gets murkier. I've been a bridesmaid in five weddings in the past four years, and my married friends are stable and happy and...not lonely on Sunday afternoons. I..." Her voice cracked, and she wanted to kick herself. "I just wasn't lucky in love like you were."

He looked at her, silent.

"I mean, I know you weren't *lucky*. But you did have that one great love. You know what it's like and..."

"Is it possible you didn't really love him? You just wanted him to be the right guy?"

She considered that and didn't like how close to right he was. "I loved things about him," she said. "He wasn't...perfect."

"No, that's for sure." He took a bite of food, looking down, ending the conversation.

"But it's nice that you care. You know...like a kind older brother."

He snorted softly, chewing, then wiping his mouth with the napkin, looking hard at her. "Nothing I feel around you is brotherly."

Heat started low in her belly, clutching her. "Oh. That's..." *Exactly how I feel.* "Interesting."

He gave a sly smile. "Isn't it?"

She looked down at her own plate, not remotely sure

where this was going, but like some of those left turns she'd made today…she wanted to risk it.

"So why don't you go after the Casa Blanca account and start your own boutique ad agency?" he asked.

The question threw her, making her fork freeze mid-bite. "What?"

"You heard me."

She blinked at him, the idea so…amazing and far-fetched and frightening she couldn't quite respond.

"I mean, I don't know a lot about advertising, but if creative is the low point on that account, and that's what you do, maybe you should talk to Lacey and pool your resources and take the business right out from under your ex's snotty nose."

"You *really* didn't like him, did you?"

"You have no idea." He took a deep drink of wine. "But, seriously, Em. You quit your job because of him and what he did, and now he's losing the account because you're gone."

"I don't hate that idea, but…" She tried to eat, but couldn't bring herself to take a bite. His suggestion just fell all over her chest like a warm coat on a cold day, and she really didn't want to like it so much, but… "No."

"Why not?" he asked.

"Really? You need the list of reasons? How about I don't have the experience? I need working capital. I don't know the account management side. I might get sued by East End Marketing for poaching a client. And…and…"

"And you're scared."

She stared at him, giving up a bite for a drink of cold water for her surprisingly parched throat. "Yes," she said after a moment. "Spitless."

"Then it's another fear we'll have to conquer."

She laughed. "Get three clients and I'm an agency."

"Damn straight," he said, his own appetite appearing to improve with the turn of the conversation. "You have the experience, and you probably picked up more about management than you realize." He took a bite, then pointed the fork at her as he chewed and swallowed. "I'd finance your working capital and, honestly, that loser doesn't have the nads to sue you. I'd bet my life on it."

And he'd probably be right. "You'd finance it? I don't think I could accept that offer, but thank you."

"Hey, I saw you in action today. When you want to come up with something creative..." He leaned forward and lifted his brows. "Everyone will *sway*?"

She laughed. "It worked, even if Jasper was only slightly horrified at first."

"But you persuaded him, and isn't that the whole idea of advertising? You have skills, and I'd invest in them."

"Thank you, but that would..." *Complicate the hell out of my life.*

"What if we win the dance competition?" he asked. "You could have my half. Then you'd have ten grand to start."

She stared at him, not sure if she wanted to throttle him, kiss him, or laugh in his face. "You're serious."

"Dead."

"Why?"

He shrugged and cut the tail off a shrimp. "Because I want to. This is how I live now. *Carpe diem*, you know?"

"What do you mean 'how you live *now*'?"

He took a second to gather his thoughts, then said, "The one thing I learned from my darkest days is that life is short, unpredictable, and only as good as what you make it during the time you're given. As much as I wanted to roll around and feel sorry for myself and drink myself into a stupor after Julia died, I refused to."

"That's why you took a chance on selling the company and spend your time jumping out of planes?" Emma asked.

"It's why I do everything wholeheartedly and with passion. I never doubt my ability to at least try. And I never, ever let a golden opportunity pass me by. And this? This is your golden opportunity."

A slow heat built in her belly, a combination of wanting to agree and just…wanting *him*. "You think so?"

"I know so. You should pitch Lacey while you're here. Talk to her, tell her who you are…"

"Oh, that'd be a fun conversation."

"We'll be straight and tell her everything," he said. "She'll understand why we're pretending to be engaged. Why don't we arrange a time for you to sit down and talk to her about the business and—"

"Whoa." She held up her hand. "I didn't say I'd pitch her. I'm not ready to do that. And what's this *we* business, anyway?"

He gave her a teasing look. "Hey, I spied for you tonight. I'm invested in the outcome, okay?"

"Okay." She smiled, the thought of his investment— emotional, financial, even time—was like balm on a heart that had gotten surprisingly bruised today.

"So talk to Lacey," Mark said. "What can it hurt? I mean, if you don't want to—"

"I do," she said. "The more I think about freelancing an account or even starting my own little shop, the more I love the idea." Like, *really* love it.

"Owning your own business and being your own boss is just like driving a Porsche," he said with a smile. "You got power, control, speed, and it feels good."

"And it costs a fortune and could send you flying right over a bridge."

He laughed at that, shaking his head. "*Carpe diem*, Em."

For a long moment, all she could do was stare at him. This handsome silver devil who'd found her on a doorstep weeping such a short time ago and now believed in her so much, he actually made her think she could do this.

"How did you do that?" she asked on a whisper.

"How did I do what?"

She searched his face, imagining a thirty-two-year-old man mourning the loss of his beloved wife. "When your wife died, you became better, not bitter. Of all the things you've done, that's the one that I envy the most."

"It's a choice you make." He leaned back and took a drink of water. "So? What are you going to call your new agency?"

And right then, under the pale moon with a man she barely knew, Emma felt her whole heart and soul slip, slide, and stumble toward something she'd never felt before.

Mark believed in her, and because of that, she believed in herself.

How was it she'd planned to marry a man who'd never made her feel like this...and she was going to walk away from this one, who did?

Chapter Fourteen

Mark woke around three thirty in the morning with a crick in his neck from the only thing that wasn't truly luxurious in the villa—the pullout sofa bed. Whose stupid idea was it to sleep on this thing?

But the door to the villa's only bedroom stayed firmly shut. Emma had spent the rest of the night chatting about the possibility of her own business, and while Mark had really enjoyed her growing enthusiasm, she'd ended the night with a warm hug and a platonic good night.

What the hell had Plato been thinking with that bullshit, anyway?

He pushed off the throw blanket and got up, trying to decide if he wanted a real drink or coffee. Since this hour didn't really qualify for either one, he settled on an ice-cold bottle of water and took it out to the patio where the air was cool, salty, and inviting.

Shirtless with nothing on but thin sleep pants, he stood at the railing and looked at the pinpoints of stars, the moon risen too far to leave much of a silver river on the bay. The sand was empty, the tide low, the surf too gentle to hear from this distance.

He took a deep breath and waited for the inevitable. The

kick of an old ache that never, ever failed to land its steel toe in his solar plexus during a contemplative moment. Grief. Loneliness. A black hole of hurt.

But he didn't feel it.

Come on, he chided himself. It would be wrong to look at stars and feel the breeze and listen to distant surf and not think of Julia, right? She'd love this. She'd say...she'd say...

What would she say?

Good God, he couldn't even conjure up the memory of her voice. What the hell?

"Julia," he whispered. "Where are you?"

But nothing, not a sound, came to mind. Not her laugh, not her sighs, not a teasing joke or insightful comment.

His chest felt numb and heavy. He'd forgotten her. How had that happened? Was it because he'd met—

"Hey."

He turned at the sound of a different woman's voice, this one soft and sweet and a little tentative. Emma stood in the French doors that led to the bedroom, a sleep shirt grazing the tops of her thighs, her long hair tangled and mussed.

"What are you doing up?" he asked.

"I can't sleep. Same problem?"

"Probably for different reasons." He rubbed his neck. "Sleeping on a pullout is for college students, I'm afraid."

"Oh, Mark." She took a few steps closer, out of the shadows into the soft moonlight. "I'm sorry."

"The sleeping arrangements were my idea."

"Everything's your idea," she agreed, her bare feet padding on the pavers as she approached him. "Fake engagements, opening new businesses, competitive dancing."

"Hey, the dancing was *not* my idea." His laugh caught in his throat as she reached him and he could see her face.

Damn, she was pretty. Her golden-brown eyes always had a light in them, and her lashes, even when she didn't have makeup on, were long and reached up almost to the arch of her brow. And her skin was like whipped cream, with lips just pouty enough to make him think about kissing them every single time she wasn't smiling. God, he couldn't stop looking at her. There was something precious and feminine about her features, but arresting and sharp, too. She was damn beautiful.

"It's a pretty night, though," she said, looking out to the blackness of the Gulf of Mexico. But his gaze stayed on her, dropping over the thin sleep shirt, impossible not to notice the sweet tips of her breasts, her nipples hard in the night air.

His body tightened and reacted, blood instantly moving south.

"You want to take a walk?" she asked.

Yeah, right back to that bedroom. "Not particularly."

She sighed, joining him at the railing.

"Drink?" he asked, holding out his water bottle.

"Yeah, thanks." She put her mouth against the open top and lifted the bottle, and he made no effort not to stare at the exposed throat and her half-closed eyes. When she finished, her lips were moist from the water and parted.

He took the bottle and set it on the table. He needed his hands and mouth free...for her. He had to touch her. Kiss her.

And he wasn't going to stop there.

"Emma." He reached to her face, touching that sweet skin and moving his hand into her silky hair.

She looked up at him, her eyes wide, her lips almost quivering as she drew in a slow breath. "Mark."

"You know, I gave you a big lecture tonight over dinner."

"*Carpe diem?*" she asked. "It worked. I'm seizing. Or at least thinking about seizing."

144

"So am I." He inched closer, threading her hair around his fingers. "And what kind of man would I be if I told you that I never miss an opportunity or skip a chance or refuse to try to get whatever I want…and let you slip out of my hands into that big bed alone?"

She looked up at him, very slowly angling her head, like a kitten nestling into a petting hand. "So you seize the day *and* the night?"

He didn't answer for a long time, lost in her eyes and the sound of her voice. Emma's voice. Not Julia's.

"I've been with women."

She laughed softly. "I bet you have."

"Not extraordinary numbers," he said, not sure why that particular truth was important, but it was. "But enough."

"And your point is…"

Being with a woman had never made him feel guilty before. Or at least it hadn't made him feel like something inside him had changed. But Emma did. She made him feel like he was breaking the bond with his soul mate…the one whose voice he couldn't even remember.

"Mark, what is it?"

He just shook his head, slowly pulling her into him and easing her head against his shoulder and chest. Just to feel her there. Just to feel her body press against his and give him…comfort.

Why the hell did he need that? Why was she able to give it when no one else had? Because their connection, brief and new and crazy, was emotional and not just physical.

Although, right this minute, it was all physical.

He felt her warm breath on his bare skin and closed his eyes, not caring that the simple contact did exactly what a woman's breath on a man's chest should do…made him hard.

The tiniest whimper of a response caught in her throat, but she didn't move.

"This could get complicated," she whispered without looking up.

"It could." He stroked her hair and let his hand drag over her back, enjoying each curve and muscle, finally setting on the small indent right above her ass. He felt her inhale a steadying breath, the move pressing her breasts against him just enough to make him grow stiffer against her. "In fact, it already is," he said. "Complicated."

She finally lifted her head and looked up at him, the tiniest smile pulling at her lips. "Is that what you call it?"

"Complicated and, um, hard."

She laughed softly, but didn't pull away. "You really can't resist a good sex pun, can you?"

"I'm sure you consider them the laziest form of verbal play."

"The worst." Smiling, she arched enough for their bodies to rub in a way that shot a gallon of blood to his already aching lower half. "But you make it cute and, let's be honest, we're both thinking about it."

"Mmm. Constantly." He punctuated that by lowering his head and taking the kiss he wanted so much. She lifted her arms and wrapped them around his neck, one sure hand on the back of his head, digging into his hair, angling him where she wanted the kiss.

And she wanted the kiss. Her mouth opened to his, inviting him in, taking his tongue for a playful thrust against hers. She tasted like mint and sweet woman, her lips so insanely soft, he let out a moan for how much he loved the feel of them.

She moaned softly, too, breaking the kiss and lifting her face to let him press his lips on her jaw and throat. He turned so her back was against the railing, bracing them so he could add pressure and feel her woman's body fit perfectly into his.

He slid his hands up her sides, moving the shirt higher and letting his hands still at the sides of her breasts. He wanted to touch them so badly. He wanted to fill his hands with her body, strip the shirt off, and taste every inch of her.

Fire shot through his veins and made him throb against her.

"Mark," she whispered as he dipped his head so he could kiss the skin exposed by the vee of her sleep shirt. "It's still complicated."

"And getting harder."

She chuckled a little, but that slipped into a moan as she dropped her head back, eyes closed, surrender in every cell of her body.

He looked at her like that, studying the lines of her face, her throat, and...he had to touch her.

He moved his hand over her breast, both of them hissing in a breath when his palm covered her budded nipple. He thumbed it, the flimsy fabric like a shield from what he really wanted—her skin.

"This would probably be a good time to tell you another one of my fears." She opened her eyes and looked at him. "Except who knows what you'd make me do three times."

Oh, he knew. "We can stop anytime you want." Except he continued to caress her breast, which was round and tender and perfect.

She let out a little whimper of uncertainty and pleasure. "I don't want to stop, but...I was engaged to another man two weeks ago."

And the bastard went on a ski trip with Rachel.

The reminder that he hadn't told her everything made him pull back an inch and move his hand.

"And that's enough to make you stop," she surmised.

"I don't want to stop," he told her. "I think you can feel that I don't want to stop."

Her breath already tight from lust, she bit her lip and considered that. "I just...I didn't think I'd be with someone so soon," she said.

"I didn't think I would be with someone here, this week. God knows, it was the last thing I expected. And we can stop at any point."

"Oh, Mark." She reached up and put her hands on his face, pressing his cheeks. "You are an amazing and awesome man."

Amazing and awesome? Wouldn't an amazing and awesome man tell her the truth? This woman whom he'd promised he'd be honest with in this villa?

But what good would it do her to know that her ex had cheated on her? She'd just—

"You're thinking too hard," she said, a tease in her voice as she added pressure to her touch. "And I don't know why, but you're not entirely sure about this, either. I mean, this isn't sure." She tapped his temples. "The rest of you feels quite certain."

And once again, she nailed it.

"Em, I'm damn near fifty years old. I know how this goes and what's involved. And with that maturity comes discipline and self-control. And the sense of when the time is right and when it's not."

"You know, that's pretty sexy, too."

He lowered his head and placed a light kiss on her lips. "We have the rest of the week. Let's take it slow."

She sighed in agreement, a mix of relief and disappointment. "But I am not sleeping in that comfy bed tonight."

"You're not?"

She slipped away from the railing, taking his hand and pulling him with her. "You are. There's no reason why I can't take the couch, at least every other night."

"No, I wouldn't hear of that."

She tugged him toward the French doors. "You are going in there. Alone." She didn't sound exactly happy about that, but maybe a little relieved. "And I'm sleeping in the living room. No arguments."

She had him through the doors now, onto the cool marble floor. The bed was unmade and inviting, draped with sheer fabric that screamed sex.

"Sleep with me," he said gruffly, pulling her into him. "Just sleep, I swear."

She snorted softly. "Yeah, right."

"We can try."

"We would fail."

He wrapped his arms around her for one last kiss. She complied, kissing hard and with her whole self, wrecking him when she stepped back.

"I totally get the whole self-control and discipline thing," she said, her voice breathless and rough. "But I'll be on the other side of that door if yours crumbles."

"Same."

She blew him a kiss and slipped away, going through the French doors to the patio, closing them behind her.

How long could he last? The night?

Maybe. Long enough to be completely sure he knew what he was doing, because this didn't feel...standard. If it had, they'd be on that bed right now. But it didn't.

He climbed into her bed, which already felt a million and a half times better than the one he'd been on, stretching out on her sheets, inhaling the faint floral scent of her all over the bed.

Which did nothing to get rid of his raging hard-on.

He closed his eyes and rolled over, wishing like hell she was there and he didn't have so much freaking self-control.

His breathing evened out and his body settled down, and he tried one more time to remember Julia's voice, but the only thing he heard was the sound of Emma's sweet sighs.

And for the first time in sixteen years, he fell asleep wanting a different woman in his arms—someone who wasn't Julia.

Chapter Fifteen

Everything was different. *Everything.*

From the moment Emma woke just after dawn, an hour she rarely saw by choice, she sensed the change in her world. Not only did the sky seem brighter and bluer, and the coffee taste richer and better, but her whole attitude felt...fiery.

Was it the new idea for her career that had taken hold of her heart?

Or the man who'd kissed away her cynicism and bitterness, promising more and making her...*optimistic*?

She wasn't certain if she was just hopeful they'd have a great session at the dance studio or that there would be a lot more of what they started last night, but she felt like someone had taken a foggy layer of plastic off her world and the new view was beautiful.

That's the power of...love.

The music thrummed through the studio. "Twirl right now, Emma!" Jasper called out. "On the *pow* of power! Try it again."

Before they could breathe, he'd started the segment of music again, and Huey Lewis belted out his anthem while Jasper clapped. "Five, six, seven, eight."

Without even blinking, Mark reached out and took her hand, following the admittedly simple steps Jasper had taught them. They moved left, right, one, two, repeated it several times, then added the twirl on the *pow*, ending with her body right smack up against his.

The studio door popped open, and another dance instructor stuck her head in.

"Jasp! Need help for a second."

"Coming."

"You're going to help the competition?" Emma teased.

"Under this chest of steel and ink is a heart of gold," he said, sweeping by them. "Let's break for ten! Somebody probably needs a lesson in how to do a plié."

He disappeared out the door…but Mark and Emma were still body to body.

"You're on fire today, Em." He didn't let her go. The room still crackled, and both of them worked to steady their breath, a sheen of sweat on their skin, hearts hammering in perfect unison.

Dancing. Who knew it was just like sex?

"I'm on *something*," she agreed. "Someone planted big ideas in my head last night." *And kisses on my lips.* She looked up, not at all opposed to the idea of another one while they were alone.

"When do you want to talk to Lacey?" he asked. "There's a committee meeting this afternoon I was hoping to avoid, but if you come with me, you could get some time with her."

"Today?" she almost choked.

"Well, you only have a week," he said. "And you're here on the property. You could put some ideas together and pitch them to her before the reunion."

But would that mean an end to this lovely interlude?

Maybe not if they convinced Lacey to keep their secret. But if she refused…

She stomped the thought away, refusing to allow anything into her head that didn't fit with today's sunny optimism.

"Today is so soon." She started to pull away, but he was having none of it. In fact, he drew her closer.

"Are you scared?"

Only of losing this. Of the inevitable solitude of a Brooklyn apartment after dancing days and moonlit nights. "I love the idea of starting my own business and getting Casa Blanca as an account," she said, sticking to the subject and not her mental copywriting.

"You could spend more time down here, since you love it so much."

"I do, and I'd like that." She'd love that, in fact.

"Then come with me to the meeting and talk to Lacey."

She took a deep breath. "I don't know."

He angled his head and looked at her. "What the hell do you have to lose, Em?"

She let that breath out on a whoosh. "We'll see."

His expression changed enough for her to know she'd disappointed him and that bothered her. She wanted to impress him.

Which was just crazy. Almost as crazy as hitting a soon-to-be-former East End Marketing client up for business. But there it was…motivation so strong she could taste it.

"I'll go to the meeting," she said. "And take it from there."

He lowered his head and got his mouth near her ear. "And after you set up a meeting with her, we'll celebrate by conquering the champagne popping fear and…"

And drink it naked, she hoped.

He didn't finish the sentence, but placed his mouth over hers, taking a soft, slow kiss.

"Mmmh." She sighed into him, sliding her hands into his sweat-dampened hair and lifting up on her toes to get the full effect of a perfect kiss.

"That's it!" Jasper's exclamation, and the smack of his hands nearly threw them apart. Except Mark didn't let go, holding her firmly in place, close to him.

"That's what?" He ground out the question, clearly not happy with the interruption.

"That's how we'll start *Endless Love*." Jasper marched over. "You come together at the end of *Power*, then we do a hard break in the music, perfectly silent while you kiss, then…we start *Endless*. Now, do not move. Not one muscle. Not one hand. Not one little tippy-toe, Miss Emma. And do not, for the love of Isadora Duncan, take your eyes off each other. Stay exactly like that. Frozen."

They obeyed, except for their lips, which twitched and threatened to smile as they endured the scrutiny and demands of their dance instructor.

"You know where we are now, don't you?" Jasper started to circle them, slowly.

"In a dance studio?" Emma asked, still looking into Mark's blue eyes.

"In the story!" Jasper almost cried in frustration. "We're in the middle of a love story, 1980s style."

Mark blinked a little, a quick move that Emma would never have noticed if they weren't supposed to be statues at the moment.

A love story, 1980s style?

Sometimes she forgot what he had to be experiencing, here on this island, with this music, and all the memories. He was so adept at hiding it. She gave his neck the tiniest stroke of one finger, a silent move of sympathy, and his eyes flashed a little. Again, nearly imperceptible, but she knew…they'd just communicated in utter silence.

And that was somehow sexier than his hard, warm man's body pressed against her.

Jasper moved in closer. "So we've had *Call Me* when this whole thing started, and then your kiss was on his list. Are you following me, kids?" He circled to the other side, staring at their joined bodies. "Then, things got serious, and we realized we wanted to know what love is, followed by our celebration of what a feeling it is. Are you with me? Do you see where this thing is going?"

Yes, Emma nearly cried out. She could see where it was going and, God help her, no matter how quickly it ended, she wanted to take this ride. Mark never moved his gaze, but his hands pressed a little harder…and they did it again.

Oh yes, everything was different. Because not one time in her whole life, not in the most intimate of moments with any man, had she ever had that kind of full and silent communication.

Jasper clapped, breaking the spell. "And at the end of this anthem to the power of love, we are going to move into the big, romantic, physical, sexual celebration of love that does not end!" His voice was echoing through the sound chamber of the studio, drowning out the thumping blood in Emma's veins.

"*Endless Love* is our next song, and that, my dear engaged couple, is what it is all about! Our story is about to reach a climax, if you will please excuse the pun."

They just exchanged a look, and Mark's brow twitched in a flash of a tease, an inside joke…another silent bond.

Jasper circled again, putting his hands on their backs. "You two are going to open this segment exactly like this and like I found you, kissing—full open mouth with tongue, please—and then you will slowly, slowly melt apart and then come right back together again as if being apart is just too painful to bear."

Emma bit her lip to keep from laughing at the crazy dance man, but Mark's expression stayed perfectly serious. Like…he was buying this story. Feeling it, even.

"Then you will come close again just when the note goes really high on 'endless'." He stuck one hand high in the air and sang. "Ennnnnndlesss love. And yours will be endless," he insisted. "You will be there on the dance floor, showing everyone that love has no time—they'll love that—and space and ending. This is it. Soul mates forever."

She heard Mark suck in a tiny breath, as if the words hit him a little too hard.

"Perfect!" Jasper said, pirouetting away to start the music. "Stay just like you are."

"Are you sure you want to do this?" she asked softly.

For a moment, he didn't answer, and all she could see in his eyes was something…something like what she sometimes saw in her own. Fear.

Oh yes. Everything was different now.

Mark recovered with a cold shower and a long stare-down in the mirror. What the holy hell was going on, he demanded of the man staring back at him.

A man who'd had his chance…his *one* chance.

It happens only once in a lifetime.

Wasn't that what he and Julia believed? From the beginning, when they were teenagers, just a couple of kids in the same algebra class, they knew. They knew they were different, they knew they would make it, they knew no one else could ever be their soul mate.

They'd talk about it late at night out on her back patio after her parents went to bed. They'd lay pressed against each other and the hard plastic straps of a cheap chaise lounge by the pool, admitting that they didn't care if they never kissed another person as long as they lived.

And they *meant* it.

Even then, they knew they weren't just love-struck kids. Their love was the real thing.

Then they built a life on it, and a business, and the idea of Mark feeling anything beyond sexual attraction for another woman, beyond the appreciation of good company, was impossible. Unthinkable. Preposterous.

Yes, he'd dated since Julia died. Gone through the motions and gotten friendly with a few women, some for weeks or even months at a time, if he was in one place that long. But none—not a single one—had had a snowball's chance in hell of getting inside his heart.

That space that belonged to Julia Coulter Solomon.

But he couldn't deny that something really unnerving was happening with Emma DeWitt. It had to just be chemistry; from the moment he'd met her, they'd had a nice connection. And lust. Obviously, the woman hit him hard below the belt, and a lot of this would simmer down once they stopped fighting that and spent the night in the same bed. It was the right time, right place, right music, right atmosphere...but it was not *the right woman.*

Or was it?

He shook his head, gave a swipe of the towel over his hair, and dressed, as he'd gotten used to doing now, from the pile of clothes he'd brought into this second bathroom when he magnanimously gave up the Moroccan-style master bathroom big enough for two.

Maybe tomorrow he'd shower in there. With her.

That would get things back into perspective, wouldn't it? Or would sex just make it all more complicated and worse?

"Hey, doesn't your meeting start soon?" Emma's voice came from the other side of the door, making him realize how much time he'd wasted thinking.

"I'll be right out." He took one last look in the mirror, seeing himself as she did. A single man, feeling like he was certainly damn close to the prime of his life, willing to help her improve every aspect of her life.

She looked at him like…she was falling for him.

And normally that made him run for the highest rock to climb and escape. But nothing about this situation was normal.

He opened the door and did a little double take, so used to seeing her in beach cover-ups and dance clothes. "You look pretty," he said, not even bothering to edit the truth.

"Not too obvious?" She gave a little twirl, and the peach-colored skirt fluttered just above her knees, showing off what he already knew were excellent legs, accented by low-heeled sandals. Her top was white and draped loosely over her breasts, professional and feminine and…nice.

"Perfect," he said. "I'd give you any job you wanted."

"Well, I'm not pitching today, remember. Just checking out the situation and seeing if there might be a chance…maybe."

He leaned closer, taking a whiff of peppery perfume. "Think big, Em. If you have her attention, pitch her. She already loves your writing."

She smiled up at him. "You're incredibly good for me, you know that?"

He searched her face, trying to come up with some easy

joke, some simple banter that would keep this thing right on the fun, casual, even secretive track it started on. But all he could do was think about how much he wanted to taste that shiny lip gloss.

"And you're good for me," he said quietly.

"I will be," she promised, taking his hand and leading him to the door without further explanation of what that meant. But he thought about it while they walked down the brick path toward the main resort building.

In the lobby, he spotted Law and Ken talking outside the hall that led to the conference room, deep in conversation. Law looked over and gestured for Mark to join them.

"Let's go talk to those guys," Mark said.

"You go," Emma replied, stepping away toward the frosted-glass doors of the spa. "I know Eucalyptus was the centerpiece of the latest ad campaign, but I didn't get to work on it. I did write the brochure before I left, but I'd really like to get a feel for what it looks like in person."

"That's a great idea. Go ahead. I'll be with those guys."

She gave him a quick smile and slipped away and...he watched, damn it. Couldn't take his eyes off her for half a second.

Ken approached with a sly smile. "Man, you make it look so easy."

"Make what look easy?"

"Women."

This, with Emma, *was* easy, he thought. Surprisingly easy. He shifted his attention to Ken and the comment. "Not making it happen with Beth Endicott, I take it."

"She's so cold I need a jacket when I see her."

"You only have yourself to blame," Mark said.

Ken gave him a quick look. "What do...how do you know that?"

"I meant if you'd signed up to dance, you'd get the benefits of forced intimacy choreographed by a dancing toucan."

Ken smiled. "There's no way she'd dance with me. Not that I'd blame her."

Mark didn't follow the comment but before he could ask for an explanation, Law joined them. "Where've you been the past few days, Lawless?" Mark asked. "Still hitting the local hot spots?"

"What I'm hitting is roadblocks," he said, tucking his hands in his pockets. "I've talked to everyone in this town, and no one knows who bought the Toasted Pelican. Just that it's sold."

"When you hit a roadblock, you have to move it," Mark said.

"Sure thing, Mr. Motivation. Is that a result of all that dancing, too?"

"Hey, don't knock it till you've tried it. What's on the agenda for Planning Hell today?" He glanced toward the conference room. "I mean, other than Cav's report on the flower-arranging program."

Ken laughed. "Flower people haven't met yet. And I've been on duty at the station since the last time I saw you."

"How many kittens did you rescue?" Law asked, but then he spotted something more interesting over Ken's shoulder. "Speaking of kitties, there's Chesty."

"The woman's name is Libby. Would it kill you to use her real name?" Mark asked.

"Seriously," Ken added. "You sound like you're thirteen and just realized what your dick can do."

"But *she* hasn't realized what my dick can do. Damn, that woman's hot for forty-five. Look at her."

Neither man turned to look at Libby Chesterfield, by

silent agreement and the fact that they *weren't* thirteen.

"Screw you two," Law said. "Captain Cav would spin like a top if I said Beth Endicott walked in."

Ken snorted. "Twenty bucks says she's not coming."

"She's missing it, then," Law said with a shrug. "Because I've got the kitchen bringing up samples of my killer apps, and can I just say that the walnut puffs will bring you to your knees?"

"The only caveman I know who makes walnut puffs," Ken said with a laugh.

"Fell free to scorn, son, but my nut puffs would melt Iceberg Endicott. Want the recipe?"

Ken almost looked like he'd take it. "No," he finally said. "I have a plan."

"What is it?" Mark asked.

After a second, Ken smiled. "I don't know yet, but there are no puffs involved."

"Chill, Cav." Law gave him a nudge. "She's just a babe, my friend. There are fifty more like her around the next corner."

"And there are twelve-step programs for idiots like you," Ken said.

"Not for idiots, but for everything else," Law replied. "Trust me, I've been through them all."

One of the women on the committee joined them and started talking, but Mark shifted his attention in the direction of the spa, waiting for Emma to come out. He wanted this to succeed for her. Wanted her to find her direction *and* beat that little prick who broke her heart.

Except, if she found out he knew the truth and didn't tell her? He'd be the next prick to break her heart.

Chapter Sixteen

"Can I help you?" The woman behind the reception desk at Eucalyptus gave Emma a friendly smile.

"I'm just checking out the facilities," she said, taking in the giant cut-glass mirror that covered one wall and the simple furnishings on gleaming wood floors. The reception area was bright, welcoming, and smelled faintly of the very plant it was named for.

A glass dispenser seeped a tendril of silvery air and another aroma, drawing Emma closer for a whiff.

"Bergamot and frankincense," the woman said with a smile. "One for your heart and one for your head."

Emma gave her a quizzical look. "How's that?"

"Bergamot helps circulation, and frankincense cleans out the synapses in your brain."

She sniffed again. "Definitely could use some of that."

"It's part of our aromatherapy treatment. Would you like a brochure of our services?"

Meaning the one Emma had written? "Yes, please."

The woman lifted a trifold from her desk and, of course, Emma recognized and remembered every fight creative had had with account management.

"Looks nice," she said, glancing at the glossy stock and the image she'd fought so hard to make the cover. The outdoor massage table with a lithe model draped over it, the postcard view in the background.

Kyle had wanted the doors to the spa to capture the Moroccan feel of the place, but when given the option, the client had chosen what Emma liked. Kyle had been pissed about it, Emma recalled, remembering how the subtext of his rant was all about how a copywriter should write copy, not choose art.

The day after he made her feel subpar for not being in management yet.

It was all so different from the man who was encouraging her to start her own business and seize her own day.

The woman at the desk tapped the scheduling book. "We just had a cancellation for our Ayurvedic massage and oil treatment later this afternoon," she said. "It's a—"

"Ancient toxin-removal system," Emma said, remembering how fascinated she'd been by the concept when she wrote the brochure. "And that herbal scrub afterwards sounds divine."

The woman beamed. "You sound like you've been doing some research and need to try it."

Emma laughed. "Are the toxins just wafting off me?"

"Not at all," the woman said, standing to reach out and offer her hand. "I'm a huge believer. I'm Jocelyn Palmer, spa manager. What's your name?"

"Emma DeWitt. I'm here for..." A canceled honeymoon. A fake engagement. A dream job. Really, the list of possibilities was endless. She went with something simple. "The reunion, with my, um, fiancé."

"Oh, nice." Jocelyn stood, a beautiful and delicate woman with sleek dark hair and kind brown eyes. "You must be on the early-bird committee, then."

"My fiancé is, and we were just about to go into the meeting, but I wanted to…" She glanced around, then at the brochure, thinking about all the conversations they'd had at the agency about the spa. Not one person had been able to communicate the impact and comfort and total feeling of escape the place offered.

No wonder Lacey hadn't been happy with that last campaign. Emma hadn't worked on it, but she'd been in some of the planning meetings before she'd quit.

"You're tempted, aren't you?" Jocelyn asked, mistaking Emma's thoughtfulness for indecision.

"I *am* tempted," she said. Tempted to tell Lacey her ideas the minute she could.

Jocelyn picked up a pencil and fluttered a page of her appointment book. "If you change your mind, I can put you in for an afternoon slot, then if you can't make it, you can call anytime. No worries."

Oh, she had worries. Plenty of worries, but they wouldn't be solved with a massage and—

The back door opened, and Lacey Walker stepped out, doing a double take at the sight of Emma, who probably looked just as startled.

"Well, hello there, Emma. Nice to see you visiting our oasis. Will you have time to get some treatments this week?"

"I'm trying to convince her to get an Ayurvedic massage, oil, and herbal scrub," Jocelyn said.

"It's not taking too much convincing," Emma said with a laugh. "I'm pretty sure I've been penciled in, and there's been no argument from me."

Lacey smiled at the other woman. "Joss isn't going to be happy until she detoxes every mind, body, and spirit on the property."

"Because it works," Jocelyn said.

"I bet it does," Emma replied. "And Eucalyptus is the only spa in a hundred miles that offers the complete Ayurvedic system." Which had been a key marketing point she'd wanted to add into the brochure, but it had gotten edited for space.

Both women looked at her, surprised. "You're absolutely right," Lacey said. "But not enough people know that. Take the appointment, Emma. My treat."

"Oh, no, that's not necessary," Emma said.

"But it's done, and it makes me feel only slightly less guilty for taking Mark's time this week." Lacey winked at Joss and pointed to the book. "Make it pen, not pencil. Are you headed to the committee meeting to make sure Mark isn't signed up for another volunteer position?" she asked with a teasing laugh.

"Moral support," Emma said. "And now that I have you…"

"Yes?"

Now, Emma, *now*.

Still, she stared at Lacey, silent. Except for the pounding of her heart, which surely echoed through the quiet spa.

Carpe diem. Carpe diem.

"I have a question."

Lacey's eyes narrowed under a frown. "Please don't ask me if you can back out of the dance competition. I know Jasper can be a bit much at times, but it will be the highlight of the reunion, I promise."

"No, no. Not backing out," Emma assured her, ignoring her wet palms and dry throat as they walked to the door. "It's something different. Something…else completely."

Lacey looked at her with interest. "Oh, Emma. You're going to take me up on that offer to meet with our wedding planners. Of course, but let me warn you, they will make you want to say your vows right on the sands of Barefoot Bay. And I would love that!"

Emma just stared at her, heat rising. "Uh, no. We weren't...planning to do that." Oh, the tangled web they'd woven. It was going to strangle her for sure.

"Then what is it?"

"I...I am interested in, I mean, I have a career in advertising and marketing."

"Really? How interesting." Lacey pulled open the large frosted-glass door. "That is definitely the most challenging part of my business. I might have to pick your brain a little."

"Yes!" Emma said, practically throwing herself through both the literal and metaphorical door opening for her. "I would love that. Anytime. I have so many ideas about this resort."

Lacey's face brightened as they walked into the lobby. "Talk about good timing. Let me dig through this reunion stuff today and look at my calendar. We can squeeze something in this week, I'm sure."

Emma nearly danced with joy. "That'd be fantastic."

Just then, Mark turned from his conversation with a group of people to see Emma and Lacey walking toward them, and his eyes lit at the sight of them.

That's my girl.

"Would you look at that," Lacey said with a tease in her voice.

"Oh, I'm looking," Emma assured her, making the other woman laugh.

"He is *gone* for you," she said.

Emma suspected the look on Mark's face had more to do with her talking to Lacey than being "gone for her," but she kept that to herself. "It's mutual," she said, a little surprised at how true that felt.

"I can understand it. He seems like a great guy," Lacey said.

"He is."

A woman at the front desk came over to Lacey looking like she needed help with a problem, and Lacey stepped away. "I'll see you in the meeting," she promised.

Still smiling, Emma walked across the vast expanse of marble toward Mark, who'd left the men he'd been talking to and hustled toward her, obviously eager to hear what happened.

He cared. He cared so damn much. How had that happened?

As soon as they reached each other, he took her hand and pulled her closer to him. "So? You have the business?"

"Stop. I have a meeting. Maybe. Probably."

He pulled her into a hug. "Fantastic."

His support was as warm as his arms, his enthusiasm for her personal project so touching that she couldn't help reaching up to clasp his neck. "I *carped* the hell out of that *diem*."

He threw his head back and laughed, hugging her again as they walked into the conference room.

"Ah, young love." A blond woman sidled up next to them and gave a teasing wink. "Or young-ish love, in Mark's case."

He laughed again. "Libby, have you met my fiancée, Emma?"

"I have not." She gave a friendly nod. "Libby Chesterfield."

Law Monroe came out of the conference room just as they reached the door, doing a double take at Libby. "Didn't know you were going to make this one, Lib."

"I thought I had a meeting in town, but it got canceled." She eyed Law flirtatiously. "You leaving?"

"Not now." He pivoted and got right next to her. "You smell good."

She rolled her eyes and slipped past him. Law glanced at Mark and brushed it off with a shrug. "Fifty more babes around the corner, I tell you."

Mark didn't respond, but led Emma to two seats along the side of the conference—giving her the one right next to Lacey and treating her to a conspiratorial wink as she sat down.

Which just made her even happier.

Emma's euphoria lasted through what should, by all accounts, have been one of the most boring business meetings in the middle of her lovely vacation. But it wasn't.

Lacey kept the agenda moving and had some ideas and responses. Emma didn't have to participate, obviously, beyond being there as company and support for Mark, but she couldn't help but take a hard look at the program as it was presented to the team.

And, whoa, it wasn't good. She stared at the copy, mentally revising it, her fingers itching to grab a red pencil and make changes.

"Is something wrong?" Lacey asked, obviously noticing how long Emma held the document.

"No, I just..." She sighed. "Do you mind if I suggest some edits?"

"Please do. I tried that one on my own. I am great at management but lousy at writing," Lacey said. "Now let's move on to the highlights of the then-and-now reel..."

Lacey's voice faded as Emma concentrated on the words in front of her, changing a few phrases and instantly seeing some missed opportunities in the welcome letter Lacey had written.

After she finished, she passed the program along and looked to her left, sensing Mark's gaze on her. She caught his eye and held it, and his lips curled in a half smile.

Under the table, he gave her leg a light squeeze, and once again, they were communicating silently.

When the meeting ended, Lacey picked up the program and read the program, pausing to look up at Emma.

"This is so clever!" she said. "I love how you worked 'time' and 'timeless' into each segment. I'm sending this right to the printer, Emma. Thank you."

"Oh, it's nothing."

"I think it's something," Lacey said as she gathered up some papers and checked her watch. "I hate to cut into your private time, Emma, but would you like to have that conversation we talked about earlier right now? I have a few minutes."

"I'd love to," Emma said.

"Perfect timing," Mark agreed. "I promised Law and Ken I'd hit the gym with them for an hour." He put a possessive hand on Emma's shoulder. "I'll see you later." He added a kiss on her hair, which was like a shot of confidence and adrenaline.

A few minutes later, Emma was following Lacey through the back halls of the resort management offices. Lacey paused now and again to point something out, or introduce her to some of the employees. Right before they turned the corner, they passed a door with the words Barefoot Bay Brides engraved on a plaque next to the door.

"And here are our destination wedding planners," Lacey

said as they paused there. "Are you sure I can't convince you to sit down with them?"

Emma heard the implication in her voice, which made her even more certain she had to be honest about her relationship with Mark the minute they were alone. "Only because the Barefoot Bay Brides are without a doubt one of the most powerful tools in your marketing arsenal," Emma said.

Lacey's eyes widened. "Yes, they are. And you're getting me all excited to talk to you. In here." She finally led Emma into a spacious office, closed the door, and gestured toward one of the guest chairs. "I feel like you've fallen from heaven the week I need it most."

Emma settled into the chair, trying not to grip the armrests, but calmly resting her hands on her lap. "How's that, Lacey?"

Lacey dropped into the leather chair behind her desk that was mostly empty but for a few papers and some family pictures, including a teenage girl who had the same strawberry-blond hair and the toddler Emma had seen at the party the other night.

"I know I need to up the advertising game, but my hands are so full right now," Lacey said.

Emma looked at the pictures. "I can't even imagine how busy you are. Are they your kids?"

"Ashley and Elijah," she said, smiling with pride at the kids. "And yes, they are fifteen years apart."

"They're gorgeous." Emma picked up the picture, taking in the red hair of both kids, but stunned by how much Ashley looked like her mother. "She's a carbon copy of you."

"Only on the outside," Lacey said with a wry laugh. "Inside she's...well, she's a handful of high maintenance. She's in college now, at my alma mater, the University of Florida, in Gainesville."

"What is she studying?"

"Are fraternities a major?" Lacey joked. "No, she's in hospitality, I'm happy to say, and will someday come back and work here at the resort. If I don't kill her first."

"I'm sure she's a great kid," Emma said, handing the picture back.

Lacey smiled as she situated the frame on her desk, next to a picture of the architect husband who'd designed the resort.

"Everything can be so different the second time around," she mused. "The first time I had a baby, I was young and dumb and still in college. The second time, I was much better at the whole mother and partner thing. Of course, it helps that my husband is a dream and my ex was a dream*er*."

Emma laughed, grateful that the personal small talk had broken the ice. And wasn't the mention of husbands a perfect opener?

"But, I still have a resort to run," Lacey said before Emma could speak. "And not that I'm complaining, but Casa Blanca has grown beyond my wildest dreams. Even the wildest dreams of my big, dreaming husband," she added.

"But that doesn't mean you stop the marketing."

Lacey pointed at her. "Exactly. I've had an ad agency on retainer for over a year, and the work has been great for the most part. Great in bursts. Creatively, they can be fantastic, but the account management has always been frustrating, and I think it's time to try something else."

So she *was* firing the agency. Emma swallowed, debating whether to burst out with the truth about East End and Kyle—which could end the conversation instantly. Of course, Kyle already knew the agency was on the chopping block, but Lacey didn't know Emma had any connection there.

She had to come clean on both counts. She cleared her throat. "Actually—"

"Do you have any ideas?" Lacey asked.

"So many," Emma said with a laugh.

"Tell me one." Lacey leaned forward and dropped her chin onto her knuckles. "Tell me a good idea."

The fake fiancé? Not a good idea. The tie to East End Marketing? Another bad idea.

Maybe a *real* good idea first. "Well, I mentioned the Barefoot Brides, which is such a feather in your cap. How many places like this can offer on-site destination wedding planning that can be supported with a print advertising campaign in major bridal publications on some of the huge sites?"

"Yes!" Lacey agreed. "My agency hates print advertising and is always talking me out of it."

Because Kyle's media department sucked raw eggs when it came to power negotiating.

Emma swallowed, wanting to impress before the meeting flatlined. "But that's only one prong of the strategy," she said quickly. "Your goal has to be increasing occupancy to ninety percent year-round."

Lacey leaned back and puffed out a breath. "Exactly my goal. We're hovering at seventy-eight to eighty."

"You could help that with an aggressive social media campaign to encourage anyone who is visiting Casa Blanca to post about the experience and elevate the resort's awareness."

"I love that. I follow some resorts that are so good at that and wonder how they get that done."

"It's not hard, but it takes dedication."

Lacey smiled. "Which you seem to have. What about my market? How does a resort the size of mine find ours?"

"You blast a market-tested print and TV campaign to northern states during the winter, and a summer resident invitation-only campaign throughout Florida. You drive home that this resort is the best of both worlds—it's elegant, high-end, and exclusive with a mom-and-pop feel." She smiled and nodded to Lacey. "Even if the mom is a gorgeous redhead and the pop is your handsome architect husband who built the place."

Lacey gave a clap and a hoot. "You so get it! What about the spa?"

"The spa?" Emma practically choked. "It's competitive with anything at the Ritz or in Miami."

"I know, right?" Lacey practically squealed. "Jocelyn has made it a world-class destination. Wait until you have your treatment today. You have to go. I want you to experience it firsthand, because I want a whole campaign around that spa."

A zing of joy shot through Emma, immediately tempered by the need to be completely forthright. "But about your agency—"

"I don't want an agency anymore," Lacey insisted. "I want to bring the business in-house."

Emma just stared at her, processing that.

"I mean, I could use an agency for projects," she said. "But what I really want is a fantastic marketing VP to supervise everything and let me out of this end of the business." She leaned over the desk and put her hand on Emma's arm. "I don't know your experience, obviously, but my gut instinct is on fire right now. Would you be qualified for that position?"

For a moment, Emma couldn't breathe. "Well, there are things—"

"I mean, it's crazy even asking since it would mean

living down here, of course, which might not be something Mark wants to do."

"Mark?"

"After you're married."

Things like that.

"Oh, well, yeah. But..." The marketing VP of Casa Blanca? Was she kidding? That would be the most perfect, most amazing, most thrilling thing that ever happened. "He travels a lot," she finally said. That wasn't a lie, right? He did travel a lot.

"Obviously, this is premature," Lacey said. "But I'm going to have to do something about that ad agency, and this is what I think will be best for the resort. Can I put you on a list of candidates? We could have a more formal interview after you've had a chance to think about this."

"I might not think about anything else," she admitted.

Lacey laughed. "Then Mark will kill me."

"No, not at all. But there is something I need to tell you." More than one thing, actually. East End Marketing...engaged to Kyle...not engaged to Mark.

"Of course."

"Okay. So, I know you think that—"

On her desk, a cell phone rang, and Lacey glanced at it, obviously ready to dismiss the call, then her shoulders sank. "It's my daughter. I better take this. Gimme a sec." She tapped the phone. "Hey, Ash, what's up?" Her eyes flashed. "What?" Lacey pushed back her chair and stood. "How did that happen, Ashley?"

Emma knew her cue and instantly stood, too.

"I'm sorry," Lacey mouthed and rolled her eyes and covered the phone to whisper, "my week's insane, and I know you're leaving Sunday. Could we get together, say, Saturday morning? Would you consider that? The reunion starts later, and we could find an—hang on, Ashley! What do you think, Emma?"

She thought that Lacey was stretched to the limit and the job she described was absolutely a dream come true. "We can talk Saturday."

"Perfect. Bring anything you want, or nothing. Tell me your experience and ideas, and we'll work something out. Maybe you can be here part time and at home in…where do you live, again?"

"New York City."

"You could split your time!" She closed her eyes and grunted softly into the phone. "Ashley, I'm in the middle of a…really? Did you go to the infirmary? Do you think it's broken? I told you not to ride that scooter around campus. I swear you are more dangerous than your toddler brother."

Emma reached out for Lacey's hand. "Handle your daughter. I'll be here Saturday morning."

"Perfect. Nine a.m. I'll bring coffee." She gave Emma's hand a squeeze. "Do not miss that spa treatment this afternoon!"

"I won't, I promise." Emma practically pirouetted out of the office and back outside to the pool deck. She took a moment to inhale, filling her lungs with clean, tropical air and her heart with…hope.

Barefoot Bay had changed her life. No, no, it wasn't Barefoot Bay, she thought as she walked over the deck to the sand. It was Mark Solomon.

She paused at the stairs, looking down at the sand.

Kick off your shoes and fall in love.

Was it just a marketing slogan Lacey Walker had made up to fill her resort with guests…or the truth?

Right then, she bought the promise of the ad copy.

Bought it completely. *Just like you bought that wedding fairy tale*, a little voice whispered. *And look how that turned out.*

But she drowned out the warning, slipped off her shoes, and ran barefoot over the sand to get back to Mark.

Chapter Seventeen

Emma was practically vibrating with excitement.

And just like when she drove the Porsche, it was the sexiest damn thing Mark had witnessed in a long time.

"I could pop the champagne myself and wouldn't even flinch." In the kitchen, she swung the refrigerator door open. "And, I happen to know that every villa is stocked with some. It's in the brochure. *That I wrote*."

He leaned against the counter, just taking her in for the sheer pleasure of it. "You're a new woman."

"Not yet, but I'm getting there." She pulled the champagne out and put it on the counter, reaching her hands to cup his face. "Of course, I have to tell her everything. The truth about you, and where I used to work, and my relationship with Kyle. Before I do anything else, I have to lay those cards on the table."

"You will. You start the meeting that way on Saturday morning, and once you've confessed, you do your stuff. And every word you say will be *awash* with *alliteration*."

"Shoots and scores with another alliteration joke." She gave him a wide grin. "I love that you know me so well."

He laughed, placing his hands over hers to enjoy the softness of her skin against his. "We're getting there."

"You know what else I love?"

For a quick flash, his body tensed and braced. "What?"

She laughed. "You should see your face. Relax."

"I'm as relaxed as I'm going to get with my hands on you."

"And me talking about love," she joked. "I was going to say I love this feeling of, well, of not being scared. For the first time maybe ever, I have this sense that I can do anything, that I'm unstoppable. I love that! I think I can really make this work."

"You can."

"With the help of my new secret weapon...Magic Mark."

He chuckled, pulling her into him. "If I could do magic, I wouldn't be sleeping alone every night."

She drew back, giving him a look like they both knew that was coming to an end.

"Anyway, you had the secret weapon all along." He stroked her hair, still warm from sunshine. "But it is fun to see it unfold in you."

"I've never met anyone like you," she whispered, the sincerity of the comment darkening her eyes to a burning amber. "I doubt I ever will. You show up from out of nowhere, get my life on track in a matter of days, and infuse me with...fearlessness."

"Did I do all that?" He eased her closer.

"It's like you're not real."

He added some pressure so she could feel exactly what she did to him. "I'm real, and this is..." He leaned his face closer to hers. "Real." He pressed his lips against her mouth.

She sighed and kept her hands in his, arching her back to

let him feel the sweet tips of her breasts and the way her woman's body fit against his.

Instantly, fire shot south, fueling him.

Blood pulsed in his head, a deafening drumbeat that almost drowned out the whimpers of pleasure and desire that caught in her throat. Without ending the kiss, he pushed her against the granite counter for more pressure and leverage.

"Mark." She threaded her fingers into his hair, breaking the kiss to tilt her head back and offer him access to her throat. He took it, starved to put his mouth on her skin, to taste more of her.

He easily lifted her off the ground and slid her butt onto the counter. She laughed at the move, her loose skirt allowing her to wrap her legs around his waist.

Holding her gaze and steadying his breath, he trailed his knuckles from her temple to her jaw.

"We have more fun on this counter," he said.

"Banging the biscuit tube," she teased.

"Actually, we just have fun, Em." He pushed a few stray locks off her face. "Whatever we do." He couldn't remember the last time he felt like that. Well, he could, but...

She crushed the thought by squeezing her legs and leaning in for a kiss on the mouth. "This *is* fun," she agreed.

"Everything is with you. Faking people out about our engagement, conquering fears, driving fast cars, lining up a new job. It's all one damn good time."

She inched back enough to get a good look at him. "And yet, you don't sound a hundred percent happy about that."

That was the other thing about her. She could read him. So well. Better than anyone...since Julia. He tried to cover the impact of that thought with another kiss and a playful stroke of his hands down her sides, lingering against her breasts.

"Do I sound like I'm complaining? The only thing I'm not happy about is the fact that our clothes are still on."

He felt her shudder, but then she reached to the top button of his oxford shirt. "I guess we could remedy that."

"It's about damn time." His pulse kicked up, tightening everything, especially his jeans. He slipped his hand under her silky top, finding the curve of her breast.

On the other counter, her phone vibrated and played a melody.

"That's my alarm," she said.

He laughed into a kiss against her throat. "I know you like to sleep in, Em, but it's almost three in the afternoon."

"I have an appointment at three in the spa." She gave him a nudge, freeing her to pop off the counter. "It won't stop until I turn it off."

"Neither will I." He reached for her, turning her and bringing her back into him for another kiss. "Cancel the spa and come to bed with me."

He actually felt her dip as though he'd weakened her knees. "I...I can't. Lacey's treating me to an Ayurvedic massage. She insisted I go."

"Go tomorrow."

She shimmied away, slowly enough for him to know she was fighting the temptation to stay. "It would not look good if I canceled now, and I really do need to experience the spa firsthand."

"Experience me." He slipped his fingers into the vee of her top, grazing the soft rise of her breast. "And this hand."

With a soft whimper, she fisted his shirt. "I want to..."

"To the bedroom, Em." He slid his hand lower, caressing her nipple.

"Ohhh." She dropped her head back, then took a deep breath, obviously digging for strength. "Can we go there

180

right after my massage, oil treatment, and herbal scrub?"

He grazed the hardened peak, adding pressure against her hips. "I can do all that for you here."

"Mark...please...I *have* to go." Somehow, she managed to escape his touch, making him release a frustrated laugh.

"I created a *carpe diem* monster and am now paying the price."

She patted his chest, pressed harder, and dragged her fingers over his pec with a sigh. "I'll be back in two hours," she promised. "Chill the champagne. Turn down the bed." She added a quick kiss. "Release the Kraken."

He gave a hearty laugh. "You are such a copywriter."

She escaped him completely, grabbed her bag, and darted toward the door. "Not for long," she said in a singsong voice. "Soon, I will be..." Her eyes grew wide. "Marketing VP? Do you think it's even possible to dream that big?"

"I think it's impossible *not* to dream that big."

She grinned and blew him a kiss. "See you soon, Magic Mark." And she was gone and out the door before he knew what hit him.

He closed his eyes, his blood and breathing getting normal again, his body returning to its usual state of calm and control.

The intense silence of the villa pressed down, making him keenly aware of how empty it was without the funny, lively, electrifying woman who'd changed this dreaded week of things to avoid into six days to cherish, with the potential for...sex.

But not just sex, he mused as he walked toward the champagne she'd left on the counter and put it back in the fridge to chill. More than sex.

He froze mid-movement, blinking, thinking, and letting out a little grunt.

He'd never thought anything with another woman would ever be more than just a physical release and a good time, needs met. But this was.

Holy crap, this *was*.

Was that right?

He stayed stone still, a familiar need starting a slow burn in his gut. A different need than the one his body was battling. He tensed, listening, searching, hoping for something—someone—to answer him. But there was nothing but quiet in the villa and the distant call of a gull.

"Julia," he whispered. "Can I do this?"

Dead silence.

And suddenly he knew exactly how he wanted to spend the next two hours. He wanted an answer, a direction, and maybe, permission to proceed without caution.

Which meant he had to go face down a fear...all by himself.

When Mark drove past the front of Mimosa High, a few teenage boys hanging out on the steps gave the Porsche a thumbs-up.

"Nice whip, old dude!"

Old? And what the hell was a whip?

He revved the engine and flew around the south corner that faced the cafeteria parking lot, just to show those kids what's what.

There were more packs of teenagers back there, filing toward their cars and bikes, since school had ended at three.

He cruised passed the lot toward the auditorium where a few buses lined up. Since when did the island kids take buses? He drove on and looked out at the football field where he'd had so many great moments of glory. Well, junior year. Senior year was just moments of fun, and that miserable season hadn't mattered because...because he was so in love.

He stared at the field, which actually wasn't a field anymore. It was a small stadium, and about forty young men were practicing with sticks and visors. Lacrosse? When the hell had they gotten a lacrosse team?

Probably sometime in the last thirty years, old dude.

He stopped the car for a few kids cutting in front of him, watching a couple walking arm in arm, pausing to kiss as they crossed.

They were freaking *babies*, he thought with a jolt. And yet, he and Julia set their course together when they were that very age. What the hell did they know?

They knew they were in love. And convinced it could never happen again with anyone else.

Reminded of his original mission, he waited until the road was clear and drove down along the side of the band room where he had always parked.

The lot had been full of Toyota Corollas and Nissan Maximas as the early eighties had ushered in the rise of the affordable Japanese compacts. Now there were SUVs, hatchbacks, and no small amount of pickups pulling out of spots, all full of kids anxious to get as far away from school as they could.

He parked in one of his favorite spots, right under the giant Scorpion painted on the doors to the gymnasium. Getting out, he pocketed the key fob and walked toward those doors, knowing exactly what he'd find on the other side.

Kids practicing, no doubt. Maybe the cheerleaders

running through a routine; he sure had loitered there long enough waiting for Julia after school. The walls would be white, the bleachers faded wood, and more animated scorpions to celebrate the school's mascot.

The door opened, and he took a steadying breath, ready for whatever message Julia would send him.

Then he stared into the gym and wondered where the hell he was. The wooden bleachers were red and white plastic. The two-story concrete brick walls were gone, replaced by massive sections of glass block that let in streams of sunlight that bounced off the shiny wood floor and highlighted the oversize MHS in the middle with another scorpion over it.

Everything was new, glossy, gleaming, and different.

Center court, there was no basketball practice. About fifteen kids sat at two cafeteria tables facing each other, a woman in her forties between them with a clipboard in one hand and a stopwatch in another. As he stepped closer, the kids all turned, and the teacher looked at him.

"Can I help you?" she asked, walking closer. Then, to the kids, "Solve for the real root, Team A." She held the clipboard to her chest, frowning as she approached him. "Are you looking for your son or daughter?"

"No, I was looking for..." *My past.* "Someone."

Her frown grew distrustful as she squared her shoulders. "Did you check in at the office? All guests are required to sign in and be badged."

Since when? Since...the last millennium, likely. "I'll go there now," he said, turning away.

"Would you like me to take you there?" she said, just a little edge in her voice.

"Actually, I know where it is. I graduated from here in 1986."

Her face brightened and relaxed. "Really? I graduated in

1989. Oh, you must be with the reunion-planning people. They've been stopping by this week."

"I am," he said, happy she was no longer considering him a criminal. He reached his hand out. "I'm Mark—"

"Solomon!" she finished. "I was a freshman when you were a senior. Michelle McGrath." She shook his hand. "Well, Michelle Hutchinson now. But, oh my God, Mark, you look fantastic."

"I'm sorry I don't remember you, Michelle."

"It's okay. You wouldn't have noticed me unless you looked up at the junior varsity cheerleader section and saw the row of fourteen-year-olds with braces on their teeth and longing in their eyes. I was the captain of the Mark Solomon Crush Team."

He laughed, shaking his head. "I didn't know there was such a squad."

"Of course not," she said. "You never had much of an ego, which only made you more attractive to the freshman girls. But you only had eyes for Julia Coulter."

He sure had. But, wait. Was that the answer he was searching for when he left the villa? *He only had eyes for Julia Coulter.*

The woman's expression changed instantly. "Oh, Mark, I know she passed away years ago and that you two were married. Is it too late to offer my sympathies?"

"No, of course not. Thank you, Michelle."

"There must be so many memories for you here."

He glanced toward the gymnasium. "To be honest, it's like a different school. Everything's changed a lot," he noted.

"Well, the school's a magnet now for STEM programs, so we've had a huge influx of cash the last ten years."

"So, science and tech?"

"And engineering and..." She pointed her clipboard toward the center court with pride. "Math, in which we hold the state championship, I'll have you know. Kids come here from all over Lee and Collier counties."

Which explained the buses. "That's fantastic," he said. "Good to see this place thrive and grow."

She nodded with pride and enthusiasm. "Anyway, I better go, but I'll see you Saturday at the reunion, right?" She took a few steps back to her students.

"Yes, of course. That's why I'm here."

"Wonderful. I'll introduce you to my husband. And what about you? Remarried, I assume."

The first time he was anywhere without Emma, and the question, of course, came up. "Engaged," he said, the lie sliding off his lips a little too easily now.

She beamed at him. "Congratulations! If you are going to the office, you should go out that door and pass the new trophy hall. It's really impressive."

He thanked her and followed the directions, not sure he really wanted to stare at trophies from days gone by. Not only would his be there—regionals in football his junior year—but for two years, Julia's squad had taken awards at most cheerleading competitions.

Maybe that was where he'd find his message. A picture of his late wife shaking her pom-poms.

Go, team, go! Go all the way!

He smiled at the memory, turning a corner and stopping for a moment to get his bearings when he wandered into a wide hall lined with massive glass trophy cases.

He paused in front of the first case, frowning at the trophy of a Greek orator. The Debate Team. The next one was for the Rocket Club, the three-foot-high award topped with a golden missile. To the right, the case was dominated by those mathletes he'd just seen and, no surprise, the Chess Club.

Finally, at the very end, a few awards for the lacrosse team and a nod to the football teams of the last few years. It seemed sports was no longer king of this school.

"Looking for someone in particular?"

Mark turned at the gravelly voice, his smile pulling at the sight of a very old man shuffling into the hall using a cane. Good God, it was Wigglesworth. The former principal had stayed at Lacey's party for only a few minutes, taken by his daughter back to his home.

"Hello, Mr. Wigglesworth," he said, approaching the man. "We didn't get to talk the other night, but I'm Mark Solomon. Class of '86. Do you remember me?"

White brows creased a face that already looked like an ancient parchment map. "I ran this school from the day it was one room for a few kids of the island founders to the day I retired fifty years later. Been back every week since then. Bet I've met more teenagers than the law allows."

"Of course," Mark said, feeling a little ridiculous for thinking he'd be remembered. "But I certainly remember you, Mr. W."

He leaned forward on his cane, narrowing watery gray eyes behind thick bifocals. "Mark Solomon. Quarterback. Smart kid. Stayed out of trouble, if I recall, and had a pretty steady girl."

Mark drew back, stunned. "I'm impressed. And honored, sir."

He laughed, which caused him to cough a little. Mark waited while the man caught his breath. "Don't expect me to know what day it is or what I had for breakfast, though," he finally said.

"Still, that's quite a memory."

"And that's what you're doing here?" He waved his cane. "Looking for *your* memories?"

"Something like that."

"These trophies?" He snorted indelicately. "All that talking and adding and subtracting. School's become a breeding ground for sissies."

"And millionaires," Mark couldn't resist adding. "I'm a tech guy myself, or I was."

"Well, good for you. Come with me. I've got something to show you."

No one ignored a Wigglesworth command, so Mark followed, moving at a snail's pace to keep up with him. They walked down a short corridor and reached a metal door that Mark guessed led to the janitorial break room.

It had been, once, but now it was a storage area, and along one whole wall were the ancient scarred trophy cases that had once stood sentry outside the old cafeteria.

As he shuffled forward, he stole a glance at Mark. "A tech guy, you say. You do look quite healthy and wealthy. What are you doing with your life?"

"I started and sold a business," he said.

"Question was present tense, son. What are you doing now?"

Now? He heard Emma's voice, capturing his "career" with her clever words. *Sounds more like you escape and enjoy risking your life.*

Just how true was that assessment? "Now I travel quite a bit and do some rock-climbing, hang gliding, and skydiving."

Wigglesworth slowed his shuffle and gave Mark a look of true incredulity. "That's your job?"

"Like you, I'm retired."

"Unlike me, you're a kid. Why aren't you working?"

He let out an exhale, suddenly feeling very much like he'd been summoned to the principal's office for a reprimand. "My company sold for a lot of money. I give to charities," he added, so he didn't look like a complete loser in this man's eyes.

Wigglesworth scowled at him, unimpressed by his money or charities. "What about your wife? Didn't you marry that pretty blond cheerleader?"

Holy shit, the guy had a good memory. "I did, but she passed away sixteen years ago."

If he expected sympathy, he didn't get it. Instead, Wigglesworth's gray eyes cleared as they leveled on Mark. "Get another one?"

"Actually, no, sir. I've never remarried."

"My wife passed away, too," he said. "Almost forty-five years ago."

"Sorry to hear that." He knew Wigglesworth was a widower back in the eighties, but honestly never gave the man's life a moment of thought before this.

"I was about your age, more or less," Wigglesworth said. "And I spent the next forty-five years…" His voice trailed off, and Mark stilled, waiting for the rest. "What were we looking for again?" he asked, his eyes suddenly clouded.

Answers. Messages. Wisdom. "Trophies," he said.

"Oh yeah. Over here." He moved to the last case, the glass so dusty and smeared, Mark could hardly see through it. There were football pictures and the basketball team, but peering out from behind an oversize baseball trophy was a picture of a group of cheerleaders in a vee formation, the face at the center so familiar, he actually sucked in a sharp breath.

Julia Coulter. Just as pretty and pure and bright and beautiful as he remembered.

"Oh, I know what I was going to say," Wigglesworth continued with a victorious tap of his cane on the linoleum. "How I spent my forty-five years after Wanda died."

Wanda Wigglesworth? Emma would love that name. The thought of her sent another strange sensation through him. Like he shouldn't think about her here, in these halls where he'd first found love. "And how was that, sir?"

He gave a slow smile. "Lonely," he said.

Mark's chest tightened. "Is that so?"

"Biggest regret I have in nine and a half decades on this earth is thinking I could never replace my Wanda."

"I'm sure she was special," Mark said, his gaze shifting to the cheerleading squad. *Special.*

"Of course she was special!" he boomed. "I married her. She could cook like that French lady with the funny voice and kept the house squeaky clean and never missed church and not one time did she raise her voice to me. Not one single time."

They had different definitions of special, obviously, but Mark got the idea. Wanda had done the trick for this old guy.

"But I was stupid," Wigglesworth insisted. "I spent forty-five years telling myself I wasn't lonely. That Wanda was it for me. And that if I even kissed another lady, I'd be somehow cheating on her."

Mark swallowed, the words hitting too hard.

"So I never did kiss another woman, not for forty-five years."

Damn. "I can see regretting that," Mark said.

"Now I'm too old to remember how. Or why." He chuckled, working to keep it from turning into another coughing fit. "But you're not."

"No. No, sir, I'm not." He remembered how and why. And *who.*

"So take my advice, young man." He tapped the trophy case with the knob of his cane. "It's nice to remember your youth, but don't hang on to the past so hard you completely miss the future."

Mark didn't respond, but took one more look through the foggy glass at the tiny face smiling out at him. And he smiled back.

I hear ya, Jules. Loud and clear.

Chapter Eighteen

There was a reason they suggested clients should plan to spend forty extra minutes in the post-massage relaxation lounge before getting up and walking around, Emma decided. Because getting up and walking around after an hour and a half of having her metabolic fibers purified and rejuvenated—she was definitely going to have to reword that—would have been impossible.

Emma was mush. Complete and utter jelly, head to toe. In fact, she wasn't sure she could actually walk all the way back to the villa without collapsing in a heap.

After drinking her second glass of cucumber water, she dressed in white yoga pants and a T-shirt, then brushed out her hair and took a long look in the mirror. She already looked pretty damn satisfied. And after tonight?

She sighed again, thinking of the sexy exchange in the kitchen and all that had led up to it. Something had clicked last night. Maybe it was some kind of closure with Kyle—knowing he'd shown up at the place where they were supposed to honeymoon for the sole purpose of saving his business. Maybe it was the *carpe diem* conversation and the confidence her meeting with Lacey had infused.

Maybe it was just that she was tired of showing so much restraint.

Whatever, she was ready to sleep with Mark. Although, there'd be no sleeping, but plenty of lovemaking.

No, no. Not that. Just sex. And that was fine. That was better. That was all.

Finally gathering her things, she stepped out to the reception area and stopped short at the sight of Mark Solomon on the sofa, his long legs stretched out and crossed at the ankles, his head back, eyes closed.

When the door opened, he lifted his head and smiled at her, and all her detoxed and purified metabolic fibers shot back to tense, achy anticipation.

"What are you doing here?" she asked.

"Waiting for you."

"That's good, because I'm not sure I can walk to the villa on these massage-wobbly legs."

"Liked it, did you?" the receptionist, not Jocelyn but another young woman, asked with a teasing smile.

Emma sighed. "I loved it." She took a moment to sign for the services and added a generous tip for her massage therapist. "It was a few hours in paradise."

Mark stood and reached for her hand, pulling her to him, surprising her with the strength of his grip. "Time for a few more," he whispered.

She inhaled a shaky breath and leaned into him. "You're slaying me."

"I haven't even started to slay."

Oh boy. With a far too quick good-bye to the receptionist, she let him lead her outside to the lobby. Everything seemed bright and bold and beautiful, especially the man who had his arm around her.

"I really didn't expect you to show up here," she said.

"It was impulsive. I was out and parked the car, checked the time, and decided to walk you back."

She nestled into him, the glow of the massage and scrub along with the time in the relaxation room warming her almost as much as the muscles of his body. "Where did you go while I was getting rubbed and oiled and scrubbed and spoiled?"

He laughed. "Put that in the ad copy, okay? You are one clever woman."

"I don't know about clever, but I'm relaxed, restored, and revived." She sighed and looked at him, then around. "Look at how beautiful this place is. Heaven, Mark. Barefoot Bay is heaven."

With an arm around her shoulders, he led her toward the stone path shaded by massive palm fronds and lined with insanely colored tropical flowers.

"You'll be great as the marketing VP," he said.

"I'm beginning to think I will," she agreed. "I can just see me walking VIP clients through this section." She glanced around and made a sweeping gesture with her arm. "Our guests enjoy exquisite sunsets every afternoon that turn the blue skies to tangerine tones and offer the opportunity to take sandy strolls and dip their toes in the beautiful blue waters of Barefoot Bay."

"Did you write that already?" he asked.

"No, I just made it up."

He laughed, shaking his head. "How do you *do* that?"

"I look at the picture or scene and describe it in a way that makes it come alive."

"I would have said, 'There's a nice beach.'"

"And you would be the world's worst copywriter." She slid her arm around his waist so they were arm in arm. "Good thing you have that pretty face to fall back on. Don't quit your day job."

"Can you sell anything, or are travel accounts your specialty?"

"Oh, anything. I can sell Thin Mints to a Girl Scout and a nice big bag of ice to an Eskimo. Name a product, and I'll make it marketable."

"Okay. How about..." He looked around. "Beach umbrellas?"

"Sturdy in the sand, unwavering in the wind, Lemon Drop Umbrellas promise to protect you from a burn and cover you in comfort."

He came to a stop, his mouth opened. "You didn't even have to think about that."

She shrugged. "I told you, it's my freakish gift."

"It's amazing, really. You can do that with anything and everything?"

"Pretty much." She pointed to a two-story guest house on their right. "Bay Laurel is the crown jewel of the Casa Blanca property, your private piece of paradise hiding among the hibiscus."

"You've written that already." He gave her a squeeze. "You didn't just make that up."

"I most certainly did. I'm telling you, I can sell anything."

They reached their villa, and Mark got out the key to open the door. "What about me?"

"You."

He slid the card key in and opened the door. "How would you sell me?"

"Depends on who's buying."

Closing the door behind her, he wrapped his arms around her to bring her closer. "You're buying."

"I'm already sold." She dropped her head back to look at him through tapered lashes. "But I could write it."

He ran his hands up and down her back, looking hard at her. "What's your tag line for me?"

"Mmmh." She reached up and fluttered her fingers through the hair at his temples. "Let's see…Mark Solomon. Older. Wiser. Hotter. *Silver*."

"Older? *Silver*? Who's going to buy that?"

"Already he's a picky client." She lowered her hands so they were on his cheeks, holding his head steady to look at him. "Mark Solomon. After you've had a boy, it's time for a real man."

He grinned at her. "Now we're talkin'."

She dragged her hands down his neck and over his chest, loving the corded muscles and masculine feel of him. She stopped when her hand reached his heart, which beat with unexpected urgency.

"Magic Mark. Strong and…" Words escaped her as she felt his erection press against her belly. "Hard."

He laughed into her neck, sucking lightly. "You've lost your touch, Madam Copywriter."

"Along with my balance…" She rocked her hips. "And my mind." Pressed her breasts against him. "And my control."

"Good riddance to all three." He kissed her mouth, placing his hands on her shoulders and slowly slid them down, lower, until he covered her breasts. He stroked until her nipples hardened.

"I like that," she sighed.

"I like you," he said gruffly, pushing her gently against the door behind her. "I like you so damn much."

He intensified the next kiss, adding pressure, growing harder against her, invading her mouth with a clever, persistent tongue. His hands moved with ease over her body, covering her breasts, her waist, her hips, and over her backside.

Still boneless from the massage, she practically fell into him, stroking his chest and shoulders with the same urgency, stopping only to catch her breath, moan his name, or just appreciate how glorious everything felt.

"Come with me, Em." He led her toward the bedroom, pausing for a kiss, a touch, a searing look. He stopped in the doorway, turning her to face him, kissing her once, then putting his hands on her shoulders. "You're sure?"

"Quite."

"You're one hundred percent ready for this?"

"Completely."

"You won't have second thoughts or morning-after doubts?"

"Second times and morning-after delights, more like."

"So this is what happens when you get in bed with a copywriter."

She reached up and kissed him, slow and long and with everything she had. "No, *this* is what happens when you get in bed with a copywriter."

She went with him to the bed and, there, he laid her back on the puffy down comforter.

For a moment, he said nothing, then climbed onto the bed, straddling her. "I'm not good with words like you."

She put her hands on his hips, slowly moving in to get the button of his jeans. "This isn't about talking." She unbuttoned and let the heel of her hand press against his erection, getting a thrill from his reaction.

"But I want to say something."

She rolled her eyes and fought a smile. "If you insist."

"I insist." He lowered himself on top of her so their faces were close. He kissed her cheek, his lips featherlight, but the little bit of contact sent fiery sparks to every nerve ending. "I want you to know...there's something about you that is different from any woman I've ever known, and even though that scares the hell out of me, I want you. I want *you*. Not just...this." He glanced down at their connected bodies. "But...*this*."

A whole different set of nerves tingled. Nerves she associated with...fears. Not little left-turn fears, but big, major heartache fears.

This was sex. Or it should be. Short-term, hot, mutually agreed upon as the right time...*sex*.

Not *this*—whatever he thought *this* was.

But telling him that would kill the moment and maybe take that sweet gleam out of his eyes. She went for humor.

"Let me get this straight. It's not this, but this." She tapped his lips, purposely playful. "Word-challenged but damn cute." Sliding her hand to the back of his head, she brought his face to hers. "Now use your mouth for good."

She took control of that kiss, using enough passion and pent-up pleasure to remind them both that *this* was sex, and that was good. Anything more and the risk was far, far too great.

With every kiss, every touch, her thoughts on the subject melted along with every cell in her body. Clutching his shoulders, she pulled him all the way onto her, wrapping her legs around him to feel all of him through the thin material of her yoga pants.

Long, lean muscles. Powerful thighs. Corded, cut abs. And one sizable hard-on spearing her belly.

They rolled together and started taking each other's clothes off with slightly shaky hands. She battled his shirt buttons and he finished for her, sitting up to strip out of the sleeves. He tugged at her top, sliding it over her head and smiling down at her before he reached around, unsnapped her bra, and slipped it off her arms.

Sighing with raw pleasure, he hovered over her, torturing her with a long, slow trail of kisses from her throat to her chest, searing her skin, and then finally taking her nipple in his mouth to suck and lick it to a painful point.

Lost. Emma was lost in the sensations that rolled over her. Heat and desire that coiled through her chest. Achy anticipation tightened her lower half. Every inch of her body sparked as if his fingers held electric charges.

He easily peeled off her pants and stood to strip his own. They were down to nothing but her lacy thong and his fully engorged boxer briefs before either one slowed down for a second.

When he did, in that last moment of suspended expectation, Mark got up and pulled the bed drape, then walked around to the other side and did the same. Through the sheer fabric, she watched him open the nightstand drawer and take something out. Then he closed the final pane at the bottom and climbed in, cocooning them in their own intimate, sexy, secret world.

He set a condom packet by the pillow and slid her higher on the bed. Next to her, he moved his gaze over her, up and down, as heated as his hands. Finally, he circled his finger around one nipple, staring at the response he elicited.

"Beautiful Emma," he whispered, his finger so light it was as if he was afraid he'd break her. She looked up at him, the closed drapes diffusing the light and accenting the angles of his chest and the darkness of the hair between his pecs.

Talk about beautiful. Even she had no words.

He trailed his finger down her stomach, circling her navel and making her smile when it tickled.

"I don't want to rush this," he said.

"Kind of hard not to."

"First time should be special."

She exhaled softly. "It *is* special."

He slipped his finger into the lace band of her panties, then took it out again, drawing a line up her stomach. "You're so damn smooth."

"Oil and body scrub. Yours are the second hands that have been all over me today."

His eyes shuttered as if her statement hit him hard. "No more. Just mine." He underscored that by spreading both palms over her, then moving on top of her, straddling again. "Mine for the week. Mine for..." His gaze lifted from her body to her eyes, his blue eyes surprisingly intense.

"For now," she finished. "Emphasis on..." She lifted her hips under him, trying to let him know how ready she was. "*Now.*"

He laughed softly. "Woman, I'm going to have to teach you how to cherish the moment. In fact, I think I'll take all night and day to teach you." With a teasing smile, he lowered his face and kissed her briefly on the lips, then worked his way down, leaving a fiery trail over her body.

She surrendered to his mouth and kisses that were slow and thorough and insanely deep. He touched everywhere, exploring, licking, tasting, and blowing soft breaths on her skin until she whimpered and sighed. He finally slipped off her panties and kissed each thigh, spreading her legs to torture her with his tongue and take her right to the brink of satisfaction.

She hung there while he made his way back up. Mark let her strip him naked so she could close her hands over a thick, solid erection that pulsed with his need. She ached to taste him, too, but he gave her the condom to sheathe him. Purring with pleasure, she slid her hands over his shaft. Again and again, memorizing every inch of it.

On top of her, he pulled her legs around him, braced

himself over her, and looked at her for what felt like an impossibly long time, but was probably only a few seconds.

She lifted her brows. "Do you want me to beg?"

"No..." He let the tip inside. "I want you to feel. Everything. Every second. Every shudder. Every time I move in and out. Don't miss a thing, Em."

"Okay." She grabbed the hard muscles of his backside and tried to pull him in faster, but he laughed softly.

"Why are you in such a hurry?"

"Desperation?" Her voice cracked a little, but he just smiled.

"We have all the time in the world."

They had a week. But now didn't seem like the perfect time to remind him of that. "Mark," she whispered into a kiss. "I really want you inside me."

It was enough to put him over the edge, making him thrust in deeper. All the way, filling her, making her cry out with the perfection of their joined bodies.

He stayed all the way inside her, holding perfectly still for one second, two, three, looking into her eyes, balancing them both in midair, breathless. And then he let go, plunging in and out very slowly at first, then building to a perfect, natural, sexy rhythm. He moaned her name and groaned with need and dragged her right along to the edge of complete surrender.

And one more time he held them there, poised on the cliff of pure ecstasy, suspended, every stroke and touch one step closer to falling, falling, *falling* into his arms.

Into him.

Pleasure finally won, pulling her over waves and waves of exquisite sensations, dragging her through an orgasm so long and intense it almost hurt. He pumped, then slowed, pushed, then stopped. Then it started all over again, until there was another crash, another surrender, another cry from her lips as she came again.

And just when she thought she couldn't take it anymore, he lifted her backside enough to reposition them and drove into her with merciless command, forcing her shattered and satisfied body to squeeze out one more blinding climax.

The last one was best of all, sweet and endless and perfect, because he came with her. Eyes closed, he lost control and pumped her full of himself with sexy sounds until all he could say was her name. Over and over again. *Emma.*

Emma.

No one had ever said her name like that. No one had ever made her come three times in a row. No one had ever made her wait so long or want so much. No one...until a perfect stranger who, by his own admission, would only ever love one woman.

And that wasn't her.

Forget the ticking clock. It wasn't the short-term present or unknown future that worked against her with Mark. It was the past.

Had she forgotten what she was "up against"? The memory of his soul mate, who could never be replaced.

She closed her eyes and tried to erase the thought with the sound of her name on his every breath, wrapping her arms around his neck until their breathing steadied and their sweat dried and their hearts slowed to a normal beat.

Except, after that? Emma was afraid nothing about her heart would ever be normal again.

Chapter Nineteen

"I can only imagine how you'd describe this," Mark said, laying his head back on the marble tub while he tried to decide if it was worth it to remove his hands from the sweet, soft spots of Emma's body to get a drink of champagne from the plastic glasses they'd brought in with them.

"Take a guess," she said, nestling her back flat against his chest and lifting her long leg up to let the bubbles drift over her silky skin.

"Wet, warm, and wonderful?" he suggested.

"A little elementary, but you did incorporate alliteration. There's hope for you yet. Try describing what you're feeling."

"Umm…hard again?" He pressed against her backside so she knew he wasn't kidding.

She laughed and jabbed him lightly with her elbow. "Not in my brochure, Mr. Solomon."

He stroked her bare breast, thumbing her. "It's been a long time since I only needed a few hours to recover," he admitted. "I like it."

She sighed. "You know what I really like about you?"

He rocked his pelvis again as an answer.

"Besides that," she joked. "I like that you are one hundred and fifty percent honest."

"We had a deal, remember?" Although, a little shadow of guilt darkened the corners of his conscience. He hadn't been one hundred and fifty percent honest with her—not about her ex.

"I don't think I needed to ask for that favor of honesty, though," she said, reaching for her drink. "You're a fundamentally honest person."

"Mostly."

"When's the last time you lied?" she asked.

"Lies can be of omission, you know." He moved his hand from her breast to take a deep drink, wishing he hadn't agreed to champagne just to see her pop the cork without fear. He'd prefer Scotch for this conversation.

"Really? What haven't you told me that you should?"

Shit. Way to ruin a perfectly good round two. The minute he told her that he knew Kyle Chambers had left her for another woman, she'd spiral. Who wouldn't? She'd be hurt all over again, and she'd be ticked at him for not telling her sooner.

Maybe he should do this over food. Dressed. Pushing up, he managed to climb out of the soapy tub. "It's almost eight o'clock, and I'm starved. In or out tonight?"

She looked up at him, her gaze dropping over his body and lingering on his partial erection. One touch—hell, that look for two more seconds—and he'd be at full staff and ready to go again.

"As much as I like the idea of going out to dinner, I'm a little over the rich restaurant food," she said. "I saw some pasta and the basic makings for a salad in the kitchen. Too pedestrian for you?"

"Are you kidding? I love that idea. Let's cook dinner."

She reached up and ran her hand up his thigh, settling just below his balls. "Unless you want to try it fast and furious this time."

"Fast is for teenagers. Slow is for lovers."

She snapped her fingers and pointed at him. "I will make a copywriter out of you yet."

Laughing, he stepped into the shower and rinsed off the bubbles with cold water, which helped deaden his arousal—a little, anyway—then walked into the bedroom to grab some loose-fitting linen pants, skipping anything under them.

He stuck his head in the bathroom to tell her he was going to start boiling the water, but didn't say anything when he found her still in the tub, pressing her fingertips into her temples as if her head ached. "Stop," she whispered to herself. "Just stop."

"Emma."

She turned, startled.

"Are you okay?" he asked.

She smiled, but it was tight and didn't reach her eyes. "Never been better."

"Now who is lying by omission?" He stepped into the bathroom. "What's wrong?"

"Would it be totally breaking the rules if I lie and say the champagne gave me a headache?"

"Yes. Tell me what's the matter," he said simply, coming closer.

"Nothing," she replied.

"Emma."

"I mean *that's* the problem. Nothing is wrong...with you. You're perfect, and this is...not real, and I'm having a moment, okay?"

"Plenty is wrong with me." He sat on the side of the tub

and reached out to her wet hair. "And I really don't like when you look unhappy."

"See?" she asked, holding up her hands as if her point had been made.

"Not...entirely." He tread lightly, knowing better than to contradict a naked woman making confessions in the bath.

"I know I said no regrets or second-guessing or morning-after doubts, but..." She shook her head and looked outside, more to avoid his gaze, he suspected, than to appreciate the water view.

He stroked a finger over her bare arm. "It's not the morning after yet, and you're allowed to doubt. What brought this on?"

"The third orgasm?" she said with a crack in her voice.

"Should we go for four, five, and six? Maybe they'll cancel the others out."

"I won't be able to walk, let alone dance."

"How about we eat and talk? We need to talk." Talk...about truths. Although, if she was having doubts about having sex with him, he'd just rock her whole world by dumping the truth about Kyle on top of her. That just wasn't fair.

But *not* telling her wasn't fair, either.

"Talk about what?"

He sighed. "I haven't been honest with you."

Her eyes widened in horror. "Please, oh God, please don't hit me with something like you're married." Her voice rose and tightened. "Please—"

"Emma!" He put his hand on her shoulder. "Of course I'm not married. I'm one hundred percent single and free to do this. Put that out of your mind."

"Whew. Okay. 'Cause, whoa, liars and cheats. I can't take them."

Shit. Double shit. Son of a bitch shit, he was about to hurt her with the truth about her ex.

"Okay," she said, sounding lighter. "Go start the pasta water, and I'll shower off the suds and be with you in a few minutes."

He took her chin in his hand and leaned over, planting a kiss on her mouth. "Take your time," he said, and meant it. He'd need a few minutes to come up with how to tell her in a way that wouldn't completely destroy her heart.

How had he started caring about her so fast, he wondered as he filled a pot with water. It had been only a couple of days. A crazy charade, a walk on the beach, a few good car rides, some dancing...and one mind-blowing afternoon in bed.

But the thought of seeing her hurt tore him to shreds. He put the pot on a back burner and closed his eyes with a sigh.

"I know what it is."

At Emma's words, he turned to find her on a barstool, facing the kitchen. She wore a loose-fitting beach cover-up with no bra, the shapes of her breasts and points of her nipples evident enough to make his mouth water with the memory of tasting them.

"What *what* is?" he asked.

"What you want to tell me."

No, she didn't. She couldn't. She'd brought the half bottle of champagne they'd been drinking to the counter, and he nodded to it. "Can I get you a fresh glass? No plastic this time."

She rested her chin on the heel of her hand as she studied him, ignoring his question. "You don't want to tell me," she said. "Why is that?"

He opened his mouth to say something, but nothing came out.

"In fact, you've gone to great lengths so that I don't find out." She angled her head. "Why?"

He swallowed and braced himself on the counter, facing her. "I don't want you to get hurt."

She frowned, drawing back. "I'd be hurt if I knew where you went this afternoon?"

That's what she thought he was holding back?

"Is that why you never answered me when I asked you where you went?" she asked. When he frowned, she said, "Remember when we were leaving the spa, and I asked you where you'd been? You changed the subject."

He actually had no memory of that and hadn't changed the subject on purpose, but slowly, the possibility of telling her something that *wouldn't* hurt her formed in his mind.

Was it wrong? Was it too easy?

"I thought you might..." As he played with the words, he looked at her, seeing the flush of sex still on her cheeks, the light that never quite dimmed in her eyes even when she'd struggled with the aftereffects of amazing sex.

He'd steal that light and drain those cheeks of color if he told her the truth about Kyle.

He clenched his jaw and made the decision. He wouldn't hurt her. He just wouldn't. To what end? His first instinct on the matter was right, as usual.

She'd find out soon enough when word got out of her boss's new girlfriend, and he'd be...wherever he was going next. She'd never know that he'd had that conversation with Kyle and knew the truth.

"I thought you might laugh at me," he finally said.

Her lips lifted in a half smile. "My favorite pastime."

He chuckled, turning to the cabinet to get them fresh glasses for a hearty red wine he'd opened to go with their pasta.

"I will tell you where I went and why," he said. "But keep your mockery to a minimum, because I got the answers I was looking for."

Silent, she watched him, finally taking the bistro glass of Chianti he'd poured and raising it to him. "Here's to honesty," she said.

Right. "To happiness," he countered. He tapped her glass with his, the thin crystal rims dinging the start of a round. A round she'd lose if he were perfectly honest, so he opted for a completely different kind of honesty.

"I went to the high school after all."

She sat up a little straighter. "You faced a fear without me? I mean, if you're now willing to admit it *was* a fear."

"It was," he conceded.

"What changed your mind?"

"I went looking for advice from Julia," he said after taking a sip.

Emma's hand froze midair, the glass inches from her mouth. "Really?"

"Really. And, believe it or not, I got that advice."

"From Julia." She couldn't hide the skepticism in her voice.

"Sort of. And from Principal Wigglesworth."

She leaned against the back of the barstool and finally took her drink. "The ninety-year-old guy who was at Lacey's party?"

"Ninety-six." He checked the water to be sure it wasn't close to boiling and came around to get next to her, ready to tell her this particular confession. Her past relationship had no bearing on their future. But his did. And he wanted her to know he realized that.

She looked a little confused and uncertain. "How is that advice from Julia?"

He let out a breath. "She was there."

She gave him a look of sheer incredulity.

He laughed softly. "We were at the trophy cases and her picture was there, but...I feel like it was a legitimate message just the same."

She searched his eyes and put the wine glass down, using her free hand to touch his face. "Why are you telling me this?"

He looked back at her, searching his heart for the truth. "It was why I was able to make love to you today with so much...feeling."

He could see her swallow hard, but she didn't say a word.

"Normally, I..."

"Don't have feelings?" she guessed.

"I avoid them and escape with the next high-adventure vacation," he admitted. Then he smiled and looked down at his wine. "So you were right about that, too."

She took his chin and forced his face up. "What was this message from Julia?" she asked, her voice tight. "What did she say?"

"Nothing. It came from the ninety-six-year-old principal. He said his biggest regret in life was not pursuing another woman after his wife died forty-five years ago," Mark said, turning the barstool so Emma was facing him. "He stayed alone."

Her dark eyes flashed for a second, then dimmed. "Okay."

"Okay? That's all you have to say is 'okay'?"

"Well, what do you want me to say, Mark? Hallelujah, I have a chance?"

"What do you mean, you have a chance?"

"Against the memory of your one and only soul mate?" She shook her head, hard. "I don't want to fight that memory. I don't want to take her place. I really, really want to have sex and have fun and have my week in paradise like you promised me. But anything more?"

"Would be bad?" he guessed.

"Would be impossible."

Would it? Was he still that mired in the past? Did he have to face more fears in order to free himself for someone as extraordinary as Emma?

"Look," she said. "I think it's very sweet that I mean enough to you in this short time to want that...that approval. But you don't need it, Mark. This is just...a ruse. Remember?"

He'd completely forgotten.

"Hey." She pointed to the stove. "Your water is boiling."

And so were his nerves.

Without a word, he scooted around the counter to turn off the burner. "Yeah, you're right," he said casually and quickly. "But it was fun to see the old school."

"So what other places are you trying to avoid? If you tell me, I will drag you to them right this very minute."

"Okay." He turned and gave her a look. If this was just physical for her, then...so be it. "Bed," he said. "I'm terrified of it."

She frowned, confusion darkening her eyes until she saw him smile. "You are?"

"Petrified. So, please, Emma DeWitt, drag me back to bed right this very minute."

She slid off her stool and crooked her finger. "Follow me."

He followed, of course. To paradise. To pleasure. To yet another thrill.

Or was it just another form of escape? It was...for her. And he wasn't sure why that bothered him, but it did.

Chapter Twenty

Jasper eyed one, then the other, his hands on his hips, his platinum rooster tail pointing to the unforgiving overhead studio lights. "So what *happened* with you two?" His voice rose with playful, unambiguous intention.

Emma looked at Mark, seeing his chest rising and falling from the light exertion of *The Power of Love* dance. He lifted a shoulder, as confused by the question as she was.

"I thought we nailed it," Mark said.

"Oh, you nailed *something*," Jasper said. "Each other for the past twenty-four hours, is my guess."

Emma felt heat crawl up her neck. Was it that obvious? Jasper was right, of course. Sex happened…and quite a bit of it.

Dinnertime sex, followed by before-sleep sex—though that was really more of Emma as dessert sex. They'd stumbled through the day yesterday, attended one subcommittee meeting, sneaked in a meal somewhere, and spent the rest of the time in bed, in the pool, on the sofa…

And today there was blissful, crazy, triple-o-time morning sex. And a whole heck of a lot of soaping each other down in the shower.

When she said "just sex" to Mark, Emma was pretty sure he'd interpreted that as *only* sex. Oh, they talked, if breezy banter counted as talking, but their short-term relationship had definitely taken a turn for the physical.

"Are we dancing differently?" Emma asked tentatively.

"You're dancing like two people on fire."

"To win this competition," Emma added, unable to ignore Mark's somewhat satisfied smirk.

"Then I hope you've picked out the perfect costumes."

"Uh, costumes?" Satisfaction disappeared as Mark's face registered horror. "We're not wearing costumes."

"Then you're not winning," Jasper replied. "Find yourself something suitably eighties. Emma, rip a T-shirt and find some leg warmers to wear over black tights. Mark, surely you've got something around. A nice white Miami Vice linen jacket and a skinny tie will do the trick. Loafers with no socks. And, for the love of Pete, *practice* at home. Standing up this time. Especially that free-for-all at the end. It's sloppy."

He clapped three times, signaling the end of their lesson, and packed up his things.

A few minutes later, at the Porsche parked on the street, Mark reached into his pocket.

"Tails," Emma said, knowing the ritual already.

He flipped a quarter, caught it on the back of his hand, peeked, and grinned at her.

"You're cheating," she accused.

"I'm just lucky. And I'm driving." He gave her a quick kiss and opened the passenger door. "Let's go back to Heaven's Helper. Mrs. Reinhardt has a ton of clothes in her thrift shop. Maybe something will work for our costumes so Jasper doesn't completely disown us."

"I know, right? Complaining about our dancing." She

slipped into the seat and looked up at him. "I thought we were amazing."

He grinned at her. "I don't think we washed all the pheromones off in the shower."

"I don't know how that happened. We did everything else possible in that shower."

They took the long way—since Mark wanted extra driving time, Emma suspected—but found Carla Reinhardt behind her counter when they arrived back at the Heaven's Helper.

"Well, speak of the devil!" she cried out when they walked in.

"Someone's talking about us?" Mark asked.

The woman looked toward the fluorescent lights in the ceiling. "Oh, Mark Solomon. Half the town is talking about you, young man. Hello again, Emma." She gave her a warm hug. "No biscuits today?"

"Not this time," Emma said. "We're here to raid your thrift shop of anything that looks like 1980s clothes."

She made a face of uncertainty. "You can look. But I hope you have better luck than the 1960s people that were here yesterday. As if I have tie-dye shirts. Come on, come on." She led them through a doorway to the adjacent thrift shop, an undersized junk store with antiques, pictures, dishes, and along the back, some clothes. It smelled as dusty and worn as the goods she sold.

While Emma started skimming through the hanging items, she noticed Carla sidled up next to Mark and whispered something under her breath that Emma didn't catch. He turned and answered in a low voice, so Emma grabbed a bright pink T-shirt from the hanger.

"Is there somewhere I can try this on?" she asked, hoping to give Mark whatever privacy he was seeking.

"There's a closet right over there that you can use."

Whatever they had discussed, the conversation was finished by the time Emma came back out. Mark looked a little pale, and serious, even though Carla had found him a fairly hideous white linen sports jacket and the requisite skinny tie. She'd even scared up some ancient leg warmers for Emma.

Set for the dance, they said good-bye, and Carla leaned close to Mark and gave him a kiss. "I know you'll do what's right," Carla whispered.

They left the small shop, walking in silence, Emma waiting the whole time for an explanation.

At the car, Mark handed her the key. "It's your turn."

"Okay, now I know something's wrong." She took his hand instead and closed her fingers over his. "Are you going to tell me what it is?"

He searched her face for a long moment, as if he wasn't sure at all, then closed his eyes. "Carla saw Wayne Coulter yesterday."

"Wayne..."

"Julia's dad." He blew out a breath. "She suggested, strongly, that I see him before he hears I'm on the island and didn't visit. She almost told him, but wanted to respect my wishes."

"Don't you want to see him?" she asked.

"I know I should," he said. "I did keep in touch with her mom, but she passed, and it was just awkward anytime I called him. He was wrecked."

He scratched the cheek he hadn't bothered to shave, squinting into the sunlight. "Frankly, I didn't know he was still on Mimosa Key, still living in the same house. After his wife, Betsy, died, he talked about leaving the island. But obviously he didn't. Carla said she rarely sees him anymore."

"Is that unusual?"

He shrugged. "Could be he's a recluse now."

"Oh, that's sad. You should visit him, Mark."

He gave her a quick look and, from the shadows around his eyes, she immediately knew that Julia's childhood home would be one of those places he wanted to avoid. And who could blame him?

She put her hand on his arm. "Let's go together. Right now."

He looked at her, astonished. "You'd do that with me?"

"In a heartbeat."

He brushed his knuckles along her jaw. "Emma, you don't have to."

"I know. But I want to."

His shoulders sank a little. "I don't want to lie to him about this whole engagement thing." He looked away, his face etched with pain. "I didn't think this plan all the way through when I suggested it."

"You don't have to lie. We'll tell him the truth. We'll tell him we're friends and we're purposely letting people think it's more to protect you from the onslaught of questions about Julia. I'm sure he'll understand."

He looked at her, obviously thinking about the suggestion, but slowly, he shook his head.

"No? You don't want to tell him the truth? Or you don't want him to meet me?"

"I can't believe you."

She felt her eyes widen. "What? I haven't lied to you."

"No, I mean I don't believe...*you*. This." He placed both hands on her cheeks again, the touch gentle, light, and precious. "I never expected...I just didn't think...I'd ever feel anything like this again."

"Oh." She exhaled the word, nothing else possible as emotions hit her hard. Dismay. Hope. Relief. Joy.

And the big one. The one she didn't even dare think.

"You just amaze me, Emma."

She tried for light. "Oh, well, that's just the sex talking."

"No," he insisted. "It's not. It's this." He put a fist on his chest. "This…thing."

She smiled. "Thing?"

"How would you describe this heart that has been numb for sixteen years and is suddenly feeling things again? What would the copywriter say?"

"I guess I'd say…*wow*." And that he was breaking their unspoken rules. "You left the copywriter speechless. That's impressive."

"You're impressive," he countered. "Would you really come with me to do this?"

"Would you have let me plow through a dangerous left turn or smack a biscuit canister all alone? You already faced fear number one by going to the high school. Visiting Julia's dad and seeing her childhood home will be number two. What's three?"

His gaze moved over her shoulder, and she turned to follow it…to the church. Hope Presbyterian.

"Let's start with your father-in-law," she said softly, taking the keys from him. "Tell me how to get there."

If the number hadn't been on the mailbox, Mark wasn't sure he'd have recognized the little one-story Old Florida house at 121 Skyview Drive just a few blocks north of Pleasure Pointe in south Mimosa Key. To be honest, none of the houses looked much like they had thirty years ago.

Shingle roofs had been replaced with barrel tile; brick homes were mostly covered in earth-toned stucco. Laurel oaks lined the street, some reaching three stories high, and many of the houses had been landscaped to show off queen palms and explosions of purple and pink bougainvillea.

He didn't remember this warren of simple houses between town and Pleasure Pointe as being so pretty.

"I guess that's it," he said, indicating the second to last house on the right. "Although I don't remember a brick driveway or windows with arches."

She threw him a smile. "Time marches on, big guy. You ready for this?"

"As ready as I'll ever be."

"Why are you dreading it so much?" she asked.

"I don't want to see Wayne on the old plaid sofa, wearing slippers and a robe, surrounded by photo albums and empty bottles." He gave her a soft smile. "You know. There but for the grace of God and all."

"You wouldn't live that way, Mark."

He might have if he'd stopped moving long enough to feel the pain of what he'd lost.

"I'm just so grateful you're here, Emma." He reached over and put his hand on hers. "After this, let's go for a nice long drive. I want to see you open this baby up. There's a deserted road on the way to the Everglades if you want to hit a hundred."

"I don't want to hit anything but you for suggesting that."

He laughed, opening the door. "Let's do this."

Holding her hand, they walked up to the door, taking in a lawn trimmed with deep-brown mulch and decorated with a bird fountain that sure as heck hadn't been there the last time Mark visited.

Even the front door had been painted a cheery red, giving

him hope that poor old Wayne still cared about maintaining his home.

No one answered their knocks or the bell after they'd tried several times. The garage door was closed, and there were no windows to see if a car was parked in there, so he didn't know if Wayne was home and sleeping, or out.

Now that he was here, Mark really didn't want to have to come back or call to schedule something official.

"Maybe he's in the back," Mark said, taking Emma's hand to lead her around the side of the house.

The yard had been neatly manicured, and the driveway paving stones extended all the way along the side. He glanced at the kitchen door, remembering that was how he always got in, never knocking.

He peeked through the window, blinking at the granite and dark wood of a completely remodeled kitchen. No yellow linoleum, no white cabinets, no...Julia sitting at the little table doing homework.

He waited for the kick from that memory, but there was none.

In the back, the screened-in pool area was different, too. The old plastic chaise, the site of so many make-out sessions, had been replaced by upscale rattan outdoor furniture, and someone had added a fire pit.

"What a pretty house," Emma said.

Pretty...different. "Well, I certainly don't feel ghosts lurking in the corners," he assured her. "Not a thing looks familiar to me."

"You want to leave him a note?"

He puffed out a breath, considering that, but then they heard a car door slam in the front. "Maybe he's back." Still holding Emma's hand, they returned to the front of the house where a late-model Jaguar had pulled into the driveway, a woman climbing out of the driver's seat.

And there was Wayne, stepping out from the passenger's side. Instead of pajamas and slippers, he wore an expensive polo and crisp khaki pants. His gray hair was cut short, and his previously bordering-on-dumpy body looked fit and healthy for a man deep into his seventies.

"Hello, Wayne," Mark said, approaching that side of the car. "It's nice to see you."

The older man did a double take, slightly unsteady for a flash, then his wide smile pulled. "Mark! So it's true. You are in town."

Damn, he'd already heard. But before Mark could apologize, Wayne reached out and met Mark for a hearty embrace, patting his back with genuine warmth and pleasure, as if to show how happy he was to see his daughter's husband.

"This is the famous Mark Solomon?" The woman came around the car, lifting sunglasses to get a look, her face remarkably unlined for a woman who was probably the same age as Wayne. Her hair was dyed dark, her clothes fashionable, and her smile warm and genuine.

"This is Linda Everhurst, my fiancée," Wayne said.

His *what*? "Nice to meet you, Linda."

"The pleasure is mine. And this must be *your* fiancée," she said, turning to Emma.

"This is Emma DeWitt," Mark said, physically unable to say *my fiancée* as an echo to what he'd just heard.

"Of course it is," Linda cooed, giving Emma a hug. "I was in Beachside Beauty yesterday, and two of the women from the reunion were getting their nails done and, of course, we gossiped." She clasped her hands as if delighted. "So lovely to meet you. You must come in, now, and see the house. And catch up." She had an arm around Emma. "I hear you are an adventurer like Mark. So exciting. Have you jumped from an airplane?"

She swept Emma away toward the walkway, leaving Mark and Wayne a few steps behind.

"She's a bit of a human whirlwind," Wayne said with a soft laugh. "She moved in and took over my life two years ago. Remodeled the whole damn house like we were on some kind of home makeover TV show."

Mark just stared at him, barely able to take in how fantastic he looked. How happy he seemed. "You're doing so great, Wayne."

The other man gave a tight smile. "Does that bother you, son?"

"Not at all," he said. "I just…imagined it was tougher."

Wayne's hazel eyes softened. "It *was* tough. Losing Julia, and then Betsy. But after a few years, I was just plain tired of being sad and lonely. So you know where I went?"

Mark shook his head, having no idea.

"Well, where would you go if you were sad and lonely?"

To the highest mountain, in the fastest car, down the steepest rock, through the roughest white water. That's how he detoured around *sad* and *lonely*.

"LoveInc.com!" He gave Mark's arm a punch. "How could I go to any other website than the one that bought my daughter and son-in-law's company?"

"You went…online? For a relationship?"

Wayne chuckled. "Hey, you practically invented the concept."

"I didn't invent it, but…" He sure as heck hadn't expected his father-in-law to use it. But, then, why not?

"I went looking for a change in my life, and look what I got." Wayne swept his hand toward the house.

"Redecorated?"

"I got Linda, and isn't she something? She's a Realtor over in Naples, and she took one look at this house and knew how to fix and flip it. I decided to let her. She redid the whole thing, top to bottom, and while she was at it, we just got closer and happier and, I don't know. *Better*."

Better, not bitter, Emma would say. But Mark wasn't bitter. He was...still running, he realized with a jolt. Running from memories. Running from pain. Running from the fear of what they would do to him.

"When it was all done," Wayne continued, oblivious to Mark's personal epiphany, "I asked her to marry me and forget flipping the house. It's a new home, new life, new family inside. We're staying."

"Wow." Mark inched back, taking it all in. "That's amazing, Wayne. I'm really happy for you."

He patted Mark's back. "And I'm happy for you. Betsy and I hoped you'd remarry."

"You did?" He'd always suspected it would break their hearts if he had.

"Julia wanted you to be happy, and it looks like you are." He peered at the house, where Linda and Emma had disappeared. "She's a fine-looking woman and, knowing you, she's got a heart of gold."

"That she does." No way he was getting into a truth-telling session now. And if he knew Emma, she'd wait for him before she spilled any beans.

Weird to think that after only a few days, he did know her and trusted her already.

During their visit, a silent communication went between Mark and Emma, sealing the fact that they weren't about to share their secret. It would end up all over Beachside Beauty, anyway.

After some iced tea and small talk, which was centered

almost entirely on the process of remodeling the house and the booming real estate market on Mimosa Key, they made their way to the door, Emma and Linda chatting like fast friends.

As they were saying good-bye, Wayne put a little pressure on Mark's shoulder and steered him a few steps back. "Son, I have something I want to give you."

"Okay."

"Come with me for a moment." He led Mark down a hall that used to lead to Julia's bedroom, a sanctuary he was rarely allowed to enter in high school, though he had a vague memory of pale blue walls, white bifold closet doors, and a mauve carpet he recalled Julia hated.

Now, it was cream and wood with walls of built-in cabinetry and a sleek pedestal table in the middle with two laptops.

"This is our office now," he said as Mark looked around.

"It's nice."

"I know what you're thinking."

Mark gave him a look. "You do?"

"Not much of a shrine to my daughter, who spent many happy hours in this room."

"No." Mark shook his head. "I'm not thinking that at all. On the contrary, I'm impressed with how you've moved on and put your life back together. Differently and quite well."

Smiling, Wayne opened one of the cabinets on the wall. "I did, didn't I? I think Betsy would be so proud."

"Proud?" The word slipped out before Mark could catch himself, but Wayne glanced over his shoulder.

"Of course proud. It was Betsy who taught me to overcome adversity. Betsy who showed me how to accept Julia's death. Betsy who made me a man who understands the value of a great woman. She'd managed as well as could

223

be expected after Julia died, until that heart attack we just never saw coming. She was healthy and then, wham. Gone. But I know she didn't want me to be holed up in here crying in my Jack Daniel's."

"No, I guess she wouldn't."

"Here it is." From inside a cabinet, he pulled out a thin envelope, yellowed with age. "This was stuck behind the baseboard where Julia's bed used to be. The contractor found it, gave it to me, and, well…it's obviously meant for you."

On the front, in a girlish, curly-cue handwriting he instantly recognized, was his name. With an upside-down heart for the *a* in Mark, the way Julia had written it all through high school. Even after they were married, once in a while she'd leave him a note around the house with that upside-down heart.

Damn it. He really didn't want to read this. "I don't…" He looked up at Wayne, unable to tell him he didn't want it. "I don't know what it could be."

"Probably nothin'," Wayne said. "But it has your name on it, and I thought if I saw you, I'd give it to you."

Another message from Julia? Two in one week and the ring before he got here? She must really have something to say.

But what if it didn't say what he wanted to hear? What if it flat out hit him over the head with a fact they'd both agreed on, a fact they'd based their marriage on: There is one and only one soul mate.

Right now, this week, Mark didn't want to face that fact. Not that he'd changed his opinion, but…

Not entirely sure why, he folded the envelope in half and slipped it into his back pocket with absolutely no intention of reading its contents, at least not this week. Maybe another time, another place. But not now.

Chapter Twenty-One

Emma's fingers hovered over the keyboard of her laptop late that night, where she'd been since she and Mark finished dinner. It was Thursday night now, and the meeting with Lacey was Saturday morning. So, Emma sought time to prepare, but not give up too much time with Mark, as time had grown...precious.

After dinner, Mark had gone to hang out with the lone males on the planning committee to watch Chef Law in action at the resort kitchen as an excuse to avoid the Favor Committee meeting. That gave Emma a few hours to concentrate on the mock advertising materials she wanted to take in to impress Lacey.

But her mind drifted as she looked beyond the screen to her sumptuous surroundings. Lit only by one small nightstand light, the villa bedroom looked shadowy and comforting, the four-poster draped with sheer linen, the French doors open to let in the warm night air.

Every time she tried to capture some essence of this resort in words...they just drifted into *feelings*. Blissful, beautiful, impossibly sweet emotions that settled over her and carried her from euphoria to peace all day and all night.

How did she capture that magic in a brochure? She looked down at the computer open on the bed, the words she'd written blurring like the past few days in Barefoot Bay.

Each day here, she and Mark had languished over late mornings in bed, since Emma had taught him the joy of sleeping in—though there hadn't been much sleeping involved. He hadn't been kidding when he said he was a morning person; he woke every day with one goal and purpose, and she relished every moment of sunrise sex.

Their time had been spent at the beach, in the pool, or making pathetic attempts to practice their dance routine, which usually ended with an open bottle of wine and long conversations topped off by sunset strolls on the beach. After dinner at the resort, with great food and lots of laughter, they fell into bed again.

In some ways, they'd truly had a honeymoon. In other ways, they were both silent about the underlying feelings that, no matter how much Emma didn't want them to, grew strong with each exquisite, shattering orgasm brought on by Mark's slow hands.

Mark had given her that gift, among so many others, and when Emma thought hard about what this week had come to mean to her, she didn't know if she wanted to laugh or cry.

She'd never forget this experience, this life-changing interlude in paradise...or the man who made it possible.

And that was the problem. She'd have to forget him by Sunday when they both left, and Emma returned to life as jilted, jobless, and jaded.

Maybe not jobless, she reminded herself. And certainly not jaded anymore. Jilted? That wouldn't be how Mark's good-bye would feel.

How would it feel?

She actually didn't want to think about it. Instead, she forced herself to concentrate and use this rare time alone to her benefit.

Emma didn't want to steal her sexy morning wakeup time to work on this, and she and Mark would be at the ballpark all day tomorrow, Friday, and then there was the pre-reunion party Friday night at the Toasted Pelican. The day after that, she'd meet with Lacey, the morning of the reunion.

So she returned to the mock brochure and her power adjectives.

"Dreamy is so...unimaginative," she muttered, tapping the backspace key. "And luxurious is so overdone. Therapeutic sounds...medicinal. Maybe..." She typed a few letters. "Sumptuous. How does that sound?"

"Sounds like you're describing this platter that Chef Law Monroe personally made for you."

She snapped her head up to see Mark standing in the open French doors, holding a tray. "For me?"

"For us." He raised an oversize restaurant service platter and entered slowly. "Dessert, my dear."

"You walked back here with that?"

"Hitched a ride from a lovely housekeeper named Poppy, and I only had to tip her a strawberry."

He came closer so she could see the tray held a split of champagne, two empty glasses, a bowl of fruit, an array of pound cake, and two heated glass bowls of... "Is that chocolate?" Emma asked, her voice cracking with longing.

"And salted caramel."

Her jaw dropped wide open as she looked from Mark to the feast to Mark and back again. They were equally delicious.

"I could kiss you," she said, leaning closer.

"That's the general idea." He held the tray out of her

reach. "Bathtub, poolside, or right here on the bed? Lady's choice."

She closed the computer. "I'm in a sleep shirt. Let me put my bathing suit on, and I'll meet you outside."

"Don't bother with that. You're not going to be in anything for very long." The words, spoken low and deliberate, sent a chill through her.

She pushed the computer to the side. Forget work. Forget brochure copy. Forget the rest of the world existed. Just like she had from the day she landed on this doorstep, she followed him like he was the Pied Piper and she was mesmerized.

Outside, he set the tray on the ottoman in front of the rattan sofa where they liked to lie together after dinner and look at the moon and stars.

Sitting next to her, Mark put his hands on Emma's cheeks and held her face. "Missed you." And kissed her.

She sighed into his mouth, which was tastier than any treat he could have come back with. Intensifying the kiss, she reached up and tunneled her fingers into his hair. It was all familiar ground now. Familiar and...wonderful.

"Did you get any work done?" He leaned forward and got a strawberry, dragging it through the chocolate and letting that drip.

"Not enough."

With a napkin under the strawberry, he brought the gooey concoction to her mouth and fed her. Sweet, dark, bitter chocolate filled her mouth, followed by the bright freshness of ripe fruit.

"Oh my God," she moaned around the bite, closing her eyes. "That's not chocolate. That's sin on a strawberry."

He laughed, dabbing the napkin on her lip, then finishing the job with his tongue. "Law has really underplayed his

228

culinary skills. Guy's a kitchen beast. He was throwing orange zest and spices in that chocolate, melting caramel, and making some kind of pastry. He really needs his own restaurant."

"What's going on with that place in town he was trying to buy? The one we're going to after the game tomorrow night," she asked, finishing the perfect bite with a sip of sparkling champagne.

"He still can't find out who owns the place, no matter who he charms for information."

"He *is* charming," she agreed.

He gave a teasing elbow. "Hey."

"But not as charming as you," she added.

Grinning, he helped himself to a bite of cantaloupe. "Anyway, you'll get a chance to see the Toasted Pelican yourself tomorrow night."

"How about Ken and Beth? Any progress there?"

"Listen to you," he said, laughing as he swallowed. "You've come to like these people."

She had gone to every meeting with him and, it was true, she was fond of all of them. "I've come to like everything about this," she admitted, leaning into him a little. "Especially my fake fiancé."

He didn't answer, studying her for a moment, then reached for the tray. "Cake and salted caramel?" he asked.

"You're killing me."

"Just warming you up, baby." He gave her a sweet, fast kiss, made all the nicer for how fleeting it was. "So, Ken and Beth, yeah." He dropped back and put an arm along the sofa, scooting her closer. "I found out they'd dated in high school when he was a senior and she was a sophomore. He didn't say why they broke up. In fact, he was purposely silent on the subject. Whatever, she must still be pissed, because she's frozen him out all week and, frankly, hasn't shown up to a couple of things Ken signed up for just because he thought she'd be there." He shot her a humorous look. "Including the flower arranging."

"I wonder why." She bit a strawberry, thinking. "I mean, he's so freaking hot."

"Excuse me."

She laughed. "And he's a firefighter."

"Yeah, I guess women love that heroic stuff. Except he'd love to get married again and just hasn't met the right woman. I imagine he had fantasies of reliving the past with Beth."

She snuggled closer to him, loving the moment, the comfort, the food, the naturalness of this. "Sounds like you three shared more gossip in the kitchen than the poor women who were stuck tying bows on soaps shaped like clocks."

"We call it male bonding."

"You were in the kitchen, cooking, discussing relationships."

"*Old*-male bonding."

She laughed. "What else did you talk about?"

"Oh, just sports, cars, babes. Pure guy shit."

She gave him a gentle elbow jab. "Did you...talk about us?" she asked, maybe a little coy, but so curious.

"I didn't tell them the truth about our engagement, if that's what you mean."

"It would be super awkward now," she agreed. "And after Saturday, you'll never see any of them again. Or..."

Shut up, Emma.

She finished the unfinished thought by taking a drink of champagne.

"Or what?" he asked.

"Nothing."

"Em." He narrowed his eyes at her. "We had a deal."

"I was going to say 'or me'." But it sounded needy and clingy and dumb.

"What makes you think I'm never going to see you again?" he asked. "We both live in New York."

"For the moment," she reminded him. "I may be relocating to paradise."

"Then I'll be back," he said simply.

She didn't respond while he dipped another strawberry. Holding it over her mouth, he eased her back a little. "Open up," he whispered, the sexy demand sending a sharp stab of longing into her belly.

"Will you really be back?"

"Open up," he repeated.

In other words, get sexy, get playful, don't get serious. *He had his soul mate, remember, Emma?*

She closed her eyes and opened her mouth, waiting for the taste of chocolate and strawberry to remove the metallic flavor of fear she knew a little too well.

She was scared of losing him, and that was one fear she'd have to face alone.

Mark gave her a bite, then covered her mouth with his, licking the chocolate from her lips.

Their tongues shared the taste, and each other, then he lifted her chin and kissed his way down her throat and, somehow, she swallowed the bite of food.

Easing aside the loose T-shirt she wore to bed but usually discarded in the first two minutes there, he pressed his lips on her skin, burning her. Of course, her body reacted instantly, arching into him, offering herself, letting him lift the top off to reveal her bare breasts.

"This is all the dessert I need," he murmured, lowering her to her back so he could take the top and begin his exploration with tongue and touch. "I can't get enough of you, Emma. Every day and every night. This is all I want."

He suckled her breast and stroked the other one, pressing down on her so she could feel him grow harder with each second.

But it wasn't all she wanted, a voice in her head echoed.

She tried to silence it by wrapping her legs around him and rocking into his erection.

But her thoughts couldn't be quieted. Even when he slid down her panties and stroked her until she couldn't breathe anymore. Not as he dropped to his knees and spread her legs to taste her. And when he used his tongue and fingers to bring her to the brink of an orgasm, she still couldn't block out the truth that pounded in her brain.

She loved him.

No, Emma, no, that voice screamed, louder than ever. *You can't love him. He's had his soul mate.*

She threaded her fingers into his hair, tugging gently as he kissed her thighs and stomach, working his way back to her tender breasts. "I can't," she said, inching his head away.

He looked up and smiled. "Since when do you stop at one? Come on." He stood, pulling her up with him so her nightshirt fell back into place. "Let's do this right."

Right. The way she always wanted it to be. Not a pretend engagement. Not a fake honeymoon. Not a game.

Should she tell him that? Talk about facing down a fear. "I can't," she whispered again, her voice cracking.

He frowned, turning to her and searching her face. "Something's wrong," he said simply, sending one of those waves of affection that always drowned her. Not a question, because he knew. Not a complaint, because he'd wait. But a statement of fact, because this man *got* her.

"Yes." She swallowed and touched his face. "Something's wrong."

"What is it?"

"This wasn't supposed to happen, Mark."

He just looked at her, and she knew he knew exactly what *this* was.

"This was supposed to be fun and fake and playful and...fake."

He still didn't say a word, but very slowly, he brought his arms around her and drew her into his chest, so close she had to turn her head and rest against his shoulder. They stood silent, breathing, holding each other under the stars.

Finally, he dragged his hands up to her cheeks and inched back so she could see his expression. And it was...raw and real.

He held her face in his two strong, capable hands and stared at her. "I'm not very good with words. Not like you are. But I have something to say to you, and if you'll come with me to the bedroom, I will show you how I feel. I will make love to you...and mean it. Nothing fun, fake, or playful. Just real love."

Forget drowning in a wash of emotions. This was a tidal wave, swamping her, knocking her over, and making her forget that every time she bought into the fairy tale, it wrecked her.

The perfect family...then Dad left.

The fairy-tale wedding...then Kyle left.

And now, Mark. Magical, wonderful, spectacular Mark, who made her believe she was capable of anything. Mark promising...love.

"I'm so scared," she whispered.

He just tipped his head and smiled. "Not my Emma. She's not afraid of anything."

He slipped his arm around her and walked her slowly to the French doors and the big bed and the future that looked so bright, she had to close her eyes.

Mark knew the difference between making love and having sex. He had, in fact, known it from a pretty young age when he and Julia planned their mutual loss of virginity with tremendous thought to the details and an actual night in a real hotel, so there was no backseat of the car or quickie on the patio while her parents slept.

Those came later. But when he and Julia did it for the first time, it had been making love.

And this—

"What are you thinking about?" Emma touched his face, no doubt feeling the sheen of sweat that clung to him as he lay spent and satisfied on top of her.

And thinking about his first time, damn it. "Who can think after that?"

"Oh, you're thinking. I can tell." She added some pressure on his shoulder to push him up so they could see each other in the dim light. "When you start thinking, you breathe differently."

"I do?"

"When you start to really consider something, your breath gets shallow."

Wow. "You really…know me."

"And that bothers you."

He inched higher. "Why would you think that? Didn't I just show you what I couldn't say?"

"You did," she conceded. "Three times, and that last one

was just unfair. Like a bowl of M&M's after cake and ice cream. Is that what you're thinking about?"

"M&M's?"

"Whatever it is you can't say but want to show me."

On a sigh, he lowered himself and slowly pulled out of the nest that had become like home to him. She released him and let him roll to the side, where he immediately lined them up and didn't leave a space between them.

"Do you really want to know what I was thinking about?"

He saw her swallow. "I don't know. Do I?"

"I was thinking about the difference between having sex and making love. And I was thinking about..." He stroked the curve of her waist, the touch light and, he hoped, tender enough to take the sting out of what he was about to say. "My first time."

He felt her shudder a little against him. "With Julia."

He closed his eyes. "Yeah. And, for the record, we were already in love. We did it with all kinds of romance, and it was a great first time." He didn't open his eyes, bracing for something like... *Well, that's nice, how fun to talk about sex with your late wife in bed together. Can we go back to not talking about her in too much detail like we've managed to do for a week?*

"I would expect nothing less from you."

Emma's words hit his heart because they were so not what he expected. "It was her idea," he said. "She wanted it to be meaningful."

She didn't say anything but nodded, as if she understood and couldn't question that desire.

"That's why I was thinking about it now," he said, surprised at how thick his voice was. "Because sometime in the last few days, or hours or minutes, we stopped having sex and started making love. And it's...meaningful."

"I know," she whispered. "I felt it with every kiss and touch." She pressed her hand on his cheeks. "And I can taste your fear over that."

He gave a soft laugh. "You can? Hey, two more times and we've conquered that fear."

"Nothing is going to conquer that," she said. "You are terrified of letting go of her."

He huffed a breath and let his head turn on the pillow. "Emma, this isn't fair. I don't want to lie here in bed with you and talk about my feelings for my dead wife."

She took his chin and forced his face back to her. "I do."

"You do?"

"I want to talk about feelings. Whatever they're for. I don't want to joke anymore or play alliteration word games or talk about my new job or your last sky-diving adventure. I mean, I do," she said quickly. "Tomorrow. Later. On the way to the baseball game or over breakfast. But right now, we have to talk about feelings. That's what makes this meaningful."

He searched her face, lost in the determination he saw in her eyes. She wanted him whole. She wanted him healed. She wanted him, period. And until he became whole and healed, she couldn't have him.

They both knew that.

"You want to talk about feeling even if those feelings are for someone who died sixteen years ago?" he asked.

"Especially if they are."

He stared at her, that thickness in his throat getting worse with each second.

"Have you ever told anyone your feelings for Julia?" she asked. "Like, why she was your soul mate? What you loved about her from the beginning? Why it worked for you two? What you miss most about her?"

Each question stabbed his heart. "Of course not."

She sat up higher. "Why not?"

He pulled her back down. "Because it doesn't matter to anyone but me. I've never been close enough to tell someone that stuff, and if I was, like I am now, it would just hurt."

"Hurt who? Me or you?"

"You, of course. I just showed you the closest thing I know on earth to telling you what you mean to me, and you want me to close out the night with a diatribe about how awesome Julia was? What kind of a brute do you think I am?"

She studied him for a minute, thinking, wetting her lips, readying her thoughts. "You know what I think you are?"

"A jerk for bringing this up?"

"I brought it up," she corrected. "And I think you are one great big, incredibly handsome, ridiculously kind, impossibly wonderful biscuit can."

He blinked at her. "Excuse me?"

"And you, Mr. Biscuit"—she poked his chest—"are ready to pop from the pressure, and until you do, you're just a container of deliciousness that no one can enjoy until they get all that stuff out of you. Even if that's a little scary."

He just stared at her, on the hairy edge of laughing and crying. "I'm a...biscuit can."

She snuggled back into him, satisfied. "And guess what I'm about to do?"

"Bang me against the counter?" He couldn't help smiling.

She settled her head against him and tapped his chest, lightly at first, then a little harder, right over his heart. Then with enough force that her fingers made a thud on his breastbone. Tap. Tap. Tap. *Tap.*

And Mark closed his eyes against a sting of tears, took a deep breath, and started.

"I met her in algebra in tenth grade," he said softly. "She sat next to me on the first day, and she had knee-high socks on with a skirt, and I'd never seen anything so damn cute in my whole life."

Against his chest, he felt her smile. "It *was* the eighties."

"It sure was. She was not that great at math, so I started tutoring her on Monday nights..." He stroked Emma's long, dark hair with one hand, a steady, slow rhythm that helped pull the memories out of the recesses of his brain. With each revelation, he discovered long-forgotten moments in time that were like lost coins and paper receipts found in pockets.

He brought each one out for Emma, turned it over, and let light shine on it. She listened, appreciating each, asking some questions but mostly just letting him...pour out a lifetime of *feelings*.

She held him, and cried with him, and finally, an hour or more later, slept soundly next to him. And as he heard her steady breathing, he realized what an incredible gift she'd just given him.

Of all the rocks he'd climbed and caves he'd dived into and planes he'd jumped out of to be free of the grief...none had liberated him. Until now. Until tonight. Until...Emma.

He pulled her sleeping body closer and felt the urge to say one more thing. For the first time in more than thirty years, he needed to say the words that he'd only ever spoken to Julia.

He pressed his lips against her sweet-smelling hair, closed his eyes, and whispered, "I love you."

Chapter Twenty-Two

"I can honestly say I've never seen anything quite like this." Emma held a hand over her eyes to shield them from the sun, scanning the acres of the Barefoot Bay Bucks Baseball Complex. "A baseball stadium and...a petting zoo?"

Holding her hand, Mark guided her into the shade of a decent-size baseball stadium that held at least five thousand people. They passed vendors selling drinks and food, some baseball souvenirs, and, of course, all things goat. Goat's milk soap. Goat's milk. A sweet little stone gift shop and restaurant that looked like it had been lifted from the hills of Tuscany.

It was definitely one of the most unusual baseball parks he'd ever been to.

"When I was in high school," Mark told her as they paused at a picket-fenced area with five or six goats bleating inside, "we used to come up here to this part of Barefoot Bay on Friday nights looking for a place to hang out and have parties. This whole area was owned by an old Italian guy named Cardinale."

"It's still owned by an Italian named Cardinale." A woman with long, dark hair inside the pen knelt in front of a tiny black goat with a white blotch on its forehead. "That's me. I'm Frankie Cardinale. Well, Frankie Becker now. My grandfather was the old Italian guy who owned the land, and La Dolce Vita—which is the name of this part of the park—was his dream."

"With a minor league baseball stadium?" Emma asked.

The woman laughed, standing and brushing the remnants of goat food from her hand as she came closer. "The baseball part was my husband's dream. Well, his along with a few friends."

Her husband...Becker. Mark thought about the name and realized this woman must be married to Elliott Becker, one of the billionaires who'd dropped into Barefoot Bay almost two years ago and decided to build their dream team.

"Come on in and pet Daisy," she said, opening the gate and gesturing toward the goat she'd been feeding. Instantly, two other goats who weren't even knee high came trotting over. "Or Agnes and Lucretia."

"They're so small!" Emma got down on one knee to ruffle the fur of one of them.

"Pygmies," the woman said. "Are you a local or a tourist?"

"I'm..." Emma looked up. "Just visiting now, but..." She stood slowly. "This island is a great place. I suppose you've lived here all your life, then."

"No, just for a few years when I was growing up, then I came back to take care of my grandfather's farm, but..." She turned and smiled at a long, lanky man in a cowboy hat who was pouring water into a drinking trough. "I fell in love."

"*That's* Elliott Becker?" Mark asked with a quick laugh.

Her smile widened when the man looked up and silently tipped his hat, not the least bit fazed by the humble job he carried out.

"He'll clean up and get into the owner's box before the game starts," she assured them.

"But I have to take care of the bucks," Elliott said, dumping his water and sauntering over to them. "Have you seen the buck pen?" he asked. "When you do, be sure to check out Becker, my namesake. He's a beast, and I birthed him."

Mark chuckled at the thought of a billionaire birthing a kid goat, but he could see nothing but pride in the man's eyes, and love when he looked at his wife.

"Okay, *we* birthed him," Becker corrected. "But I was there."

Frankie rolled her eyes, but they both laughed in a natural, clearly loving exchange. The kind of thing that usually made Mark sad or a little jealous. But nothing felt sad today. He couldn't conjure up a shred of sadness and jealousy.

He tucked Emma closer to him, shooting her the hundredth smile of appreciation today.

Becker's goatherd wife was pretty, but Emma? He glanced down at her and pulled her closer, getting a warm smile in response, her eyes glinting like they had in bed a few hours ago.

"So have a blast while you're here," Frankie said. "Enjoy the game and be sure to go to the store and get our romance line of goat's milk soaps. Perfect favors..." She gestured toward Emma's left hand. "If you're planning a wedding."

"I named every soap we have," Elliott added. "Even the corny ones."

Frankie tapped her husband on the arm, nudging him back to the trough. "Quit bragging and get going. The game starts soon." She looked over her shoulder at Emma. "Best of luck to you two."

Alone, they shared a look. "We can't keep lying to strangers," she whispered. "Half the time I forget we're supposed to be engaged."

Really? Mark thought. Because half the time he couldn't think about anything else.

He stared at her, the sun beating down, the goats circling, the crowd cheering as the pregame festivities got louder inside the stadium. If this wasn't the stupidest place to make a declaration, he didn't know.

But everything was different today. He was different. They were. Who cared if they were standing in a petting farm?

"It doesn't have to be a lie," he said, his voice surprisingly raspy.

She just looked up at him, her mouth opened into a stunned little o shape.

"Emma, I really—"

"Emma! Mark! There you are!"

They turned to see Lacey Walker, with her husband, Clay, and a red-headed toddler between them hanging on to their hands.

"Hi, Lacey." Emma sounded a little less than enthusiastic to see her possibly future boss. "We were just…"

Getting *real*, Mark thought. He tamped down his own disappointment. He'd find the right moment, and they wouldn't be surrounded by goats or people.

"Hey, bud," Mark called to the little boy. "You want to come and pet the goats?"

"Go ahead, Elijah," Lacey said, opening the gate. His face brightened as he came barreling into the pen. "You better stay with him, Clay," she said to her husband, who was already following his son to the pygmies.

"Yep," he said. "I got this."

She reached out a friendly hand to Emma. "I'm so glad I saw you. I didn't know if we'd get a moment to talk today. Want to walk to the soap store with me, you two?"

Emma threw him a quick look, and he read it instantly. She was torn, but duty—or the chance of it—called.

"Sure," he said. "The goats are all yours, Clay."

The other man laughed but was on the heels of his lightning-fast son, while the three of them left the petting area and made small talk on the way to the store.

It didn't matter that his moment had been squashed. He'd tell her tonight. In the villa, in bed, alone, together.

But he didn't want to horn in on Emma's opportunity to forge that personal relationship with Lacey right now, either.

"Actually, I'm going to wait out here," he said as they reached a split-rail fence that surrounded grass outside the store. "You ladies go ahead and buy some of that romance goat's milk soap."

Emma shot him a grateful smile as they disappeared into the storefront. Mark leaned against the rail and looked around at the crowd of tourists and locals. Mostly tourists, he'd guess. Which was remarkable. This island had really changed. It was home, but it wasn't. He could actually see himself—

"Hey, I know you."

Mark turned at the sound of a man's voice, instantly recognizing those narrow shoulders and horn-rimmed glasses. Son of a bitch, it was Kyle Chambers.

"Lacey's judgmental friend." Kyle took a slow step closer, a woman next to him looking at Mark as if he was one of the animals in the petting zoo.

"Hi," she said with a friendly smile. "I'm Rachel. How do you guys know each other?" She was tiny, not five-two, with blond curls and big blue eyes. She looked like a Kewpie doll, all bright and cheery.

"We don't," Mark said, his mind spinning through all the options for how to get out of there, with Emma, and away from these two.

"What is your problem, man?" Kyle asked, not moving but looking hard at Mark. "Are you some kind of spy for Lacey Walker?" A whiff of beer came at Mark, and reddish eyes narrowed.

Great, the lying scum was drunk.

"Nope." Mark took a step closer to the door, eyeing the opening to make sure Emma didn't walk into the middle of this.

"Every time I turn around, you're there," Kyle said, coming too close. "What is up with that?"

"Gosh, Kyle, you don't have to be a jerk," Rachel said. "He's just standing here minding his own business."

Mark moved away, walking purposely inside the store without making another second of eye contact. Surely the woman would lead Kyle away, and Mark would keep Emma in the shop as long as he could.

The store smelled like a woman's lingerie drawer, a mix of sweet and spicy fragrances. He glanced into the crowd, past groups of people around bins and stacks of soaps, spotting Lacey and Emma at a display near the door.

"Hey," he said, putting his hand on Emma's back. "I decided to look around a bit after all."

She turned, surprised, and maybe just a tad annoyed at the interruption, which he couldn't blame her for. "Why?"

"For a gift," he said quickly, hating that it sounded like the lie it was. "I thought maybe we can find something for Linda and Wayne."

"Oh, okay."

"They have great gift sets in the back, Mark," Lacey said. "I'll show you."

"Come with me," he said, adding pressure to Emma's shoulder. He could hide her in the back if Kyle walked in.

Emma gave him a strange look, but let him guide her along with Lacey.

He cursed himself the whole way. Why the hell hadn't he told her about Kyle? Now it could all blow up in his face. And Emma's. Shit, her job and her heart could implode in one random meeting, and it would be all his fault.

"This way, Mark," Lacey said, gesturing him around a six-foot-high display to a wall in the back. Perfect. "They have samplers in different fragrances."

He glanced over his shoulder to check the door, aware of Emma looking at him.

"Is something wrong?" she asked.

"I just…don't want to miss the beginning of the game."

She drew her brows together. "But you want to buy a gift."

Then, over her shoulder, he saw Kyle and Rachel enter the store.

Son of a bitch. How could this be happening?

"These are really cute," Lacey said, pointing at some soap. "Who is the gift for again?"

"Kyle," he whispered, trying not to stare at the man.

"Excuse me?" Emma asked.

"I mean, um, Wayne. My…my former father-in-law. And his fiancée."

"Julia's dad is getting married?" Lacey asked.

As Kyle and Rachel came deeper into the store, Mark put a protective arm around Emma and eased her around, using the display of soaps to get her out of Kyle's line of vision.

And that move earned a quick look of *what the hell?*

from Emma, but he would have to explain later. He just didn't want them all to slam into each other. Kyle and Emma and Rachel and Lacey and *shit*.

"There's a ton to pick from," Lacey said, pointing to another stack of soap. "But I have to run and grab my guys before the game starts. I'll see you two in there. We have a huge section in the bleachers, Emma, so maybe we can talk some more. Otherwise…" She gave Emma's arm a quick squeeze. "See you tomorrow."

Lacey stepped out from behind the display just as Emma peered up at him. "I was kind of making progress with her."

"I know, I'm sorry, but I had to—"

"Lacey Walker! Imagine seeing you here!"

The man's voice from behind the display was like a hammer to Mark's head. But his reaction was nothing compared to Emma's. First, she blinked, startled.

"I can't believe I'm running into you here, Lacey!"

"Oh, hello, Kyle."

Then Emma paled, as her first impossible thought was proven right.

"I saw him outside," Mark mouthed to her.

"Let me introduce you to my girlfriend, Rachel Howell."

Then her jaw dropped and hung wide open. "His—"

Mark put a finger on her mouth to silence her.

"Lacey, about our conversation the other day," Kyle said. "Do you have a second?"

"I don't, actually."

"But I just need to tell you one thing."

That instant, Rachel popped around the display and saw Mark. "Oh, it's you," she said, her pixie face brightening. "I'm sorry my boyfriend was rude to you before. I—"

"Hey, Rach, come here, honey," Kyle stepped around the display. "I want you to tell Lacey what…" His voice trailed off as he glanced at Mark, then he turned as pale as Emma when his gaze moved to her. "What...are you doing here?"

And then, just to ice the cake, Lacey joined the party. "Oh, do you all know each other?" she asked brightly.

Mark could have sworn Emma swayed a little.

Chapter Twenty-Three

Surreal.

It was the only word that popped into Emma's head as she tried to process the dreamlike sequence of events, but nothing would register as reality.

It couldn't be real.

Blood pumped in her head so loud she couldn't hear what anyone was saying, even though everyone seemed to talk at the same time.

She had to manage her way out of this, but she didn't quite know what she was in or how bad it could get.

"Wait a second," Lacey said, pointing from Kyle to Emma. "You know each other?"

A little bad.

"She worked at my agency," Kyle said. Not, *we were engaged to be married.* Which stung, but—

"You did?" Lacey's eyes widened. "Why didn't you tell me that when I interviewed you?"

"You interviewed her?" Kyle choked. "Nice, Emma. Anyone tell you it's slimy to poach business?"

Okay, more than a little bad.

"What?" Mark shot back, his shoulders tensing as he inched a little closer into Kyle's face. "Anyone ever tell you it's slimy to have a girlfriend two weeks after you leave your fiancée at the altar?"

Lacey gasped. "The altar?" she asked, voice rising. "I thought you were engaged to Mark."

"So you're the ex I had to steal him from," Rachel said, eyeing Emma with a mix of suspicion and curiosity, then attempted a sympathetic smile. "Sorry."

Emma felt pressure squeeze her chest. Rachel *stole* Kyle?

"Wait a second." Kyle stepped closer, his gaze slicing Mark. "So you knew who I was when I told you I left Emma for Rachel and didn't say a word."

And that's when bad went way down to worse, the very instant the truth punched through Emma's fog, more sickening than the sweet smell of patchouli that hung in the air.

Mark *knew* this?

"Whoa, whoa, *whoa*." Lacey stopped the avalanche like a referee. "I'm either in a bad sitcom, or the joke's on me. You all know each other? And you..." She pointed from Kyle to Emma. "Were going to get married?"

"And honeymoon at Casa Blanca," Emma said.

"And you didn't tell me this?" Lacey's voice had an understandably sharp edge, and Emma knew that trying to defend herself would just make her sound worse.

"She planned to tell you tomorrow, Lacey," Mark said, putting a hand on Emma's arm. "She didn't have the opportunity before, but—"

Lacey cut off the defense with a swipe of her hand. "It sounds like you all have sort of a personal mess here that doesn't really involve me, but..." She leveled her gaze at Emma. "You lied to me."

You wouldn't let me finish a sentence. Your daughter called. You were all enthusiastic about my ideas. I was helping Mark and...

I was scared to tell you.

There was the truth, all ugly and real. The rest were just excuses for a lie of omission, and it all left a bitter taste of self-loathing in Emma's mouth.

"No wonder your ideas were so spot-on," Lacey said with a dry laugh.

"You gave her *ideas*?" Kyle interjected.

"I planned to tell you everything tomorrow," Emma finally said. "Everything."

Lacey's eyes shuttered as she slowly shook her head. "Let's, uh, reschedule that."

Emma's heart dropped.

"Lacey," Mark said. "If you let us explain, it will all make sense."

She looked up at him, no warmth in her expression. "You lied, too, Mark."

Just then, a loud cheer came through the open doors and windows of the shop, and a noisy stadium organ started screaming out loud notes.

"And the game's starting," Lacey said. "A different game," she added, giving Emma a look of disappointment that she probably used frequently on that problematic college daughter of hers.

Three beats of silence passed before Kyle leaned closer. "I can't believe you tried to steal my—"

Mark's hand rose involuntarily. "Shut up and get out of here before I slam my fist through your teeth."

Kyle shook him off, fire in his eyes. "Who the hell *are* you?"

"Emma's fiancé," he said.

Something in Emma's head popped, a little white explosion of fury and frustration and fear. "No," she said. "That was just a...game. A charade." She closed her fingers over the ring on her left hand, trying like hell to yank it off, but it stuck on her knuckle.

"Emma, come on." Mark put his hand on her back, but she jumped away from his touch, still fighting with the ring.

"No." All her anger and misery and resentment and sadness bubbled up and made her want to rip the skin off if she had to.

Rachel grabbed something from a bin next to her. "Do you need some soap?"

Emma choked at the offer, glaring at the little blonde. Deep inside, hadn't she suspected all along? Hadn't she known there was someone else? Hadn't she refused to face it? Way down, in her own hidden place, hadn't she known Kyle was just like her father?

Finally, the ring popped over her knuckle, and she took it off and held it in the middle of the three of them. "I don't want this. Any of you can have it."

She dropped it on the ground, pivoted, and marched out of the store, fighting tears.

"Emma!"

Outside, she held up her hand to silence him. "Don't even think about talking to me. I mean it. Just let me go, Mark. Let me go."

Mark saw Emma run off to a tiny cab stand outside the stadium. He didn't want to, but his gut told him to respect her request and let her go alone.

He left Kyle and Rachel—and the ring—behind in the store. He stood in the sunshine, watching her take off, regret strangling him. Why didn't he tell her? Why did he avoid the very things he knew he shouldn't?

The question pounded in his head as he walked across the grass toward the parking lot as *The Star-Spangled Banner* rose up from the stadium behind him, building to a land of the free and home of the brave crescendo.

He didn't feel very free or brave, he thought glumly. He had last night and today, but all that freedom had disappeared, and he felt very much alone.

And not in the way he was used to or liked…more like lonely.

Which would be the downside of falling in love, and losing.

Why *didn't* he tell her the truth? To protect her from pain…or to protect himself from possibilities?

Shit, now even his thoughts sounded like her. How had she climbed into his brain and heart that way?

He reached the Porsche and opened the door, half hoping to find her sitting in the passenger seat, waiting for him. But she wasn't there.

He could beat her to the villa in this car, easily, he thought. He even knew a back road, but he had to give her some time alone, some time to process every betrayal and loss.

Kyle lied to her.

Lacey pulled the job.

And Mark had let her down when he had promised her from day one that he would be nothing but honest.

He couldn't silence his guilt, not even with the growl of a great engine. He burned a little rubber getting out of the parking lot, earning a look from an attendant and security guard having a conversation.

Windows open, he let the spring air whip through the car,

waiting for the punch of memories. And they hit him, all right.

Not Julia...but Emma. Driving in this car. Laughing. Touching. Falling for each other. A thousand minutes packed into one week.

One lousy week.

Except it had been anything but lousy. It had been amazing. Fun. Hot. Perfect. And unforgettable.

He reached the intersection of the beach road. Taking a right would lead to the resort, where Emma had probably gone. Left would take him toward town. The future or the past, Mark Solomon?

For a long moment, he sat at the empty intersection, staring at the blue on blue horizon of Barefoot Bay straight ahead. The fact was, he couldn't turn right until he turned left.

There was one more thing to do. One more fear to face before it was completely conquered.

He swung left and cruised down the road toward town, stopping at the light and glancing over to the Super Min, revving the engine on Center Street, slipping down a road behind Miss Icey's, and arriving at the parking lot of Hope Presbyterian.

Parking the car, he turned off the ignition and stared at the Spanish-style building where he'd enjoyed one of the happiest days of his life, and endured one of the worst.

It's just a church, he told himself. *Go in and make peace. That's what it's there for.*

The front door was open, and he stepped into an oversize foyer built for after-church mingling and pastor greeting. The changes were subtle, but he saw them, just like he noticed evidence of time marching on all over Mimosa Key.

The linoleum floor had been replaced by creamy tile, and

the resource desk had been updated, and a small ATM for electronic tithing was tucked next to a selection of CDs and books.

Here's where he'd stood sixteen years ago, shaking hundreds of hands, hugging dozens of shuddering shoulders, and saying "thank you" more times than he'd thought possible.

He closed his eyes for a moment, twisted by an unexpected slap of grief, the deep kind that he had long ago learned to manage and subdue. He hadn't felt grief last night reliving his romance with Julia. He hadn't been sad, not really. He'd actually felt joy to have known that kind of love.

But he felt grief now. The heavy, aching, breath-stealing grief that used to be his constant companion.

Determined to fight it, he walked to the glass doors that led to the sanctuary, peering down the very aisle that Julia had walked down on Wayne Coulter's arm in a hastily purchased white gown and a pearl necklace that had been her grandmother's.

He grabbed the door handle, half hoping it would be locked and he wouldn't have to do this. But the door swung open, and he stepped into the hushed chapel.

What was he doing here?

No one was going to help Mark Solomon except Emma DeWitt, so why didn't he go to the resort to hound her, apologize, grovel, beg her to forgive, forget, and look forward?

Instead, here he was, mired in the past. Why?

Because he'd never really said good-bye. Oh, he'd gone through the motions and carried on, but what he'd really done was…avoid reality, escape the pain, seek a thrill, and wait for his late wife's next message.

And then he imagined he'd gotten one. Like the class ring that sent him here.

He slipped into a pew a few rows from the front, sitting down and staring ahead. He could still see the flowers his bride carried...and the rows of bouquets that had been sent for her funeral. He could see an eighteen-year-old girl smiling up at him, that secret gleam in her eye because they were soul mates...and the two-foot-high poster of Julia Solomon on an easel during the process of sending that soul to another place.

He could hear her voice saying her vows.

But he couldn't hear her voice saying anything else anymore.

"Can I help you, sir?"

Mark turned to see a young man with an athletic build and a tentative smile in place.

"I'm just..." *Letting go.* He shrugged, unable to come up with any plausible reason for sitting in an empty church.

"I'm Matthew Cooke, the assistant pastor. Would you like to talk or pray?"

He searched the man's earnest blue eyes, thinking he was so incredibly young to be a pastor and looked more like a ballplayer than a preacher.

"Not really," Mark said. "I haven't been here in a long time, and I thought I'd see the church."

"Are you with the reunion people?"

Mark gave a soft laugh. Yep, Mimosa Key was still a very small island, despite any changes. "Yeah. And my parents went here years ago. I was, uh, married in this church."

"Really?" He brightened at that. "How many years have you been married?"

Thirty years, minus sixteen. The math wouldn't make sense and would just set off a series of questions he didn't want to answer. "A long time," he said vaguely, standing up. "But I'm leaving now, Pastor. Thank you."

"You're welcome to stay as long as you like."

Mark shook his head, done with the heavy memories. He had to get back to Emma. "It's good, thanks."

He walked by the man and out to the lobby, crossing the space with brisk steps. He should have made a right at that intersection.

"Excuse me, sir?"

Mark was just about to the exit when the pastor came jogging out of the sanctuary, holding a paper in his hand. "Are you…" He read the paper, squinting. "Mark?"

"Yes."

"I think you dropped this."

Mark took the thin time-weathered envelope, seeing only the upside-down heart in place of the *a* in his name. Julia's letter. He'd forgotten it was in the back pocket of these shorts. "Oh, thanks."

He took the letter out into the sunshine and stood, stone still, for a moment. Then he ripped open the top and pulled out a thin piece of paper, a memory floating back at the sight of pink and white flowered stationery. She must have written him fifty letters in high school on this paper. He'd find them in his locker, stuck in a math book, in the bottom of his gym bag.

They'd never said anything of consequence, but reminded him of how much she loved him. And he'd never written one back, he thought with a pang.

Of all the "messages" he'd imagined she'd delivered over the past sixteen years, none had ever been so obviously and truly from the head and heart of Julia Coulter Solomon.

So he read it.

Dearest Markie…

God, he'd hated when she called him that.

I'm stuck in civics behind the dandruff-filled hair of Joey

Michaels—it's snowing on my desk! I wish you weren't in bio lab now, because I'd go to any class and get you out just to give you a kiss in the hall. I'd tell them old Wiggy sent me.

He smiled at the nickname he'd totally forgotten for the principal. What would she say to learn Wigglesworth still roamed the halls of MHS all these years later?

Anyhoo, I just wanted to say I am super excited about Friday and can't wait to go to the SOB before the Spring Fling. A dinner date like grownups!! Even if Allison and Josh are coming and all they do is fight. Oh, I'm going to wear jeans (of course) and that new yellow top you like so much. (Easy buttons!)

He chuckled softly, remembering the top he'd managed to find his way inside frequently. He could just about hear her sweet voice in every word, her light tease, her warmth. There was no punch of pain, no choking grief. Nothing but fond memories and good thoughts.

He skimmed the rest of the letter, full of more high school nonsense, then his gaze dropped on the signature.

I love you, J.

Under it was a turn-the-page arrow. Flipping the paper, he found a postscript.

P.S. I can't stop thinking about our talk. Yes, I want babies. A couple of them, I hope. And, if you insist, I will name our boy Daniel, since you love Dan Marino so much. But I get to pick the girl's name, okay? And I already have. Emma. Emma Solomon. Isn't that the most beautiful name you've ever heard?

His breath caught and his heart kicked as he stared at the words his late wife had written thirty-one years ago.

Emma Solomon. Isn't that the most beautiful name you've ever heard?

"Yes," he whispered, vaguely aware his feet had already

started moving, even if his brain was stuck in the past. Emma Solomon was the most beautiful name he'd ever heard, and this was a message he was not going to ignore.

He yanked the Porsche door open and threw himself behind the wheel, tossing the letter on the seat next to him.

Was he crazy? He'd known the woman less than a week and, right now, she was rightfully pissed at him. He'd wrecked her job, her heart, her trust, and her week in paradise…but he'd make it up to her.

Because when they went to that reunion tomorrow night—and they would go and they would dance and they would win—she would be his fiancée, and there would be nothing fake about it.

Emma Solomon. *A beautiful name indeed, Julia.*

Would she take him seriously? Would she laugh in his face?

The questions plagued him all the way back to the resort, but he smashed every doubt with confidence. They had something special. They were…soul mates.

Good God, could that happen twice in one lifetime?

He parked the car and hustled across the lot, the path to Blue Casbah suddenly seeming a hundred miles long instead of a pleasant walk along the beach. As he reached the first villa, an electric golf cart came humming up behind him, and he turned, greeted by the smiling face of the world's friendliest housekeeper.

"Poppy, can I have a ride?" he asked impulsively.

"You sure may, Mr. Solomon. Blue Casbah? You skipping the baseball game, too?"

"Yes." He hopped in. "Do you know where everyone is all the time?"

"I try to," she assured him. "I know a little bit about everyone who's here."

He peered ahead as if looking for the villa could get him there faster.

"For instance, I know you're not engaged to that woman you've been staying with."

He swiveled to look at her. "How the hell do you know that?"

"Hey!" She held out her hand. "There's a fine for cursing in my cart."

He stared at her in disbelief. "I just came from church," he said. "Does that pay my fine?"

"This time." She turned her hand and patted him on the thigh, easing into the curve right before the villa. "And I only know about the engagement because she told me a few minutes ago."

"She told you?"

"No worries. Getting people to tell me stuff is my gift. Here you go. Blue Casbah."

"Thanks." He swung his feet out and hit the bricks, the first tendril of something not right twisting around his chest. "Did you bring her back to the villa when the cab dropped her off?" he asked.

"The other way," she said, pointing over her shoulder. "To the lobby. With her bags."

And that tendril tightened to stop the next beat of his heart. "Her bags?"

She lifted two pitying eyebrows. "Sorry to be the one with the bad news, but she just took a cab to the airport."

He opened his mouth, but nothing, not a single word, came out. He just nodded and backed away, then turned to go into the villa.

Except, he already knew what he'd find.

Still, hope had a way of rising over all that certainty, driving him to stick the card key in the door and step into the entryway to see her, hear her, smell her, touch her...kiss her...and tell her...

Emma Solomon. Isn't that the most beautiful name you've ever heard?

But there was nothing but a heavy, still silence that told him he'd never get to ask her that question.

Chapter Twenty-Four

This was travel hell. Emma would have to wait an hour, then make two connections in Charlotte and Pittsburgh, and shell out a small fortune to Uber for the final leg after landing in Newark. But if weather and winds were in her favor, Emma would be home in her Brooklyn apartment before the clock struck midnight.

Jilted, jobless, and jaded…even more than when she'd landed here six days ago at the junior-size regional airport that had the audacity to call itself Southwest Florida International.

In a restaurant that smelled like cheese and beer, she plopped down at an empty two-top table that looked out at the six people bustling by on the concourse.

"Bitter," she murmured as she tucked her suitcase under the table. "I am so bitter."

"Bourbon and bitter did you say?" A waitress stood next to her table with an order pad in one hand and a pen in the other.

Emma gave a soft laugh. "That might just be strong enough, but no. I'll have a glass of white wine. Do you have…" She thought of the crisp, dry wine from a vineyard Mark liked and instantly her heart sank. No, she can't wallow over him, but she could at least re-create the wine experience. "Sauvignon blanc?"

Lips that were just pink enough to have been covered in lipstick many hours ago curved up. "I could tell you it's souvy...whatever blank. But it'll get poured from the same bottle of lighter fluid we give anyone who wants white wine."

"Thank you," Emma said, thudding her elbows on the table, eyeing the woman's name tag. "You know what the problem is with this world today, Joelle?"

"Bad wine?"

"Not enough people are just flat-out honest. It's all I want. Am I asking too much? Just tell the truth. So it might not be what someone wants to hear. So it might not sell your product or increase your bottom line. So what, I say. Be honest. Even if there's a price to pay. Even if you break a woman's heart. Tell the truth, please."

The woman just looked at her, but Emma's blood was bubbling now, and the tears she'd fought since she'd left Casa Blanca swam in her eyes.

"I can handle the truth," she continued. "I'm not a fragile little thing with a tender heart that needs to be lied to. And not telling someone something is just as bad as lying. People benefit from the truth. They grow. They have their eyes opened. They get what they really wanted in the first place."

The waitress tapped her pad. "Which would be..."

"A beer," Emma said on a sigh. "Just something cold on tap. No lighter fluid."

"Good call." The woman disappeared to the bar, leaving Emma to drop her head onto her palm and sigh.

She'd left Barefoot Bay as impulsively as she'd arrived. This time, she'd had the airline schedule on her phone while she was still in the cab. Packed in record time, grabbed a housekeeper's golf cart to the lobby, and was in a cab before Mark Solomon could figure out what hit him.

Because if he'd come back to the villa, *she* would have hit him.

No. She would have cried more, and he would have explained his compelling reason for not telling her that Kyle had cheated on her—Kyle, that black-hearted, two-timing bastard—and then Mark would have lured her into bed with his clever hands and sexy mouth and *lies*.

Well, he'd never lied about their relationship, but then, they didn't have a *relationship*. But she'd started to hope...

And then she went falling face first for the biggest lie in the history of mankind: the happily ever after lie. Again! How stupid was she?

Stunningly stupid. A first-class fool who should know better than to think that kind of happiness could happen to her.

"What was his name?"

Emma looked at the cocktail napkin that had just been placed in front of her, then up at the waitress, mid-forties, most likely, a weathered but warm face with deep-brown eyes and wiry blond hair. "Mark," she said simply.

"Nice name. Good and strong." She took a foamy beer from her tray and put it on the table. "Don't tell me. Another woman?"

"Not this one," she said, wrapping her hand around the icy glass. "That was the guy before him."

"But he lied, and you cried."

Emma snapped her fingers and pointed to her. "That's good. Have you ever considered a job writing advertising copy?"

"What? And leave all this?" She gestured toward the nearly-empty concourse and the restaurant that wasn't exactly overflowing with customers. "I didn't mean to be poetic, but you look wrecked. Beer's on me."

"Really? It's that obvious?"

Joelle glanced at the bar and the back of a bored bartender who was watching CNN on the TV. Then, she pulled out the other chair at Emma's table and dropped into it. "How do you think I ended up here, working in an airport bar?"

"An international airport bar," Emma joked.

"Exactly, because as you can see…" Joelle gestured to the empty restaurant. "We are a beehive of exotic international travelers."

Emma snorted. "See what I mean? Lies. One flight probably got rerouted from South America on its way to Miami and they called an emergency marketing meeting to change the name."

The other woman laughed. "Hey, we serve Canada and Germany, but I guess this place is small compared to Kennedy or O'Hare. But, seriously, honey girl, don't let one bad experience sour you on all men. And airports."

"It was two bad experiences. Consecutive. Three weeks ago, I was jilted at the altar. Have the cancellation fees and unresellable Vera Wang gown to prove it."

She cringed. "Ouch."

"Then I come down here for a little R&R, and my villa's taken by some…some…" Perfect, funny, sexy, wonderful man. "Slick-tongued silver fox who…" She shook her head. "Never mind."

"Like hell never mind." Joelle leaned closer. "This is getting good. What happened?"

Emma angled her head and gave the waitress a "what do you think happened" look.

"You didn't."

"I did." Emma punctuated the admission with a slurp of foamy beer.

"Please, oh God, please, please, please don't tell me he's married. The number of married asswipes that come through this—"

"No," Emma assured her. "Not married. Worse. So much freaking worse."

"Broke? Abusive? Boring with a small dick? The possibilities are endless."

"A widower who believes there is only one person for everyone, and he already met, married, and buried her."

Joelle dropped back and let her tray hit her lap. "Ohhh. That's harsh. But was the sex good?"

"Ridiculous." Another gulp, and she finally hit beer. "Slow, sweet, sensual…satisfying."

Joelle laughed. "Sounds downright poetic."

"It was."

"Then don't complain." She pushed up and pressed her round tray to her chest. "You had good sex and a nice vacation. A girl can't ask for much more than that."

"Can't she?"

The woman started to throw back another quip, but something stopped her, and it came out like a sigh as she dropped back into the seat and put her hand on Emma's arm. "Is he worth fighting for?"

Emma just stared at her for a moment. "I've honestly never met a man more worth fighting for, but—"

She hushed Emma with a flat hand in the air. "No buts. If you're worth it and he's worth it, what are you doing running away?"

"I'm…" She swallowed. "I'm afraid of losing the fight."

One well-drawn brow lifted. "Oh, honey. Fear is the enemy."

"So I've heard." She picked up the beer and stared into the bubbly top. "Gotta conquer those three times. So maybe the next time I meet a man, he'll be my soul mate."

"You know what I always ask myself when I'm afraid of something?"

"What's the worst that could happen?" Emma guessed, and got a massive eye roll in reply.

"That's a loser, quitter, slacker mentality. I ask myself, 'What's the *best* that could happen?' And that makes me want to kick fear in the nuts. So, what's the best that could happen with this slow-hand widower named Mark?"

She thought about it, sinking into the idea like it was a puffy white cloud of comfort. The best that could happen? Forever. Soul mates. Partners. Laughter. Fun. Adventure. Tears. Sex. Together. Emma and Mark. "Everything I ever wanted."

The waitress tipped her head to the side and gave a smug smile as she headed back to the bar, calling over her shoulder, "Let me know if you want another one."

Another drink...or another chance?

The question echoed in her head for an hour as Emma sipped her beer, checked her phone—her silent phone—and replayed every minute of the past week. What had she learned from Mark Solomon, if not to fight her fears?

Hadn't she also learned that men couldn't be trusted? That they're just selling the same thing everyone else is—sex?

"You need anything else?" a man asked, pulling her from her sad reverie. It was the bartender, holding a check. So much for the beer being on Joelle. Maybe she'd lied, too.

"No, I'm good." She grabbed her wallet and took out some money, then another ten-dollar bill. "Can you do me a favor and give this to Joelle?"

He frowned. "Who?"

"My waitress, Joelle."

Still frowning, he turned and looked over his shoulder, then back at her. "We don't have a waitress named Joelle. You mean Julia?"

Julia. She felt a little blood drain at the name. "Is that her...real name? The woman who waited on me?"

"I don't know who waited on you. My shift just started five minutes ago, and Julia called in sick today."

There had to be an explanation. "Then who..."

Or not.

She gave him all the money anyway. "Thanks. Keep the change. I have a plane to catch."

Chapter Twenty-Five

L aw Monroe put both elbows on the table and scowled at Mark. "So, let me get this straight. You just *met* her this week?"

Next to him, Ken leaned in closer. "And you told everyone you were engaged?"

"Including your former father-in-law?" Law added, lifting a glass of club soda to cover the fact that he was about to crack up in laughter.

"Don't forget the dance." Ken elbowed Law. "Now he's going to have to put on his Don Johnson jacket and dance alone."

The two men shared a look and laughter won out over any sympathy from his newfound friends.

Mark set his rocks glass hard on the table, looking away at the huge crowd mingling on the beach for the cocktail party and dinner that kicked off the evening's festivities. "I'm not going to dance. I'll forfeit."

"What?" Now Law looked appalled, but Ken shook his head, and his attention drifted across the reunion crowd, too.

"Seriously, what are you going to do?" Ken asked.

"About the dance?"

"About Emma," he replied.

"Yeah," Law added. "Why didn't you go after her for the big movie moment in the airport? Could have broken through security, gotten on one knee in front of the crowd, and made the rest of us schmucky bastards look bad."

He'd considered it.

"Hey, A-Team of Planning Committee Men." Libby Chesterfield came up from behind Mark, slipping into the empty chair next to Law. "Not a single one of you showed up at the baseball game yesterday. The bleachers were a sorry place without you."

"Hey, Chesty." Law lit up a little at the arrival of a pretty woman, and Mark silently thanked her for the distraction.

"It's Libby to you, Monroe. What's your sad excuse?"

"I was working on the menu for tonight and made two hundred pork tenderloin crostini. That's my excuse."

"You made the tenderloin crostini?" She smacked her lips. "Little orgasms for the mouth, I say."

"I don't know what that means, a 'little' orgasm," Law joked. "I only give big ones."

She rolled her eyes and leaned closer to Mark. "What's your excuse for missing the day at the ballpark? You and Emma have a meeting with the destination wedding planners, by any chance?"

He glanced down at his drink, hating that he'd made the decision to tell everyone the truth. Everyone. Even those he'd rather not deal with.

"Mark was busy, too," Ken said quickly, filling the gap of silence.

Mark gave him a quick look of thanks for the assist, but then shook his head. He was done lying. That decision had cost him enough.

"I wasn't busy, actually." He met Libby's gaze. "Emma left. She was never my fiancée. It was just a ruse to ward off people asking me about my late wife." And to ward off women hitting on him, but he didn't need to add that.

Her jaw dropped so hard it was a wonder it didn't hit her double D's. "A ruse?"

Law leaned closer. "Do you know what that means?"

She gave him a playful tap on the arm. "Shut up. I still haven't forgiven you for standing me up junior year."

"I didn't stand you up, Chesty."

"Then what happened?"

"My best guess? Booze. Weed. My usual high school distractions of choice. I'm sorry if you weren't on the list of people I asked to forgive me, but I thought I covered that step in AA."

"I could forgive you. It was twenty-eight years, two ex-husbands, and one lifetime ago." She leaned closer, her deep cleavage inches from his face. "But I think forgiveness is highly overrated."

She turned back to Mark. "Did you really think that was necessary? Why not just tell us you'd rather not talk about her?"

Hell if he could even remember now. Emma had made him realize just how stupid that whole avoidance business was. "I don't know," Mark said. "It was kind of a spur-of-the-moment decision, and she was all in, and next thing we knew..." *We were falling in love.* "She left."

"What?" Libby's voice rose in outrage.

"Mark screwed her," Law added.

"Not literally." Yes, literally. "We had a..." Misunderstanding? "I wasn't completely..." *Honest with her.*

She leaned in. "Did you behave in a dicklike manner?" she asked sweetly.

Ken snorted, and Law threw his head back and barked a

laugh. But Mark looked right at Libby and nodded. "Guilty as charged."

"Oof." She threw up her hands. "Burst my bubble, why don't you? Here I thought you were perfect."

"Far from it," he assured her.

"So far," Law added, sharing knuckles with Ken.

"Perfect is in another ZIP code," Ken agreed.

"But what about the dance?" Libby asked. "You and Emma are partners!"

"He's forfeiting," Ken said.

"Speaking of dicklike behavior," Law added.

"That's preposterous!" She pushed her chair back as if the news propelled her into action. "You know the steps, right?"

"No, no, Libby," Mark said. "I'm not going to dance..." With anyone except Emma. Ever, he thought glumly.

"Of course you are."

"I can't teach it to you now. The dance competition starts as soon as we wrap up dinner and go into the banquet room."

"The eighties can't lose, Mark!" She was dead serious. "We are the best decade, right?" She looked at Law.

"If you say so."

"Hey, the nineties weren't bad," Ken added. "And I don't think he wants to dance with anyone."

Mark threw him a grateful glance, but Libby tapped the table. "He won't dance with anyone. He'll dance with *everyone*. There's strength in numbers, I say."

All three men looked at her like she'd lost her mind. "Stay here, enjoy your dinner, relax. I've got this." She stood up and peered down at Law. "For the record, Law Monroe, I was going to do you so hard that night. You should have picked me over whatever demon won the evening."

271

All humor left his face. "I know that now, Lib."

When she left, the three men were quiet for a moment, and Law picked up his club soda in a mock toast. "To all the women I lost because of booze."

"Hey," Mark said. "You're a new man now."

"Wait, if you don't drink," Ken interjected, "why are you trying to buy a bar?"

"You heard the lady. Demons. I try to keep those devils close and under control."

"Speaking of women lost..." Both men looked at Ken, whose gaze moved into the crowd. Then he picked up his beer and shifted his attention away, disgusted.

"Beth?" Mark spotted the attractive blonde in a red halter and a short white skirt that showed off legs from here to tomorrow. After a beat, she turned her head slightly and zeroed right in on Ken like she was locked on a target. "You sure you lost her?" Mark asked.

Ken looked, and she instantly turned away. "The Titanic hit a smaller iceberg," he said quietly.

"So melt her," Law said. "Come on, let's hit the buffet. It's a thing of beauty, if I say so myself."

An hour later, sated with dinner and listening to someone at the podium list a string of accomplishments and memories, Mark realized that all he'd done all night—for more than twenty-four hours, to be honest—was hope that Emma would come back.

But as the evening moved toward the dance competition, that hope grew from a warm ember to a cold chunk of stone residing in his heart. That feeling he'd been most familiar with for a decade and a half.

Loss. Loneliness. An ache that felt like a black hole that had been filled by laughter and love—oh man. He *still* sounded like her.

"Whoa. *Whoa.*" Law sat up straight and stared over Mark's shoulder. "Brace yourself."

Emma?

He whipped around and disappointment kicked at the sight of seven women, including Libby, walking arm in arm toward their table, some faces familiar, some not. They moved in unison like dancers or...cheerleaders. Instantly, Mark recognized a few, like Margot the dancer who'd offered to be his partner, and realized he'd seen many of these ladies' teenage faces in a trophy case the other day.

Everyone looked...right at Mark.

"Holy shit, you weren't kidding, dude." Law laughed. "You're like catnip."

Allison Breyer was on the right, a glimmer in her eyes as she tossed back her sassy streak of white hair. "Solomon," she said.

He swallowed. "Yeah?"

"Scorps don't forfeit."

A few of them laughed, along with Mark and his friends. "Is that so?"

"Scorps sting!" The whole line crouched down a little, dropping their joined hands so they could shoot the right one over their heads, shouting, "Sting 'em, Scorps!" in perfect unison.

A cheer went up from the entire crowd, including Law and Ken. Another table yelled the same thing, and soon the Mimosa High Scorpion battle cry was being shouted all over the sands of Barefoot Bay. Which was probably what was supposed to happen at this event.

"You're the cheerleading squad," Mark said as he realized who and what they were.

"From 1980 through 1989," one of them called out.

"And eighties ladies don't mess around," Libby added. "We got the playlist, and we know these songs."

"*Know* them?" one of them called out. "Some of us have *Flashdance* tattoos."

Mark just dropped back in his chair and started laughing. "I give up."

"Oh no, you don't." Allison grabbed one hand, and Libby took the other, pulling him out of the chair. "We've already talked to the committee chair. We're doing this. Let's go, big guy. Dance competitors are behind the curtain in the banquet room."

"Haul that sexy ass," Libby added with a yank.

The next thing he knew he was flanked by the very women he'd hoped to avoid all week. All smiling, laughing, teasing, and, God, cheering. Each one was beautiful in her own way, and not one of them mentioned Julia or threw herself at him.

What the hell had he been so worried about?

They dragged him into the back of the resort, and for the briefest moment, he forgot his sadness while they took him behind the curtain that blocked off a large stage at one end of the large ballroom. A number of other couples were back there, donning "costumes" and practicing moves. Enough booze had been imbibed that no one cared that Team Eighties had seven women; they weren't going to win, but with this crew? They sure as hell weren't going to forfeit.

Libby ran the show, and Mark could have kicked himself for the wrong assumption he'd made about her when they'd first met earlier in the week. She was no pampered socialite or, if she was, she was bright and funny and clearly a woman who knew how to get stuff done.

In moments, Libby had assigned each woman a song, taking *Endless Love* for herself.

"No fancy steps," she said. "Whatever you learned at that studio, you can forget, Mark. We're all just going to dance the way we did at Mimosa High at every Spring Fling."

Julia's letter flashed in his head for a moment, but he had no time to think about it, because a few hundred slightly inebriated and way-too-old-for-Spring Flinging guests started filling up the banquet room, much noisier than when they'd arrived and checked in.

"How are we doing back here?" Lacey Walker slipped behind the curtains, holding a wine glass and wearing a relieved smile. The dance contestants hollered at their leader, some gathering around her. She greeted a few, but her gaze cut through the crowd to Mark.

"You're here," she said, stepping closer.

"With my squad." He gestured to the women around him who responded—*of course*—with a perfectly timed "Woo-woo-woo!" and synchronized fist-pumping like they were on the sidelines of the big Friday-night game.

Instantly, inexplicably, he loved them all for the support and attitude. Man, he'd judged people wrong.

Lacey nodded slowly, a light in her eyes that had certainly been absent the last time he'd seen her. Late last night, he'd called and told her everything and made one more pitch for her to consider Emma for the job. She'd left it hanging, but doubtful.

"Are you dancing to the same songs?" she asked.

"One each," Libby offered. "With a grand *That's What Friends Are For* finale. Please join us on stage for that, Lacey."

"I'd love to," she said enthusiastically, raising her glass. "One more of these and I'll be leading the show."

"It's been a tough week," Mark said.

She rolled her amber eyes and pushed some strawberry-blond curls away from her face. "Tough but great fun. This is definitely going to be an annual event. But I'm not chairing it ever again." She narrowed her eyes at Libby. "You're pretty good at it, you know."

"I'll chair," Libby said easily. "But I get to handpick my team." She turned to the group. "Starting right here."

"Count me out," Mark said. "I'll be in China next spring."

"You might come back to Barefoot Bay," Lacey said. "You never know."

He'd never step foot on this godforsaken rock again. One too many memories. But that sounded rude, so he just smiled. "You're right, Lacey. You never know."

Music quieted the crowd, and a coordinator moved all of the dancers to the back of the stage and lined them up in order, youngest to oldest. An old married couple, the Bentleys, who met while they were in the class of 1956, were seated on a sofa, surrounded by their kids and grandkids. They'd be last, of course, and the stars of the show as the oldest alums at the event.

The first couple, twentysomethings who'd graduated ten years ago, ran off to the opening notes of a song Mark didn't know, but he heard the words "tonight's gonna be a good night" over and over again. It *would* have been a good night, if he hadn't been an idiot.

When they finished, the crowd applauded, and on went the thirty-year-olds from the 1990s.

Libby gathered her girls around Mark for a huddle and hug, and he played along, knowing it would be a disaster and he'd be a laughingstock, but he couldn't care less. He'd get through this without Emma, thanks to these new friends, then he'd leave the party, pack up, and get out of town tomorrow morning. Back to Australia, maybe, or maybe Bhutan to hike up to the Tiger's Nest Monastery.

Where he supposedly got engaged to Emma.

He closed his eyes to kick the thought away, and when he opened them, the nineties dancers were running behind the curtain to wild applause.

"Ladies and gentlemen, we have a small change from what's in your program for our 1980s dancers."

The women gave a cheerleadery squeal, and Margot, his partner for *Call Me*, sidled up on his left, sliding her arm through his and giving him a smile.

"We'll do great, Mark, no worries."

Another woman he'd misjudged and made wrong assumptions about. "I know we will," he said easily, but his comment was partially drowned out by the announcer.

"This tribute to the decade that gave us *Miami Vice*, Reaganomics, shoulder pads, yuppies, and MTV—" He was cut off by the crowd's reaction of cheers and boos. Mark shook his head as he laughed, and realized, with yet another boot to the gut, how much Emma would have enjoyed this.

"This dance number," the announcer continued, "was supposed to be danced as a great love story, but I've received word from backstage that it's changed."

The crowed "awwwed," and Margot squeezed his arm. "You should have had more faith in us, Mark," she whispered.

He should have. He was wrong to assume they were manhunting with every breath. Wrong and ashamed. "I'm…sorry." And he meant it.

She laughed lightly. "No need to grovel to me, but there might be a woman out there who'd like to see you suffer a little."

But she *wasn't* out there, and that was making him suffer more.

Lacey interrupted, coming over to deliver the good-luck hug she was giving to each couple before they went on.

"You're a lucky man," Lacey whispered in his ear as their cheeks touched.

Lucky? "I don't know about that," he said, adding a sad smile.

"But you are."

"All these women, you mean?"

She lifted a brow. "Twice in a lifetime. Most of us only get one chance for something like that."

Twice? "No. One chance is all I had."

Her lips curled up, but before she could answer, Margot pulled him through the opening of the curtains while Blondie wailed. Almost immediately, his body started the moves he'd learned from the yellow-haired choreographer. As Mark turned, he saw Jasper on the side, a friendly arm around the young dance teacher he was competing against.

Mark gave him a nod and mouthed, "Sorry," as Margot started moving maniacally around the stage and Mark did his best to dance. He heard Law hollering at the top of his lungs and the hysterical laughter of a well-lit crowd watching others make complete fools of themselves.

He let go and danced, as one crazy-ass fortysomething woman after another came out and danced through every song on the playlist, taking them up to the *Flashdance* song, which brought the house down. Then they rocked out to *The Power of Love*, all the while every note made his heart ache for Emma.

Every note had a memory or a moment. A laugh, a trip, a touch, a kiss. Right there, as they reached the end of that song, the very moment that he and Emma were supposed to kiss and start *Endless Love*, he felt a tap on his shoulder.

Libby, of course. This was her song.

How badly he wanted it to be Emma. What he wouldn't give to turn around and see her. He wanted it so much, he didn't turn until the first few notes started, because the disappointment was going to hurt yet again.

A woman's hand snaked around his waist, the fingers spreading possessively. If only—

He felt warm breath on his neck and the pressure of a body against his back.

A few people made catcalls and hooted suggestively.

The song started. *My love, there's only...*

"You in my life."

The woman's voice floated into his ear, softer than Lionel Ritchie and so...familiar.

"And you," she sang breathlessly, "will always be..."

Emma.

He turned slowly, as if the spell would be broken if he moved too fast.

And there she was, looking up at him, light in her eyes, her lips parted in a half smile of hope.

"My endless love," she finished, taking his hand and drawing back exactly as they'd practiced.

"You're here," he whispered.

She winked. "Jasper's watching. Dance."

Dance? He wanted to lift her up and spin her around and kiss her until everyone and everything disappeared. "Emma, I'm so—"

"Dance," she ordered, moving to the song as they'd learned. This had been their favorite song to practice at the villa. It always ended by falling into bed and making...

God, he *loved* her. Did she know that?

"You have to dance," she insisted, taking the lead and turning. Muscle memory kicked in, and they got through the next minute arm in arm, eyes locked, silent, certain, and as happy as he'd ever felt.

The chorus built to a crescendo, but Mark barely heard the music or the crowd. Every sense was focused on Emma, reading the look in her eyes and seeing forgiveness and her irrepressible humor and…love.

Was he imagining that?

He finally took his gaze off her to see his seven friends, huddled like women do, excited and happy and wiping a few tears.

They'd been in on it.

Lacey came up behind them, and they pulled her into their circle, all of them beaming at him. Did she know, too?

"How did you do this?" he asked Emma.

"That's what friends are for," she teased as the music to the song of the same name started. But instead of their usual positions, Mark and Emma stepped side by side, and the women came rushing out, forming a line on either side of them, and the whole lot of them started swaying to familiar words with a powerful message.

This was what friends were for.

In no time, hundreds of Mimosa High alums, ages twenty-five to God knew what, slid arms around the waist of the person next to them and swayed and sang as loud and off-key as only a room full of tipsy, maudlin, happy people could.

But no one was happier than Mark, with his arm around Emma where it would stay as long as she would have him. And he hoped that was forever.

As the song ended and cheers rose and the room rocked, he turned her in his arms and pulled her into him. "Not letting you go, Emma DeWitt," he whispered.

"Not leaving you again, Mark Solomon," she shot back.

He drew back, still unsure that this could really be happening.

"I can't believe you're here. What about Lacey? Can you still talk to her?"

"I met with Lacey this morning. I'm on the short list for the job."

His jaw dropped.

"Your call really greased the skids last night, so thanks. She was awesome, and so are you for thinking of that first."

"Emma!" He couldn't help grabbing her tighter and lifting her off the ground for a celebratory twirl, which just sent the cheering section into a frenzy.

"Get off the stage, you two!" Jasper came running across the stage, ushering them to the other side. "Go make out in private. You can be sure you didn't win ten grand today."

"We won everything," Mark said, leading her off the stage, where the cheerleaders and matchmakers parted with hugs and pats on the back for both of them.

They managed to escape, slipping out a side door into a wide corridor where it was hushed and cool and secluded.

He barely whispered her name before kissing her on the mouth and getting the same enthusiasm in return.

"I missed you," he murmured into the kiss.

"Mmmm." She inched back, eyes closed, smile wide. "Me, too."

"Emma." He closed his palms over her face and held it, her warm, soft cheeks like heaven in his hands. "I have to tell you something."

"I know you're sorry, Mark—"

"I love you."

"You do." It wasn't a question.

"I love your heart and your humor and your…"

"Give me another h-word and I'm yours."

He laughed, dropping his head back for the pure joy that the feeling sent through him. "I love you," he said again. "It's all I have. No alliteration, no epic groveling, though I owe it to you, just plain love that I want to share with you for the rest of our lives."

"Oh, Mark. I love you, too." She choked on the admission. "I knew it the moment I left. I made it as far as Charlotte, spent the night in the airport and got on the first flight back to Florida. My luggage is…somewhere. I met with Lacey, and she told me that when you called last night, she really understood everything." She glanced in the direction of the banquet room. "And she even gave me clothes to wear. When I arrived at the reunion, I was planning to find you, but I ran into Libby, who already knew the truth, so those girls helped me cook up the whole thing."

"Those girls." He laughed ruefully. "I shouldn't have been so terrified of them."

"No, but after they heard why you were so afraid to be alone at this event, they decided to embarrass the hell out of you onstage."

"I deserved it," he admitted, pulling her into him and toward a back beach exit. "Let's go home," he whispered. "Let's make love."

"All night."

At the edge of the sand, they stopped and looked down at their feet.

"You know what the marketing says," Mark teased.

"Kick off your shoes and fall in love."

Mark toed off his loafers, and as he bent to pick them up, he kissed her cheek. "Done and done."

Arm in arm, they walked along Barefoot Bay, the music of the sixties still audible from the banquet room.

"So, what changed your mind, Em?"

"Not what. *Who.*"

He slowed down and turned to her. "Who?"

"I met a woman who made me think. She made me realize that a man like you comes along once in a lifetime, or maybe twice." She wrapped both arms around him and laid her head on his chest. "And she made me realize I have nothing to fear with you."

"She was right." He lifted her chin to look into her eyes. "Whoever she was, I love this woman."

"Yeah," she said with a sly smile. "You'd have loved her."

"But I love you, Em." He took her hands and stepped back, holding her gaze. "And you get to pick the place. Name it, and I'll make it happen."

She frowned. "What place?"

"The romantic proposal of your dreams. You want the Champs-Élysées? The Tiger's Nest Monastery? Skydiving? The moon? Where do you want me to pop the question?"

She reached up and touched his face. "The place I'm going to call home and so will my husband if he's not running from anything. Barefoot Bay."

Placing his hand over hers, he pressed her palm to his cheek, then turned his head to kiss it.

"I'm not trying to escape or run from anything anymore," he said. "You've grounded me. Right down...to the sand." He dropped to one knee and held on to her hand. "Marry me, Emma DeWitt. And be my soul mate."

She looked at him for a long time, hesitating long enough that his heart actually slipped in his chest.

Finally, she pulled his hand to her mouth. "Yes. Yes. A thousand million times yes!"

He was up and kissing her in an instant, spinning her on the sand as she called out, "Yes!" as loud as she could.

He scooped her up, unable to wait another minute to get her home.

"Emma Solomon!" She dropped her head back and laughed. "Isn't that a great name?"

"Yes," he agreed, scooting her higher for one more kiss. "Emma Solomon is the most beautiful name I've ever heard."

. . . Sneak Peek . . .

Barefoot

AT MOONRISE

Barefoot Bay Timeless #2

roxanne st. claire

Chapter One

Ken Cavanaugh charged into burning buildings on a routine basis. He faced life-threatening emergencies, unforeseen crises, and potential disasters almost every day with titanium nerves and steady hands. He led a crew of fearless, tough, muscle-bound mavericks who turned to him for wisdom, guidance, life-or-death decisions, and changes in their shift schedule. And, icing on his résumé cake, Captain Cav was the fan favorite to lead the fire station tours because women and children loved him.

So why the *hell* did his feet feel like he was wearing iron boots? Why did his pulse thump as though he was seconds from stroking out? All he had to do was walk across a banquet hall in the middle of a high school reunion and talk to a woman, but he couldn't bring himself to do it.

Because Bethany Endicott had frozen him out this week no matter how he'd tried to thaw her. Of course, he might have had that coming, considering their past.

But twenty-five years had passed since he'd been a grieving, angry eighteen-year-old who wanted to hurt anyone named Endicott...including his girlfriend.

All he really wanted to do was put that dark day—all those dark days, in fact—in the past and clear the air.

He *had* to talk to her before this week went up in smoke and he could do nothing but watch his chance burn to the ground.

For one week, during the interminable "planning" of this reunion, they had yet to have a substantive conversation. There was plenty of eye contact, all kinds of accidental brushes, and a low-grade simmer that stretched his nerves—and libido—to the limits. He'd caught her gazing at him on more than one occasion, but any time he'd initiated a conversation, she managed to be suddenly pulled away or busy.

Who could blame her? He could rationalize what happened between them all those years ago for the rest of his life, and the fact was, he'd said things that had to hurt, and now he just wanted to apologize.

Wasn't that kind of what high school reunions were for?

But time was running out, though, leaving tonight, the night of the all-class Mimosa High reunion at Barefoot Bay's swanky resort, for Ken to make his move. After this, they'd go back to their regular lives, and another twenty-five years might pass before they saw each other again.

This was his last chance.

"Come on, Cav. Tap that powder keg."

Ken didn't even turn to give Lawson Monroe a dirty look when the man sidled up next to him. Law was three years Ken's senior, and they hadn't known each other in high school—though Ken knew of Law's reputation for trouble—but this week the two men had had no choice but to hang out together at the various reunion-planning sessions. In the process, Ken grew to appreciate Law's irreverent sense of humor and signature sarcasm.

He'd let Law and Mark Solomon, who'd rounded out the trio of Y chromosomes on the planning committee, think his interest in Beth Endicott was physical—which wasn't a lie. She still got him fired up with one look. But there was more to his need to get Beth alone. Much more.

"Seriously, Captain Cav, what are you waiting for?" Law needled. "A kick in the ass? A glass of courage? I'm so pleased to provide both." Law offered a glass of beer. "For you, since I don't drink."

Ken took the beer and sipped. Let the man think all Ken wanted to do was hit on a pretty woman. He couldn't tell them the truth. He could never tell anyone the truth, but that was something he'd accepted years ago.

He could still apologize to Beth, and wanted to.

Looking around, he considered his next opportunity to get Beth alone. There would be desserts and after-dinner drinks back on the beach following this. Could he talk to her there?

"When is this dance contest thing over?" Ken asked.

"When the thousand-year-old couple keels over."

Ken smiled, taking in the seventy-seven-year-olds who'd stepped onto the stage to close out the decades-themed dance competition. Decked out in 1950s costumes for a jitterbug, the married oldsters were surrounded by a few more generations of their family cheering them on. "They met at Mimosa High, class of 1956," he mused. "Married forever."

Law grunted like the very thought pained him. "Damn, that's a long time to ride the same love boat every night."

"Seriously. How the hell does a guy get so lucky?" Ken avoided Law's cynical expression to steal another glance across the hall. The crowd broke enough for him to get a glimpse at the short, white skirt that flared over Beth's thighs, showing off her heart-stopping legs and killer red and white high heels. She loved her high heels and short skirts, and wore them just as well now as she had in 1991.

She was watching the show, checking her phone, and occasionally glancing at the exit to the deck behind her.

He had to *move*.

"Boredom sets in fast," Law said. "I need variety."

"Variety gets boring, too," Ken replied. "I'd rather have something steady."

"Shoot me now," Law joked. "Two-point-five and a minivan in the driveway is my idea of hell on earth. Anyway, I hate to burst your bubble, but I heard your Beth is the poster girl for I Am Woman, Hear Me Roar."

His Beth. If only. Ken's gaze drifted across the room, catching her checking her cell phone for the sixtieth time that hour. Who the hell was she waiting to hear from?

"Weren't you a freaking Navy first responder before you became a firefighter?" Law demanded. "Failure isn't an option for you life-saving types."

No, failure wasn't an option. Not in his line of work, not in his life. But where Beth was involved? It had been a fail all those years ago, and starting to look like a fail tonight.

"Pretend the place is on fire and you have to evacuate her to the nearest...bedroom." Law took the beer back. "Don't make me show you how it's done, son."

Ken checked out the couple on the stage, twirling—slowly—for their big ending. Everything in his gut told him Beth would never stay for dessert on the beach. She'd been half checked out all week long, barely showing up for any of the committee crap he'd agreed to do when he saw her name on the list.

Maybe it wasn't a man who had her glued to the phone. Maybe it was work. Maybe it was...*him*. Ray Endicott. He knew only that she was in some kind of housing and real estate business, so it was more than likely she worked for her father.

An old, familiar metallic taste filled his mouth when he thought of the coldhearted bastard responsible for shattering Ken's world. No conversation with Beth would ever change the truth of that, but *she* wasn't responsible, and he wanted her to know he didn't blame her.

"All right," he said. "I'm going in."

"Get 'er done, Captain."

Ken gave a quick nod and made his way across the room. Being six-two made it easy to see over most heads, but the crowd was thick with huggers and dancers and drinkers. To avoid them, and the possibility that someone would stop him to talk, he swerved toward the perimeter of the room. Staying locked on that golden hair spilling over bare shoulders and a sleek red halter top, he was steady and sure now.

Beth's gaze drifted over the crowd and settled on the spot where Ken had been standing with Law. Blue eyes narrowed, and a slight frown creased her forehead. She angled her head a bit, and her shoulders dropped as if she'd sighed.

As if…she was disappointed that he'd left.

Buoyed by that, he powered forward, slipping between two people with a quick, "'Scuze me."

"Oh no, you don't!" A woman's fingers snagged his elbow and squeezed, jerking him to a stop. "Ken Cavanaugh, if you don't remember me, my heart's going to break into a thousand pieces."

He turned quickly toward a petite woman with frosted-blond curls and glasses, with zero recognition of her face. "I…uh…sorry…I'm—"

"Chrissie Bartlett!" she exclaimed, her voice rising along with her wine glass. "Spanish 1? Freshman year? Señora Norton's class?"

Oh yeah. He remembered the name. Remembered that she hadn't given him the time of day in Spanish class back then. "Hi, Chrissie."

She came a little closer. "You've changed, Kenny."

Kenny. The only person who'd ever gotten away with calling him that was…inching closer to the exit. "It's been a long time," he said, trying to move away. "We've all changed."

"For the better," she added.

Yeah, because now he wasn't from the wrong side of Mimosa Key.

Another woman joined them, a three- or four-drink gleam in her eyes. "I don't think we ever talked in high school," she said. "I'm Marta Burns."

Marta Burns? No, they'd never talked, because Ken worked construction jobs after school while they were busy with clubs and crap to pad their college applications.

"I hear you're a firefighter. And the captain, no less." Chrissie added a squeeze to his bicep, blocking Marta from getting any closer. "Impressive."

"Yeah." He glanced back to Beth, catching her making a quick scan of the room as she moved toward the door. Was she looking for him?

"Excuse me, Chrissie, but I—"

"Hey, Chrissie, why'd you slip away?" Another man approached, much shorter than Ken and with way less hair. He threw a look at Ken, who gladly stepped away to let him flirt with Chrissie. The whole thing took two seconds, long enough for him to lose sight of Beth.

Damn it. He made a few comments, shook a hand, threw out one more excuse, and finally got away, muscling through the rest of the crowd to reach the side exit that led out to a large wooden deck.

But it was empty, with no sign of Beth.

Swallowing a dark curse, he took a few steps toward the railing, and then spotted a pair of red and white high heels tucked by the stairs that led to the sand.

He couldn't help smiling, because, hell, this was better than Cinderella. She'd left only one shoe.

All he had to do was follow the footprints in the sand.

Books Set in Barefoot Bay

The Barefoot Bay Billionaires
Secrets on the Sand
Seduction on the Sand
Scandal on the Sand

The Barefoot Bay Brides
Barefoot in White
Barefoot in Lace
Barefoot in Pearls

Barefoot Bay Undercover
Barefoot Bound (prequel)
Barefoot with a Bodyguard
Barefoot with a Stranger
Barefoot with a Bad Boy (Gabe's book!)

Barefoot Bay Timeless
Barefoot at Sunset
Barefoot at Moonrise
Barefoot at Midnight

The Original Barefoot Bay Quartet
Barefoot in the Sand
Barefoot in the Rain
Barefoot in the Sun
Barefoot by the Sea

About The Author

Published since 2003, Roxanne St. Claire is a *New York Times* and *USA Today* bestselling author of more than forty romance and suspense novels. She has written several popular series, including Barefoot Bay, the Guardian Angelinos, and the Bullet Catchers.

In addition to being an eight-time nominee and one-time winner of the prestigious RITA™ Award for the best in romance writing, Roxanne's novels have won the National Reader's Choice Award for best romantic suspense three times, as well as the Maggie, the Daphne du Maurier Award, the HOLT Medallion, Booksellers Best, Book Buyers Best, the Award of Excellence, and many others.

She lives in Florida with her husband, and still attempts to run the lives of her teenage daughter and 20-something son. She loves dogs, books, chocolate, and wine, but not always in that order.

www.roxannestclaire.com
www.twitter.com/roxannestclaire
www.facebook.com/roxannestclaire

60202994R00183

Made in the USA
Lexington, KY
30 January 2017